BURIED ON AVENUE B

Also by Peter de Jonge
Shadows Still Remain

BURIED ON AVENUE B

A NOVEL

PETER DE JONGE

HARPER

An Imprint of HarperCollinsPublishers
www.harpercollins.com

HarperCollins books may be purchased for educational, business, or sales promotional use. For information, please write: Special Markets Department, HarperCollins Publishers, 10 East 53rd Street, New York, NY 10022.

FIRST EDITION

Grateful acknowledgment is made for permission to reprint from:
    "Hot, Blue and Righteous"
    Words and Music by Billy F. Gibbons
    Copyright © 1973 Music Of Stage Three.
    Copyright Renewed.
    Worldwide Rights for Music Of Stage Three Administered by BMG Rights Management (US) LLC.
    All Rights Reserved. Used by Permission.
    Reprinted by Permission of Hal Leonard Corporation.

Drawings by Joseph de Jonge

Designed by Lisa Stokes

Library of Congress Cataloging-in-Publication Data has been applied for.

ISBN: 978-0-06-137355-8

12 13 14 15 16   OV/RRD   10 9 8 7 6 5 4 3 2 1

For my mother

You don't want to see these guys without their masks on

—*the Mountain Goats*

PART I

CHAPTER 1

DARLENE O'HARA SITS on her rug and gazes at her twenty-one-year-old
son stretched out on her couch, his red beard tilted up at one end, his pale
feet hanging off the other. Two hours earlier, Axl Rose O'Hara showed
up unexpectedly at the door of her Bronx apartment. He put down his
overstuffed messenger bag and Fender Stratocaster, announced he had
momentous news, and promptly nodded off, and as the quiet Sunday afternoon fades into a quieter evening, O'Hara steals glances across the room,
stunned by the pleasure it gives her to watch her long, beautiful kid sleep.

Due to the cost of airfare, Axl, a senior at the University of Washington, hasn't been back in New York for five months, and to see that
he feels so comfortable in his old home that he is snoring in minutes is
gratifying in itself. Knowing that he's safe and sound and out of danger
is even better, and when can a mother of a six-foot-three-inch manchild
know with certainty that that's the case, except when he is sleeping six
feet away on her own living room couch? There's a third advantage to
their modest interaction. With Axl asleep, she can actually enjoy his company. She doesn't have to worry about saying the wrong thing, or the right
thing in the wrong way, or the approximately right thing at precisely the

wrong time, and see him grimace as if he's just taken a mouthful of rancid food. No, son asleep/mother watching is about as good as it gets, and she knows it.

Axl twitches and readjusts his limbs, and as her terrier mutt Bruno finds another niche on his flank, O'Hara marvels at how well her son has turned out. A minor miracle, considering she was fifteen when he was born, then stacked the deck even further by giving him the name of her favorite sinewy front man. O'Hara isn't fooling herself. She knows her mother deserves most of the credit, and at five-foot-four, she certainly didn't give Axl her height, which came courtesy of the neighborhood lothario who knocked her up. But still. She must have done something right.

Six hours later, Axl shows no signs of waking. O'Hara covers him in a light blanket and pries off Bruno for his walk. O'Hara's apartment is on the top floor of a three-family house in Riverdale, less than a mile from the Hudson, and as she and Bruno stroll past an empty playground, the dog's rubbery nose is alive to every emission of the summer night. She lets him walk nearly to the water's edge before she reins him in and points him back toward home. Although O'Hara is curious about Axl's impending announcement, she isn't overly concerned. What seems epic to a twenty-one-year-old usually isn't, and based on the guitar, she figures it has to do with his music. A couple weeks earlier, Axl e-mailed her a file containing three songs recorded in a bathroom in his dorm, and he has talked about starting a band. Maybe they've landed a gig. If so, she'll call her old partner Krekorian, who just got transferred to the robbery squad, and some old friends from the 7, and try to rustle up a crowd.

When O'Hara and Bruno reach the top of the hill and climb the three flights of stairs, Axl hasn't moved, and the next morning, he still hasn't. That's pushing fifteen hours straight, but who knows how long the kid had been up, and she takes Bruno for another walk. This time when they return, Axl is not only off the couch, he's made coffee. Not only that, he pours her a cup.

"Darlene, I've started a band." Because of their relatively minor age difference, Axl has always been more comfortable calling his mother by her first name.

"That's great. I really liked those songs. No bullshit."

"We're called the Flat Screens."

"I like it."

"Good," says Axl. "The name's important."

O'Hara wonders if that's true. Or if every band name sounds slightly ridiculous until you fall in love with the music.

"So you formed a band, and you're called the Flat Screens. That it?"

"Yeah . . . except that I'm moving to Bushwick."

"Really? You're not going back to school? You only have one year left."

"I've made up my mind. I'm going for it. Actually, there is one other thing."

"What?"

"Can you lend me three thousand dollars?"

CHAPTER 2

AN HOUR LATER, at 8:07 a.m., O'Hara restarts her day with a grapefruit juice and vodka at a downtown dive called Milano's. Six months ago, after the tabloids allotted O'Hara her fifteen minutes for making a collar in the murder of NYU student Francesca Pena, O'Hara was transferred to Homicide South. Homicide South, or as it is sometimes referred to, "Homicide Soft," is housed in the 13 on East Twenty-First Street. Milano's is in a tenement on Houston between Mulberry and Mott, which means that in addition to being among the handful of bars open this early, it offers a workable ratio of discretion and convenience, neither too close nor too far from her new headquarters.

Although this is O'Hara's first visit, she'd heard how narrow Milano's is. When she leans back on her stool, her shoulders brush against the side wall. It's so tight, thinks O'Hara, a drunk couldn't fall down if he wanted to, at least not until he reached the street, where he became someone else's problem, i.e., a cop's problem. More than its cozy confines, O'Hara is taken by the delicacy of the light and the lovely sense of remove, both from the pedestrians hustling by on Houston and from time. Instead of the news, the TV is tuned to an old black-and-white on Turner Classic

Movies, and from overhead come disembodied snippets of sixty-year-old dialogue. Leaning against the register is a twenty-pound dictionary, a hernia-inducing relic from an age when every dispute of spelling or geography wasn't settled on some dipshit's iPhone.

As her eyes take in more of the space, she sees that every square inch is covered with old crap, and every square inch of old crap, including the pretzels and chips, is covered with layers of grime. Although O'Hara could take or leave the photos of JFK, Sinatra, and old Yankees in pinstripes, and could certainly do without the toy fire engine on the register, one more ode to the heroics of FDNY on 9/11, she appreciates the quiet efficiency of the pretty brown-haired barkeep and takes it as a good omen that she's wearing an AC/DC T-shirt. In O'Hara's considered opinion, AC/DC is not only the rockingest band in history but also one of the best T-shirts.

There are two other patrons in the bar, and both were in front of O'Hara in line when the doors opened. On her left is an attractive overweight woman, her bag, suit, hair, and makeup immaculate. In fact, everything about her, except for the fact that she is at a bar at eight in the morning, is in perfect order. To her right, just beyond where a *Times*, *Post*, and *News* lie untouched in a neat stack, is a flamboyantly dressed middle-aged man, his Louis Vuitton man purse on the bar beside his Jack and Coke. O'Hara makes the woman as midlevel corporate, the man as a rather successful drug dealer, and although she would insist that her observations are based on more than racial profiling, she also notes that, of the three of them, he's the only one drinking after rather than before work.

O'Hara takes another sip and reminds herself that someone who names her kid Axl Rose O'Hara shouldn't be shocked when he drops out of school and forms a rock band. Particularly when his mother's idea of a bedtime lullaby was "Sweet Child of Mine" or down-tempo Stones like "Wild Horses" and "Angie." One reason she feels so undone may be that picking up the tab for her son's tuition was her way to make up for the other things she couldn't or didn't do. O'Hara toted him back and forth from high school for nine months, concealing the growing bulge beneath ever looser hippie blouses, and suffered the eye-opening indignities of childbirth, but from then on her own mother pretty much took over. And on those dark Irish days when she turned on herself and her deficiencies as a mother, she at least had those canceled checks to the University of Washington to hold up in her defense. It's almost funny, she thinks. They say education is something no one can take from you, but Axl just took it from her.

Mostly, though, O'Hara is scared for her son. She wants Axl to have a comfortable life. She wants it to be a stroll in the park, a piece of cake, and what are the chances of that as a musician? O'Hara wanted a professional job for her son—lawyer, accountant, teacher, etc.—because with those, being competent is generally good enough. Everything else, you've got to be brilliant or lucky or both, just to slip through a crack into the middle class. Of course to your kid, that kind of hedging comes off as an insult: "So you don't think I'm that good after all. You didn't really like those songs. That was just more of your condescending bullshit." In fact, that's not the case. She thinks the songs are wonderful. She just doesn't like the odds.

A couple more sips, and O'Hara is reminded of another point in favor of an unabashed dive. They don't stint, and however fleeting, a generous pour on an empty stomach provides a measure of perspective. O'Hara concedes that as a name, the Flat Screens is growing on her, and as she slides her $7 Ray-Ban rip-offs over her freckled nose and steps into the glare of an August morning, she reminds herself it could have been a lot worse.

He could have told her he was becoming a fireman, or a singer-songwriter.

CHAPTER 3

HOMICIDE SOUTH IS buried in a warren of windowless rooms on the third floor of the 13. Just off the elevator is a lonely cubicle.

"Morning, Ray. Anything?"

"A kid got stabbed outside Rocco's on Delancey," says Hickey and hands O'Hara a printout. "They took him to St. Vincent's. Listed in critical."

Hickey works the overnight, between 1:00 and 9:00 a.m., an inglorious assignment known as the wheel. If all hell breaks loose, he calls Kelso, the lieutenant, and wakes him up. Something less urgent, like an assault that may or may not get upgraded to homicide, he fills out an unusual and hands it off to the detectives when they arrive for their morning shift. If you're working the wheel, you did something wrong and got caught. In Hickey's case it was knocking over a cyclist in a bike lane—or, more precisely, being captured on the cyclist's girlfriend's cell leaving the scene. Now he's strapped to the wheel as if it were a giant rock.

Unusual in hand, O'Hara continues into the squad room and sits at her desk beside her partner, Augustus Jandorek. Jandorek is in his mid-fifties, natty and thin, with closely cropped gray hair and beard, a late-career detective who's cast himself as Prince of the City. His gray tropical wool suit actually fits. A gold bracelet dangles at the cuff.

"This whole thing is about pepper flakes," says Jandorek. Although his copy of the unusual is on his desk, he is preoccupied by something on his computer screen.

"At four in the morning, two guys step into Rocco's for a slice. One is built like a refrigerator, six-five, two-ninety. The other, like a hotel minibar, five-seven, one-fifty-five. The smaller man reaches for the pepper, which might suggest he's eaten at Rocco's before, because their pie needs all the help it can get, although the guy at the counter swears he's never seen him. As he reaches for the jar, he knocks the shoulder of the larger man. The smaller man apologizes, even offers to buy him a second slice, but the refrigerator won't let it slide. Apparently, when he was upstate, he read Emily Post cover to cover and is a stickler on dining etiquette."

"He is unappeasable."

"You got that right, Dar. The motherfucker is nothing if not unappeasable. He invites his fellow diner to step outside, and when the man shows no enthusiasm, he insists. Once outside, the little guy stabs the big guy, Ted McBeth, in the abdomen. McBeth is at St. Vincent's. The perp remains at large."

"So much for etiquette," says O'Hara.

Despite the way her day began, O'Hara is invigorated by the possibility of catching a homicide, a rare occurrence in Homicide South. On the far wall is a blackboard listing the eleven individuals unlucky enough to have been murdered below Fifty-Ninth Street in '07, ten of whom have a blue line running through the middle of their names. The only name that doesn't belongs to a man who choked on a hot dog in April. When the ME determined the choking was the result of damage to his esophagus sustained in an assault fifteen years before his last meal, the death went from a tragic case of underchewing to a homicide. To Kelso, who is obsessed with the squad's closure rate, it has become a blemish that will never go away, and every time he looks up at the board, he feels like the frank is repeating on him.

To detectives in the Bronx and Brooklyn or even Manhattan North,
eleven murders in seven months is laughable, and the reason Manhattan South is called Manhattan Soft. Even compared to the 7, the pace is
maddeningly slow, and not long after O'Hara arrived, Kelso, sensing her
restlessness, sat her down for a little heart-to-heart.

"Manhattan South may have a small caseload," he said, "but there's
a flip side. When someone gets killed here, people, as in the media and
brass, actually give a fuck, which is why we get assigned the best detectives in the system." Kelso's office is just beyond Hickey's cubicle, and
seeing it over Kelso's shoulder felt like a warning. "Our closure rate has
been the highest in the city five years running. Hell, three of the last four
years it's been perfect, and if it weren't for that motherfucker who forgot
to chew, we'd be at a hundred percent this year too. It's not quantity, it's
quality. The detectives in Homicide South are the last adults in NYPD,
and when you come here, that's what's expected—adult behavior."

O'Hara got the message, and Hickey's cube, which seemed even scar-
ier for being empty, reinforced it. Over time, however, O'Hara has also
come to see that in homicide, *adult* is synonymous with *old*. Every detective in the squad, except for her, has got their twenty years in, or even
their twenty-five. After that long, the job is like elevator music, what's
playing in the background while you're thinking about something else.

"We heading to St. Vincent's?"

"You in a rush to catch SARS? Or Ebola? Or West Nile? You must not
have seen that waiting room lately. I made a call. McBeth is still in surgery. We won't be able to talk to him for hours."

"We could talk to the nurses. He might have said something as they
wheeled him in."

"It's possible," says Jandorek as he stares at his computer screen, "but
let's sit tight. Besides, there's something I want to ask you. There's this
kid, maybe the best cop softball player in the country. I went to his Face-
book page, and he's posted a ten-minute video of himself working out.
Does that strike you as gay?"

"Yeah."

"Me too. But my buddy who knows him insists he's not, and swears he gets more tail than anyone."

"Okay, then. Maybe I'm wrong. Maybe he's just a little off. Maybe he's a scientologist."

Jandorek looks up from his screen and shoots O'Hara a quizzical look, and O'Hara knows she has to be careful. For Jandorek it's all about cops, being part of the fraternity—that's why he's checking out the Web site for the NYPD softball team rather than the one for the Yankees or the Mets—and determining whether the best cop softball player in the country is gay is not something to be taken lightly.

"I don't think you are wrong, Dar."

"I don't think I am either. But let me ask you something. Why do you give a fuck?"

"That's a very good question. But it's a completely different question than the one I'm addressing right now. By the way, you might want to consider brushing your teeth."

"That bad?"

"Yes."

As O'Hara fishes in her drawer for her toothbrush, Lauricella, the desk sergeant from downstairs, approaches her desk in the company of a tall black woman in her fifties.

"Paulette Williamson," he says, "this is Detective Darlene O'Hara. Ms. Williamson wants to report a possible homicide. She asked to talk to a woman."

Two potential hommies in one morning, thinks O'Hara. In Homicide Soft. What the hell?

"Please," says O'Hara and points to a chair.

"I'm a home health aide," says Williamson. "I take care of an elderly man on East Third named Gus Henderson. A couple weeks ago he caught the flu, and for a few days it looked bad." Williamson is about fifty, pretty and well-spoken with a trace of Caribbean lilt. She exudes the patience needed for her line of work.

"We thought he might pass, and I think he thought so too because one night he asked me to close the shades and light a candle. There was something he wanted to get off his chest." O'Hara doesn't have to look over at Jandorek to know he's rolling his eyes.

"Gus tells me that seventeen years ago he killed someone, stabbed him to death in a fight, then buried the body."

"He mention where?"

"He said it was under a tree."

"He say anything else about the victim—his name, age, physical description?"

"A big black guy," says Williamson, "only he didn't say it like that."

"He used the N-word?"

"Correct."

"Your client, how old is he?"

"Sixty-seven, but he seems older. He was a drug addict for a long time."

"How about mentally? Is he playing with a full deck?"

"He has good days and bad days."

Was this a good one or a bad one? thinks O'Hara. At this point, she's heard enough, but if Williamson could let Gus get it off his chest, O'Hara figures she can do the same for Williamson. It's that or talk about softball.

"I was going to ignore it, too," says Williamson pointedly. "Thank goodness, Gus got better, and yesterday on our way back from the doctor, he stopped the cab at Sixth Street and Avenue B. He made us both get out, so he could point into the garden at a spot by a tree where he 'buried the big black nigger.' Since it would take you people about five minutes to find out if it's true or not, I thought I should come forward."

As Williamson sits beside her, O'Hara types "Gus Henderson, 67" into the system, and in seconds calls up an endless rap sheet of low-level offenses. Talk about focus and endurance. As she scrolls the lowlights, she sees that his first arrest, for possession of narcotics, was at seventeen in Tompkins Square Park, and his last, for the same offense, barely two blocks away on Second Avenue and St. Mark's Place, was forty-five years later, at the age of sixty-two. In between were some hundred and fifty other arrests, the overwhelming majority in eight square blocks of the Lower East Side and East Village. If they gave a lifetime achievement award to junkies, thinks O'Hara, this guy would be tough to beat.

Then O'Hara turns to Williamson. "Paulette, I'm going to run your name too. Before I do, is there anything I ought to know about?"

Williamson stares hard at O'Hara, then wearily shakes her head, as if telling herself she should have known that this would be her thanks for walking fifteen blocks on her own time.

"At one point, Detective O'Hara, I had a drug problem myself. Eight years ago, I cashed two stolen checks. Since then I've been clean. A year ago I made full restitution, every last cent."

O'Hara runs her name, and what comes up corroborates her story. Her last arrest was in '99.

"Those checks totaled almost eleven thousand," says O'Hara, looking at the screen. "That's a lot of money. How'd you pay it back?"

"I worked," says Williamson, although it sounds more like "Fuck you." "Are you going to look into this?"

"I doubt it," says O'Hara, "but thanks for coming in."

Williamson gets up to leave, then hovers over her chair and looks down at O'Hara. "I had a problem, Detective. It's true. But at least I dealt with mine."

MCBETH MAKES IT through his first surgery, and two hours later he is wheeled back in for a second. When O'Hara and Jandorek step into St. Vincent's ER, it's almost 7:00 p.m. The office of the admissions nurse has a glass window overlooking the dreaded waiting room. Above it is a sign informing arrivals that patients will be treated based on the seriousness of their condition, not the order in which they arrived. Jandorek refers O'Hara to the second sign, which reads, "Don't Spread Germs! Please cover your mouth when you cough."

"You think these motherfuckers cover their mouths when they cough? Not a chance in hell."

They are informed that the nurse in charge of the intensive care unit is on her way down, but twenty minutes later she still hasn't arrived. Being in a hospital with Jandorek reminds O'Hara of the events that made him a legend among fellow detectives. A dozen years ago, Jandorek was working in homicide in Queens when he was appointed to be a union rep, a full-time position that supplants all your responsibilities as a detective. Careerwise, a stint with the union can work for or against you, but if you're already in homicide and essentially guaranteed to make grade, there's not much upside. Nevertheless, Jandorek took the job, and proved to be an effective rep, but one incident elevated him to the pantheon. About ten years ago a Brooklyn detective, after a long night of drinking, ran a stop sign and broadsided another car. Although the detective had only suffered minor injuries, a couple broken ribs, both passengers in the other car—a kindergarten teacher and her husband—were killed. Jandorek got the call in the middle of the night. He told the detective not to say a word before he got there, and more importantly, not to blow a Breathalyzer. "Tell them you're in too much pain," he said, "that you can't breathe." Both Jandorek and the DA arrived at the scene within minutes. The DA wanted the detective bad, which was understandable—he drove drunk and killed two human beings. But Jandorek refused to let the detective blow a test, said he'd got three cracked ribs, he could barely breathe, claimed it was unconscionable to even ask an officer in his condition to blow, that it was jeopardizing his life. Without the failed test, the only thing they got him for was running a stop sign, and a year later, the detective retired with a full pension. But brass was pissed, and now Jandorek is the only longtime homicide detective in the city who hasn't been promoted to first grade and probably never will be.

Finally the head ICU nurse, Evelyn Priestly, deigns to brief them. Like Williamson, she is a tall, handsome Caribbean, and compared to the chalky complexions of the men and women slumped nearby, her cheeks and forehead glisten.

"Detectives, I assume you're here to check on the condition of Ted McBeth," she says, "who was admitted to the hospital early this morning. I have good news, although from your point of view it might not be. The young man came through his second surgery extremely well and is no longer in danger."

"Can we talk to him?" asks O'Hara. "Even if he didn't succeed, someone did his best to kill him."

"He asked not to be disturbed."

"Maybe tomorrow, then."

"He told us he doesn't want to talk to the police while he's in the hospital. And I don't have to remind you about the HIPPA rules, which mandate that his wishes be respected."

"Thanks," says Jandorek. "We appreciate it, particularly the attitude."

Two blocks from St. Vincent's, Jandorek stops at a Rite Aid and comes out carrying an over-the-counter elixir called Sambucus. When he gets into the car, he rips off the packaging and takes a long swig directly from the bottle. "Immune syrup," he says, "made with elderberries and echinacea. My buddy in Brooklyn Homicide, he swears by this stuff."

CHAPTER 4

WHEN O'HARA PARKS her old Jetta in front of a hydrant on Sixth Street, there's less than ten minutes of light left in the summer sky. She drops her NYPD placard on the dash and walks across the street toward a tall gate that runs half the length of the block along the west side of Avenue B between Fifth and Sixth Streets. The entrance is locked, but there's enough light to read the sign—"The Sixth Street and Avenue B Community Garden"—and make out at the top the decorative pattern of children's hands stamped out of the green steel. At waist level, near where an iridescent yellow-green bike has been bolted to the gate, another decorative piece of metalwork bears the year the garden was founded, 1983. At least the garden existed when the old man claims to have turned it into a burial ground.

In the thickening dusk, O'Hara walks the perimeter and peers through the untrimmed bushes and evergreens that push out against the gate from inside, as if trying to escape. What little she can see of the garden is not nearly as lovely as the gate that surrounds it. Crowded into a quarter square block are scores of individual wood-framed plots the approximate dimensions of a queen-size bed. Everything else—over, around, and in between—is visual and vegetative chaos. The damp night is pungent with urban rot, the smell of everything growing, sprouting, and dying all at once. In the past couple weeks, a malty nausea-inducing odor has wafted over lower Manhattan, and she wonders if it started here.

The night is dropping quickly. O'Hara can't see with any detail more than twenty feet. In the dim space she can penetrate, the horticultural free-for-all suggests a Montessori cemetery. Stone walkways start promisingly, then stall or disappear, as if the pavers lost interest, suffered a falling-out, or stopped to smoke a joint, and stuck into the ground between two trees is a broken ladder leading nowhere—four rungs and then nothing. It's such a tangled mess, a person could wander in and never find their way out.

In the center of the garden, there's just enough light for O'Hara to make out some tables, an archway, and a bigger structure of some kind. For a second she thinks she spots a figure in the shadows. He or she resembles a garden gnome, but O' Hara can't tell if it's human or inanimate. When she rubs her eyes and squints, it's gone. To the north of the tables and in front of the larger structure is the willow tree that Williamson described. It is by far the largest and thickest tree in the garden. Backing up on the garden are four brick tenements, in which only a few windows look out on the garden. The only other windows with facing views are in a couple apartments in the higher floors of the tenements on the north side of Sixth Street.

By now O'Hara can barely see a thing, but that is also a kind of answer. After dropping Jandorek at the precinct, O'Hara stopped at the garden to see if she could rule out the old junkie's confession as implausible if not impossible, but she can't. On a summer night when the growth of the trees and bushes was as thick as this, a quiet gravedigger could easily plant a corpse under that tree without being seen. Seventeen years ago, when there wasn't a bar on every corner, he could have buried a dozen.

CHAPTER 5

THE ASSAULT ON McBeth may not have blossomed into a homicide, but it's still attempted murder, and O'Hara spends the next morning on follow-up. She returns to St. Vincent's, where she gets more pushback from Priestly, and a terse message from McBeth's old-school mom. Her son, she says, has no intention of cooperating with the police on this matter—i.e., he'll handle it himself—and since McBeth just came off parole, O'Hara doesn't have the leverage to change his mind. Jandorek spends the morning looking for MTA video of McBeth's assailant ducking into a subway after the attack, but also comes up empty, and at 1:15 he inquires if O'Hara is interested in lunch. "I was thinking of a nice piece of fish," he says.

Thanks to Jandorek, O'Hara's diet has undergone a massive upgrade since leaving the 7. Instead of a slice on a paper plate or a carton of Chinese, it's cod grilled in rice paper, penne arrabbiata, pork bellies, and roasted beets. As far as O'Hara can tell, it works like this. Jandorek goes to a restaurant, has a glass of wine at the bar, and gets to talking to the owner, a lonely, overworked immigrant who may have arrived from Macedonia or Belarus or Albania twenty years before, but feels like one foot is still in the boat. Because he works a hundred-hour week and has been fucking his tattooed waitress instead of his sturdy child bride, he has marital problems, and Jandorek gets to hear about them in considerable detail. By the time Jandorek pushes wearily from the bar, the Macedonian has a new American pal, and not just any native, but an NYPD detective, homicide no less, and for the first time in twenty years, he feels like he's rooted on solid ground. In return, Jandorek has another restaurant in his rotation, where his only cost is the tip.

Today, however, O'Hara declines. Instead of grilled halibut and a glass of rosé, she picks up a turkey sandwich and an Amstel at the bodega on Sixth and B, and carries them across the street to the entrance to the garden. The weather has turned seasonally hot and muggy, and in the unforgiving midday light, the garden looks even scruffier and more chaotic than it did at dusk. The gate is still locked, but a handful of aging East Village hippies, who are presumably key-holding members, loiter at picnic tables. Eventually O'Hara succeeds in making eye contact with a man with a gray ponytail.

"Whatsa matter, you can't read? It's only open to the public on weekends."

O'Hara doesn't want to identify herself as a cop. She smiles and holds up her sandwich and beer. "Is it going to kill you to let a woman step out of the sun?"

Reluctantly, the man rouses himself and lets her in. "Clean up when you're done," he says.

Just inside the gate is a foul koi pond she hadn't noticed the night before, and the blurry structure in the back can be identified as a crude stage. Scattered among the individual plots, which are more numerous than she realized, are watering cans, pieces of green hose, and ceramic shards, as well as chipped and discolored statuary in plastic and Styrofoam of birds, turtles, cherubs, and saints. Every few trees, a bird feeder dangles from a branch, or an obsolete flyer for a performance long past is taped to a trunk, and flapping from a pole stuck into a garden pot is the flag for the People's Republic of China.

Although the place is hardly soothing to the eye, it affords some shade, particularly the willow under which Henderson claimed to have deposited his adversary. If, as O'Hara determined the night before, the garden is a feasible spot to dispose a body, then the area around the tree is the most propitious spot to do it. Not only is it shrouded by the second layer of cover provided by the drapery of branches that extend like a long skirt nearly to the ground, but the ground beneath the tree is about the only vacant piece of dirt in the entire garden.

On a nearby bench, O'Hara unwraps her sandwich and cracks her beer. From her spot she can make out the small storefronts on the north side of Sixth Street. In the ground floors of neighboring tenements are a fortune-teller and a place offering Korean reflexology, the phony occult and the quasi therapeutic side by side. A sign on the curb in front of the Korean place proclaims THE BEST FOOT MASSAGE IN THE CITY, and O'Hara is not untempted. She daydreams about foot massages almost as often as men do about blow jobs.

Despite the heat, several gardeners are at work, including a woman in her mid-twenties who tends to the bed closest to the willow. She is as lovely as she is tall, but her self-consciousness suggests she is only aware of her height. O'Hara polishes off her beer, and steps out from under the willow.

"Do you mind if I take a look?" asks O'Hara.

"Of course not. I love showing off my garden," replies the girl. "Would you like a tour?"

"Please."

Stepping closer, O'Hara is startled by the variety of produce cultivated in such a circumscribed space, and despite her education in nouvelle from Jandorek, a lot of it is new to her. "This is called jalapeño heaven," says the woman, pointing at a familiar jalapeño shape covered with tiny striations. "*Mucho caliente*. And this," referring to a pepper as big and solid as an apple, "is an orange bell, a hybrid between a red and a yellow pepper. The next section is devoted to salad greens. My favorite is this guy over here with a stippling of red over a green background, called 'Speckled Trout Back.' And here are my tomatoes, basil, and baby eggplant." The color of the eggplant is dazzling, like a deep bruise.

"How long have you had the garden?" asks O'Hara.

"Forever. My father kept it originally. I took it over when I was eight or nine."

"You got your green thumb from your dad?"

"I hope not. He's terrible at growing things. He's only good at making them."

"By the way, I'm Darlene O'Hara."

"Christina Malmströmer," says the girl with an apologetic smile, as if she's as encumbered by her name as by her height.

CHAPTER 6

HENDERSON'S PLACE ON East Third is a five-minute stroll from the garden. At the door of his basement apartment, O'Hara is greeted by a blast of ungodly heat and a nose full of spices, presumably Caribbean. When she left Riverdale the temperature was already approaching eighty. Now it's considerably warmer, and for some reason, despite the lack of AC, the large window looking up at the street is closed. But the coup de grâce is that furry aroma, and when O'Hara looks toward the kitchen, she sees the flames of the front burner licking the black bottom of a cast-iron pot. Henderson, who sits on a folding beach chair and stares at the *Post* through black plastic glasses, is dressed for the weather, if nothing else. He wears a wifebeater and boxers, his pale, acutely bowed legs ending in black tube socks and lace-up brogans. At least, thinks O'Hara gratefully, his unit is tucked out of sight. His jet-black hair notwithstanding, Henderson is as decrepit a sexagenarian as she has seen this side of the Rolling Stones. He looks more like eighty, but after forty-five years of heroin addiction, that only seems fair.

"Gus, my name is Darlene O'Hara. I'm a detective with NYPD."

"Bully for you."

"Paulette came and talked to me the other day."

"Paulette?"

"Gus, I'm Paulette," says Williamson, who sits three feet away.

Gus smiles at O'Hara. "They send some very nice girls," he says. "Of course I got to watch them like a hawk, or they'd rob me blind. Particularly the dark ones." Then in a whisper, "I used to have over twenty cars, you know."

"All gone?" asks O'Hara.

Gus nods sadly. "Every one."

"You don't think Paulette took them?"

"She has three Caddies hidden in her snatch." A three-car snatch, thinks O'Hara, like a McMansion. "You hungry?" asks Henderson. "We got a nice stew on."

"I just ate, Gus, thanks. You mind if I sit?"

"Knock yourself out."

"Gus, Paulette told me you wanted to talk about something that happened a long time ago in the garden around the corner."

"What good would talking do?"

"Talking can help. Get it off your chest, you feel a whole lot better."

"I feel fine now."

"You told Paulette you stabbed a man in a fight, and a couple days ago pointed out the spot where you buried him under a big tree."

"Paulette's a nice girl, but I don't know what you're talking about."

Sitting in Henderson's airless apartment, with its murky alternative realities and noxious odors, not all of which can be laid on the simmering pot, O'Hara feels less like a detective than a social worker trying to assess a client's mental competence. A lot of Gus's brain seems to be history, but there's a fair amount left, along with some sly wit. Although he denies it now, Paulette claims he talked about the killing on two different occasions a couple weeks apart. Maybe his current fogginess has nothing to do with Alzheimer's and everything to do with the fact that O'Hara is a homicide detective, in which case his behavior is the opposite of senility. O'Hara feels like she's jumped down a rabbit hole.

"Gus, okay if I get myself a glass of water?"

"Knock yourself out." O'Hara retreats to the sink, washes out a glass, and fills it from the tap. She can feel the heat of the pot on her arm, but is no more tempted to look inside it than she would be to peer into the abyss. O'Hara brings the water back to her seat and tries again.

"Nice place, Gus. How long you had it?"

"Thirty years. Inherited the lease from my mom. You want to know what I pay?"

"Probably not."

"Seventy-eight dollars a month." Maybe that's what Paulette is after, thinks O'Hara, the cheapest apartment in Manhattan.

"The guy upstairs pays twenty-five hundred."

"Gus, you telling me you don't remember your fight with a large black man in the garden? Paulette said you two had quite a brawl. He was a lot bigger than you, and you stabbed him."

"Paulette?"

O'Hara thinks about what happened at Rocco's two nights before and how often the smaller man pulls the knife. "What you reading about, Gus?" she asks, referring to the *Post.*

"Our asshole president."

"You think he's worse than his father?"

"All I know is he doesn't look like he does in the movies."

"Who do you think is president, Gus?"

"Who do I think is president? I know who the president of this country is. Arnold. With the big muscles and the accent."

I've heard enough of this crap, thinks O'Hara. Arnold Schwarzenegger. Big Arnold. Schwartze Nigger. The motherfucker thinks he killed the Terminator.

As O'Hara takes a last sip and prepares to leave, Williamson points at the colorful cigar box on the end table by Gus's chair. "Pretty, isn't it?" she says.

"I get them for free from a place on University," says Gus, "before they throw them out. Go ahead, knock yourself out." In fact, the box is lovely—

white with elaborate green trim, built by a brand called Montesino from the Dominican Republic. O'Hara opens it and finds Henderson's meds— Flomax, Lipitor, and two other prescriptions, Aricept and Namenda, which O'Hara is lucky enough not to have sat through a commercial for. There's also loose change, mostly American, but some foreign coins too, an old tie clasp and a couple subway tokens. Facedown in the corner is a photograph, and O'Hara can tell from the film that it was taken on a Polaroid. O'Hara flips it over. It's a picture of a tree. Then she realizes it's the willow in the garden.

"Hey, Gus, this is a beautiful picture."

"You act surprised."

"You mind if I take it?"

"I guess not. Why?"

"It's so pretty."

"Knock yourself out, then."

"Do you know where this tree is growing?"

"Of course," says Gus.

"Where?"

Henderson responds with a look of anguish.

"What's the matter, Gus?"

"I forgot something."

"What?"

"To go to the bathroom."

CHAPTER 7

COMPARED TO GUS'S apartment, the squad room is an oasis of comfort and calm. O'Hara slips the photograph from her bag and drops it on her desk. Based on the tree's foliage and the plants and flowers visible in the background, the picture was taken in the summer, but how many summers ago is impossible to know.

"It was taken with a Polaroid Swinger," says Jandorek over her shoulder. "My uncle gave me one for my twelfth birthday. In the sixties, they were cool and cost about twenty bucks. Now guys with tats and hats collect them in Williamsburg."

"I found it in a cigar box at Henderson's place," says O'Hara, "right before he pissed himself. The whole visit was a preview of what we have to look forward to in the golden years, a trailer of coming attractions. Kind of interesting, though, that Henderson has a picture of the tree. And if this camera was around seventeen years ago, it fits the time frame."

"It was around way before that," says Jandorek. "Not that it matters."

"Why not?"

"Because it's a complete waste of time. No way in hell Kelso approves homicide dollars for a backhoe because a junkie with Alzheimer's told his health aide he killed a black guy. Please. And by the way, you missed a nice piece of fish—cod, roasted, over heirloom tomatoes."

Jandorek is right, of course, but Gus and Paulette and the frigging willow have taken root in her brain. So has that quagmire of a garden. And now three distinct bits support the possibility that a body is under the tree: Henderson's original candlelit confession when he thought the end was near; his pointing at the spot two weeks later when he was better; and this photo found among a handful of meds and old keepsakes.

O'Hara Googles "Polaroid Swinger," and discovers that Jandorek got it pretty much exactly right, as usual. If the guy cared half as much about solving homicides as the location of his next piece of fish, he could shame Sherlock Holmes. The cameras were made from 1965 to 1970, went for $19.95, and became one of the best-selling cameras of all time. According to Wikipedia, "The Swinger was especially successful with the youth market due to its low price, stylish appearance, and catchy 'Meet the Swinger' jingle sung by Barry Manilow in a television advertisement featuring a young Ali MacGraw."

While the computer is on, O'Hara decides to take another look at Henderson's rap sheet and marvels again at his stamina. Here was a man who found his vocation early and never wavered. He did what he wanted as long as he could, and then stopped, and in her visit, O'Hara didn't detect a trace of self-pity or regret. Between his first arrest in '57 and his last in '02, is an endless roll call of picayune offenses—panhandling, loitering, turnstile jumping, shoplifting, public intoxication, public urination—tell me about it, thinks O'Hara—possession of stolen property, possession of burglary tools. And then there's the shit that's so stupid it's almost inspired, like when he got arrested twenty years ago, trying to pawn three full-length furs on Canal Street in the middle of July.

In his twenties, thirties, and forties, Henderson was like a slugger a manager could pencil in for thirty homers every year, only in his case it was thirty arrests. His consistency was so remarkable that what catches her attention is the three-year gap in his résumé between 1988 and 1991.

A little more research, and she learns the reason. He spent twenty-eight of those thirty-six months in Attica, his first and only real stretch of jail time, for a mugging in Washington Square, which got elevated to armed robbery because either he or his accomplice wielded a screwdriver.

When the shift ends at four, Jandorek is out the door, O'Hara pulls a Red Bull out of her drawer and continues to pore over the junkie rap sheet like a railbird studies a racing form, and if the fact that she has been known to start her day with a grapefruit juice and vodka makes her fascination with Henderson's epic addiction more than strictly professional, so be it. She is particularly intrigued by the fact that he was able to stay clean for six months after his release from jail, that he showed the discipline to sit tight and wait out his probation, not out of a desire to go straight but because he knew if he violated and got sent back, the beautiful affair between him and dope could be over. After his release from jail in the middle of 1990, it took almost a year for the arrests to start again, and from that point on, he was more careful, the arrests were fewer, and he never truly put his addiction at risk.

AT 7:30, O'HARA takes a short walk to Second Avenue and picks up some beef and broccoli from the place on Twenty-Second. She didn't think she could miss bad Chinese, but she does. Grease, sugar, and MSG has never tasted this good. She devours the carton's contents at her desk, and as she lingers over the last dripping stalk of broccoli, the date of Henderson's release from Attica catches her eye—August 15, 1990. That is seventeen years ago, almost to the day, and Henderson told Williamson he killed someone seventeen years ago.

O'Hara is onto something. There are no coincidences in homicide. If his confession was accurate, and O'Hara is becoming increasingly convinced it was, than he killed someone right after he got out. Maybe, thinks O'Hara, the killing stemmed from something that happened inside. O'Hara logs into a separate database for the Department of Corrections to see what she can learn about how Gus did his time. As it turns out, he did it very well. There are no red flags, no disciplinary actions, no evidence of a dispute. Henderson sat himself down and did his little stint like an adult. Even Kelso would have been impressed. He was such a good inmate, they let him out a couple months early.

With nothing coming out of his prison experience, O'Hara refocuses on Henderson's time on the streets and scrolls again through the breakdown of offenses and arrests. She notices that in many of his shenanigans, Henderson was operating in concert with a hapless accomplice and soul mate named Charles Faulk. From 1983 to 1988, Henderson and Faulk were taken away in handcuffs nineteen times, a streak that ended with the mugging that sent Henderson to jail.

Henderson told Williamson that seventeen years ago, he'd killed a large black man. Faulk's description: "African American, six-four, three hundred twenty pounds."

Faulk is large and black. But is he dead? Now O'Hara runs Faulk's name. Faulk's rap is similar and often identical to Henderson's. The only substantial difference is that Faulk's career in petty crime ended ten years before age slowed Henderson. His last arrest for possession or anything else was on August 11, 1990, four days before Henderson got out of jail. O'Hara takes a deep breath and reminds herself that just because Faulk hasn't been arrested for seventeen years, that doesn't mean he's dead. Perhaps he finally saw the folly of his ways, accepted Jesus as his personal savior, and is running a small ministry for wayward youth in Cheyenne, Wyoming. Or maybe he's spent the last seventeen years rotting under a willow in the East Village.

O'Hara runs Faulk through Missing Persons and finds that on November 13, 1990, his mother, Marie Scott of Monroe, South Carolina, filed a missing person report for her son and the case is still open. Again, O'Hara tells herself to chill. The missing person file could be out of date. It's been seventeen years; maybe Faulk has resurfaced. She Googles "Marie Scott, mother of Charles Faulk, Monroe, South Carolina." She gets an address and phone number, and makes the call. A woman answers.

"Mrs. Scott?"

"Speaking."

"My name is Darlene O'Hara. I'm a detective for the NYPD. I'm very sorry to trouble you about this matter. I saw that you reported your son missing in 1990. Has your son been found since then, or was there any progress in the attempt to find him?"

"What do you think?" asks Scott. "A junkie disappears, who's going to care? You're with NYPD, you know that better than me. For a couple years, I made calls to a detective in the Ninth Precinct, but eventually I gave up after I heard my son had jumped off the Staten Island Ferry. Charles had a history of mental problems and depression, and he'd tried to kill himself once before. So it could be true."

"May I ask who told you your son had committed suicide?"

"An old friend of his."

"You don't remember his name by any chance?"

"Gus Henderson. My son was gay, and I always assumed he and Charlie were lovers. Why this sudden interest in my son after all these years?"

"I'm a homicide detective, Mrs. Scott. I was just given a file on a cold case of someone who may have been associated with your son. I was hoping your son had been found and I could talk to him."

"Really? Well, he wasn't, because no one ever looked for him. Good night, Detective," says Scott and hangs up.

A couple hours ago, all O'Hara had was the alleged confession of a demented ex-junkie. Now she has the body to go with it, a body that fits the description and disappeared at the right time. To get Kelso to rent a backhoe, she still needs one more piece, a persuasive reason for Henderson to turn on his old partner: she needs a motive. Minutes later, after opening both men's files side by side on her screen, she finds it. Five weeks after Faulk and Henderson were arrested for the mugging in Washington Square, Faulk was arrested again for public intoxication. In other words, while Henderson did twenty-four months, Faulk didn't do a minute. O'Hara already knows why, but to be sure she verifies it in the transcripts from *The State of New York versus Gus Henderson*. Listed first among the witnesses for the prosecution is Charles Faulk. Henderson's old running mate flipped, turned state's witness, and ratted him out. That's all very understandable and happens every day, but sometimes payback is a bitch, in which case it's probably no coincidence that four days after Henderson is released from jail, Charles Faulk commits his last crime and, sometime very soon thereafter, takes his last breath. Now O'Hara has a confession, a missing body, and a motive, not to mention a really nice picture of a willow tree. A pretty good day's work in Homicide Soft. It still might not be enough for Kelso, but she doesn't have time to worry about that now.

CHAPTER 8

AN HOUR AFTER O'Hara leaves her desk, the Flat Screens storm the stage of the second-floor ballroom of the Ukrainian Center on Second Avenue. If all goes according to script, rock historians and MTV specials will note ad nauseam that the band's maiden performance was witnessed by only seventeen people, and that four of them, including the lead singer's mother, were current or former detectives from the Seventh Precinct. With its tiny and barely elevated stage, rimmed by plastic plants, and tables and chairs pushed against the side wall, the space evokes the best and worst of junior high, a time when it still seemed like everyone was in the same leaky boat. The band got the show through the drummer's mother who works at the center three days a week. Axl wears a white button-down shirt, lederhosen spray-painted orange, and flip-flops. He grabs the mike and growls a cappella:

Let's get the fuck out of Dodge!
Let's get the fuck out of Dodge!
Let's get the fuck out of Dodge!

Then he adds an elegant last line, whose logic is unassailable.

Because Dodge . . .
Is the place . . .
We want to get the fuck . . . out of!

As the crowd, nonplussed, watches in silence. O'Hara wonders if it's her destiny to spend both her days and nights with the mentally challenged. She also wonders if it's possible, technically speaking, to empty an already empty room. Axl takes a gulp of air, nuzzles the mike with his beard, and launches into the tuneless ditty again. By the second "Let's get the fuck out of Dodge!" three kids and two bulky detectives have taken up the chant, and by the time Axl sings again:

Because Dodge . . .
Is the place . . .
We want to get the fuck . . .
. . . out offfff!

The whole audience, seventeen strong, has signed on for the trip.

With that last clumsy addendum still hanging in the air, the Ukrainian American drummer hurls himself at his kit, the guitarists of unknown ancestry pile on, and a rock 'n' roll riot breaks out.

The sound is so ragged and Axl expectorates the words in such a rush, O'Hara can only make out a line or two here and there before everything is buried beneath the sonic rubble. Enunciation aside, Axl's voice is strong and full of feeling, equal parts outrage and dark comedy. And the songs keep her off balance, the phrases either running longer than she thinks they will or abruptly pulling up short, as Axl clings to the mike stand like a life raft, gasps for breath, and rants on.

She could be wrong, but in the second song, she thinks she hears:

Young lady, if you think one roast chicken
Is going to make up for doing my best friend on my floor
You've got a lot to learn.
That's going to take three chickens
And a side of brussel sprouts . . . beeatch.

The third song begins:

I have a friend who says she just wants to be happy.
Good luck with that, baby girl.

FIVE SONGS AND nineteen minutes later the show ends much too quickly, although thankfully without a reprise of "Let's Get the Fuck Out of Dodge." As the small but ebullient crowd pushes up against the stage, O'Hara exchanges hugs with Krekorian, Nieves, and Flannery.

"I'll say one thing," says her old partner K. "The boy has sack."

"A two-hundred-pound leprechaun in German leather," says Flannery. "It works for me. Always has."

O'Hara, herself, is overwhelmed. When did Axl, who as a fourteen-year-old was so traumatized by his first breakup she had to stage an intervention/road trip to the Grand Canyon, acquire the sack, as K put it, to live so large and loud? And when did he acquire the experience to write those lyrics? And how did all this happen without her noticing any of it?

O'Hara had naively planned to take her son out for a celebratory drink, but when she sees the crush of friends, including one very pretty girl who may or may not know how to baste a bird, O'Hara realizes that Axl is not going to be celebrating his band's first show with moms. Lucky to get a five-second audience, she pulls his ear within whispering distance and cuts to the chase.

"Not for nothing, Axl, but that was friggin' amazing."

"Thanks, Darlene."

O'Hara's former colleagues have to head to back to New City, Long Beach, and Valley Stream, but O'Hara is too amped for Riverdale. Besides, there's still work to be done, and after depositing three twenties in the tip jar, O'Hara heads for the stairs. At 11:00 on a summer Thursday, Second Avenue is a zoo. O'Hara pushes to the curb and turns around to snap a retinal image of the building that housed what will always be Axl's first New York show. Till now, it had never quite registered how Ukrainian this block is, with Veselka on the corner, and next to it the Ukrainian National Home, a shockingly ugly piece of architecture that looks as if it was airlifted from a midsize Soviet city. O'Hara had walked by the Ukrainian Center a hundred times without noticing, built into the facade, the gold bust of a man who, she assumes, is the Ukrainian George Washington.

Half a block south, O'Hara turns right onto St. Mark's. O'Hara is just old enough to remember a time when St. Mark's still packed a little transgressive thrill. Now it's low-end tourist traps—head shops, tattoo parlors, and T-shirt stalls—and dozens of small restaurants, mostly Japanese. All that's left from the bad old days of Joey and Dee Dee and Sid and Nancy are the Gem Spa at one end, the Continental at the other, and the Grassroots Tavern in between, and that's where O'Hara makes her first stop.

She takes her Maker's Mark to a small table in back, across from a pair of dartboards, raises her glass in a silent toast, and repeats to herself what she whispered in her son's ear—*Not for nothing, Axl, but that was friggin' amazing.* Over the years Grassroots has lost some of its roué charm, but makes up for it with the strongest air-conditioning below Fourteenth Street, and O'Hara wonders if the chilly draft is strong enough to affect the flight of a dart, not that she normally gives a flying fuck about darts. Then she glances over her shoulder, and when she sees that the bartender is distracted, she pulls a paper rectangle from her bag, peels off the back, and slaps it to the wall between the two boards. Bull's-eye.

Until someone is sufficiently motivated to scrape it off, every dart thrower who lets his concentration waver will come eye-to-eye with the Flat Screens. So begins a brisk hate-to-drink-and-slap-a-band-sticker-

on-your-ass-and-run pub blitz that will include successful stops at half a
dozen iconic East Village dives. In the next hour and a half, the women's
bathrooms at Holiday Lounge, the International, Lakeside, 7B, and Mani-
toba's are all installed with Flat Screens. Maybe it's guerrilla marketing,
probably it's vandalism, but without question the working conditions are
foul enough to warrant a medal and a tetanus shot.

Her last stop is Three of Cups. The basement bar below First Avenue
represents a unique challenge to a proud mother, since it already boasts
the highest concentration of band stickers in the city. The low ceiling is
plastered five, six, seven deep. Fortunately, O'Hara has become something
of a regular over the past couple years, and is able to guilt the bartender
into surrendering the best media placement in the neighborhood—the
chrome bill drawer on the old cash register, which faces out from the back
wall, among the vodkas and whiskeys. Now every sale is a ringing, open-
and-shut endorsement of New York's next great band.

After five brown drinks in two hours, O'Hara is finally coming down
off the rush of the Flat Screens' show. For the first time since she's left
the squad room, her attention drifts back to her homicide, and the likeli-
hood that Henderson's treacherous old partner Charlie Faulk is buried in
a shallow grave a couple blocks away. Persuading Kelso to let her dig him
up is not going to be easy, but she can worry about that tomorrow, and
with one last look at her handiwork on the register, she pushes from the
bar. Time, she thinks, to get the fuck out of Dodge.

CHAPTER 9

"**ANY CHANCE YOU** and I could have an adult conversation?" asks O'Hara.

"I don't see why not," says Kelso, his face registering surprise as he sits up in his chair. "As far as I know, it's still legal."

"Right now," says O'Hara, "there are eleven names on the board, and ten have lines through them. The eleventh, the guy who forgot how to chew, is never going to close. He's going to be up there till the ball drops on Times Square. Every time I see his name, it makes me sick."

"Really? I thought I was the only one who felt that way."

"Right here," says O'Hara, pointing at a spot in the middle of her chest, "Like acid reflux. Can I borrow your calculator?"

When O'Hara says the C-word, something changes in Kelso's expression. For a second, O'Hara can't interpret it. Then she realizes Kelso is listening to her. For the first time since O'Hara got to homicide, Kelso is actually paying attention to what she has to say, and when she bends over the little device and starts jabbing at it with a fingertip, he's riveted.

"Right now we're ten out of eleven," says O'Hara, "a closure rate of point-nine-oh-nine-oh-nine-oh-nine. That's barely over ninety percent. For a precinct with a hundred hommies a year that would be just dandy, but for Manhattan Soft, that's not going to get it done. Brass expects better—you've spoiled them, Lieutenant—and with our caseload, you can hardly blame them. My pal Torres says Manhattan North is over eighty-eight percent, and a Colombian narco is about to plead to those execution-style slayings in Washington Heights, which would take eight homicides off the board just like that. With a little luck, they could end the year with a better closure rate than us. With ten times the caseload."

"What are you suggesting?"

"A couple weeks ago a home health aide came to the precinct. She told me that the guy she's taking care of, who thought he was about to croak, made her pull the shades and light a candle, then confessed to a murder. Seventeen years ago, he says, he stabbed a big black guy to death and buried him in the garden on Sixth and B."

"That overgrown tangle of weeds?"

"So I look up the perp's rap sheet. I see that twenty years ago he and his best buddy, Charles Faulk, African American, six-four, three-twenty, got nabbed for mugging somebody in Washington Square. Faulk flips, and Henderson, my perp, does three years in Attica. When does he get out of jail? In 1990—seventeen years ago—and a couple weeks later Faulk disappears. His mother files a missing person report, and he hasn't been seen since. It's a ridiculous case—the perp has Alzheimer's, thinks Schwarzenegger is president, and would never go to trial—but I got a confession, a motive, a body, and the place where it's buried. All I got to do is dig him up. Now look at this."

O'Hara bends over the calculator again, jabs it a couple times, and spins it so the screen faces Kelso. "Point-nine-one-six," she says. "Which rounds up to ninety-two percent. We go from barely over ninety to well over ninety percent. And one more thing, I just got off the phone with Lucas Bradley, the forensic anthropologist they hired after 9/11. He says he doesn't need a backhoe or any other heavy machinery. Just an assistant, a shovel, and five hours."

O'Hara is spouting nonsense, but it's Kelso's favorite variety of nonsense.

"You got six hours," he says. "But that's it, because it's on our dime. So don't come running back to me asking for even five minutes more. And one other thing."

"What's that, Lieutenant?"

"Thanks, Darlene. For caring."

CHAPTER 10

THE NEXT MORNING at 6:00, Kelso, O'Hara, and Jandorek stand beneath the willow in the community garden at Sixth Street and Avenue B as Lucas Bradley makes his first incision in the downtown dirt. To thwart rubberneckers, an orange tarp went up around the tree overnight, along with a new padlock on the gate and notification that the garden will be closed for forty-eight hours so Con Edison can repair a gas leak. To give the cover a ring of truth and further impede the view, half a dozen Con Ed trucks are parked along the perimeter. The thirty-four-year-old Bradley, who has lank brown hair and the kind of open boyish face rarely seen on a native New Yorker, was hired to oversee the sifting and identifying of remains at the base of the World Trade Center towers. He made such a good impression, he was appointed the city's first full-time forensic anthropologist. O'Hara heard that he got his PhD from a department at the University of Tennessee known as the Body Farm, because of a wooded plot strewn with stiffs where students can observe them in various states of rot. To O'Hara, he looks like a kid in a sandbox, particularly when he unzips his nylon backpack and removes a Teenage Ninja lunch pail. It would drive O'Hara crazy to work with strangers looking over her shoulder, but Brad-

ley seems to appreciate an audience. As he strips away the topmost layer
of soil, he points at the hardy weeds around the base of the tree.

"Normally, you wouldn't have this much grass or weeds near the base
of a tree, but sometimes you see opportunistic growth above a grave site,"
he says. "There's no better fertilizer than a juicy corpse."

With the help of an intern, Bradley exposes an area of dirt about the
size of a picnic blanket. The outer ring of dirt is darker than the area
inside it, and according to Bradley that's another propitious sign. "When
you dig a hole and refill it, the dirt from various levels get mixed together.
Overall that makes it lighter." The intern sets aside the loose sections of
sod. Bradley opens his juvenile lunchbox and extracts a handful of plastic
chopsticks. He sticks them into the dirt about sixteen inches apart around
the border of the possible grave.

"I don't think I'll be going Chinois for a while," whispers Jandorek to
O'Hara.

"You don't eat it anyway," says O'Hara. An Asian guy would kill himself before he shared his marital woes with Jandorek.

Using the trowel like a shovel, Bradley begins to dig, and dumps
each small scoop into a basket covered by a fine-mesh screen. It's slow,
tedious work, even more so for the gallery of detectives, like watching a
man empty a bathtub with a spoon. The temperature is rising quickly, and
because of the tarp, there's no breeze. Kelso in particular grows restless.

"Any chance we could goose this up a little?"

"Excavating is a destructive process," says Bradley without turning.
"You only have one chance to do it right."

Bradley works briskly but carefully, the sweat stain on his shirt
expanding at about the same rate as the hole. It's at least half an hour
before he comes into contact with anything other than dirt, but when he
does, the sound is so sharp, everyone but Bradley jumps. "We got a body,"
says Bradley. "Naked, topless, headless. Petite."

Bradley twists on his knees and extends his arm. Lying tits up on the
trowel is a cigarette lighter in the shape of a female torso.

In the next hour, Bradley and the mesh catch one stray item after another—an old subway token like the ones O'Hara saw in Henderson's cigar box, a couple foreign coins, a marble, a folded-up $20 bill, a tiny plastic bag of weed, and then a couple larger objects: a CD, a Swiss Army knife, and a pint of whiskey. As they're found, the intern deposits them in a plastic container, and in one of the many lulls O'Hara wanders over for a closer look. They are such a motley assortment, and in an effort to make some sense of them and their possible connection, O'Hara pulls out her notebook and lists everything Bradley has unearthed so far: "1 cigarette lighter, 1 subway token, 2 coins—5 pesos, 25 yen—1 roach clip, 1 marble, $20 bill, pint of Ballantine's, 1 Swiss Army knife, 1 synthetic pearl, 1 CD, 1 small bag of weed."

Of the objects in the Tupperware, the pint of Ballantine's gets O'Hara's attention first, not because it's good and alcoholic, but because it's unopened. Why would someone throw away a brand-new bottle? That it's unopened differentiates it from the rest of the items, which seem like random urban debris accumulated over the years. But when she scrutinizes the others more closely, she notices that the tiny plastic bag of pot is also sealed. As O'Hara pores over the collection as best she can through the plastic lid, the intern adds another New York artifact—a ticket stub from Sunshine Cinema for a movie called the *The Lives of Others* dated 6/11/07. The date surprises O'Hara. That's less than three months ago, and when she combines it with the pristine condition of the pint and some of the other items, it doesn't jibe with a seventeen-year-old homicide. Then O'Hara recalls Bradley's comment about "opportunistic growth." There may be nothing quite like human fertilizer, but would it still be pushing up daisies after seventeen years? While the intern is nearby, O'Hara asks her to flip over the CD. O'Hara sees that it's Coldplay, something called *X&Y*, which according to the label came out in 2005, but O'Hara is distracted from her calculations about dates and timing by word from Bradley of another find.

"This is soft," says Bradley almost to himself. Till now, everything Bradley has found has been hard and quite small.

After Bradley climbs out of the grave, O'Hara sees that the entire length and width of the hole has been taken down more than two feet. Bradley, who is drenched in sweat, takes a long pull from a bottle of water, then goes back to his lunchbox and removes a brush and a single chopstick, this time a wooden one. Back in the hole, Bradley uses both to pick and whisk away the dirt from the soft thing he has found.

"It's some kind of fabric," he says, and a couple minutes later, "It's the bill."

He backs away to give the lieutenant and two detectives an unobstructed view. O'Hara can see that he's referring to the bill of a cap, the leading edge of it, which is pointing straight at the sky. In the next ten minutes the entire navy blue lid is revealed, then the crown, with the "NY" of the New York Yankees. The style of the hat is quite current; it's certainly not a seventeen-year-old cap. Apparently Kelso has noticed that too, because she can feel his glare on the back of her neck. But neither has long to concentrate on the other. Less than a minute later, Bradley sits back on his heels and announces, "We've got remains."

CHAPTER 11

THE YANKEES CAP rests on a yellow-brown skull. Where there were eyes are two square holes, and centered beneath them, where the nose had been, is a triangle. Between the upper and lower jaws, small teeth are visible. It's been a while since O'Hara scrutinized the human skull, and is surprised by the rounded smoothness of the shapes, which are far more elegant without the lumpy draping of skin and tissue. O'Hara feels as if even without eyes, the skull is staring at her, and despite the ghoulishness of the scene, something in the cast of the jaw suggests a smile. Kelso, however, is far from smiling. His agitation is so palpable that O'Hara resists the urge to turn and face him.

"It's not a black man, is it, Bradley?" says Kelso.

"No."

"You can tell by the opening for the nose, can't you?"

"If it was an African American, the aperture would be bigger."

"And it's not a large man, either," says Kelso.

"No," says Bradley, "it doesn't appear to be."

Working steadily from the cap down, Bradley uncovers a striped button-down dress shirt. If there were any possibility that these are the remains of what had once been a six-four, 320-pound man, it's gone by the time Bradley uncovers his jeans. From the narrow shoulders and waist, it's clear that the clothing covers the remains of a child, a small, slight one. When Bradley reaches the knees of the pants, Kelso can't contain himself. "It's not the motherfucker," he mutters. "It's not the mother-fucker. It's not the goddamn fucking motherfucker."

O'Hara has sold him a bill of goods. Not one thing she promised has come to pass. Instead of a black male, it's a white child. Instead of a victim named Charlie Faulk to whose murder another man has already confessed, O'Hara has dropped a pile of unidentified bones on his desk. And instead of a name going up on the board with a line already drawn through the middle of it and a closure rate of 0.916, O'Hara has added a John Doe, and nothing else. He watches morosely as Bradley reaches the bottom of the pants legs and whisks the dirt from a tiny pair of Converse high-tops.

CHAPTER 12

THE MEDICAL EXAMINER'S office is in a building on First and Thirtieth as ugly as the Ukrainian National Home. The decomp morgue is located in the most ventilated corner of the basement. Bradley wheels in the body, still enclosed in the orange bag in which it was transported from the garden, and parks it next to an archaic X-ray machine. It's 1:00 a.m., and Bradley moves in the deliberate manner of someone who has been awake too long. With the discovery of a recently buried white child instead of a long-deceased black junkie, all bets are off, and the six-hour time limit waived. Bradley and his assistant were still sifting, measuring, and photographing long into the night, and although Kelso and Jandorek headed back to the precinct, O'Hara stayed in the garden until the work was done, then followed the body up First Avenue to the ME's office. Bradley loads a twenty-four-by-eighteen-inch cartridge and slides the tray under one end of the bag. Then he aligns the nose of the X-ray machine and takes the first shot. "When I got here," says Bradley, "there was talk of finally getting a state-of-the-art machine. As you might guess, that conversation didn't go anywhere."

Bradley works his way down the length of the body bag, the previous image developing while the next is being taken. When he's done, the four overlapping shots, laid out on the counter, yield a composite view of the full skeleton. For the next couple hours, Bradley separates clothing and remains. He unbuttons the dress shirt and finds a black T-shirt, "The Germs" written across it in red letters. From the armholes of both shirts, Bradley pulls out the delicate bones of the fingers, hands, and arms. From the bottom and top he slides the spine, ribs, chest, and shoulders. Then he performs the same drill with the lower half, removing the bones of the feet, legs, and pelvis from the victim's sneakers and the legs and waist of his jeans, a process made slightly simpler by the fact that the victim is not wearing underwear. When he's done, the clothes are lying on one high-bordered metal tray, the bones on another beside it. To make sure the bones are all accounted for, Bradley reassembles them like a jigsaw in proper anatomical order. "An adult has fewer bones than a child," says Bradley, "because over time, bones fuse, particularly in the hands." When he's finished, the skeleton lies naked on the table, as it lay clothed in the grave.

Bradley will return to the skeleton later, but now directs his attention to the clothes. Hovering over them, he takes them in as a group. Then, although the evidence department will perform the same task in greater detail, he moves from one garment to the next, examining it inside and out; assessing its condition; looking for signs of blood, hair, or remains; and checking the contents of the pockets. In a back pocket of the jeans he finds a sodden clump of paper so stuck together that he decides to leave it where it is for evidence to tease apart, and caught in the laces of the sneakers he finds several strands of light blond, nearly white hair. "A towhead," says Bradley, showing a strand to O'Hara before sealing the hair in a separate plastic bag.

Finally he gathers each article of clothing, holds it about a foot over the table, turns it over, opens it up, and gingerly shakes it to see if anything has been caught in the fabric. When he shakes out the black tee, the early morning silence is punctured by a metallic ping, as startling as when his trowel hit the lighter. A quick search and Bradley holds a small copper bullet between his latex-covered thumb and forefinger.

"Twenty-two-caliber," he says, "the kind my grandfather and I used to shoot beer cans and bottles, as well as various critters who made the mistake of treating themselves to his vegetables. Twenty-twos aren't much good for killing anything much bigger than a rabbit, and this is a lot smaller than the urban ammo that gets pulled out of bodies here. You got to be pretty unlucky to be killed by a twenty-two, but I guess we've already established that this kid wasn't lucky."

Having found the bullet, Bradley takes a second, more focused look at the two shirts. He searches for holes and blood, but he finds neither. Then he walks to the counter where the X-rays are lined up. And after scanning the ghostly images for several minutes, points out a dark spot in the left shoulder blade or scapula. "Until the last of the flesh decomposed, the bullet was lodged in here. Eventually, it fell out into the shirt."

Bradley slips the bullet casing into a plastic bag and sets it aside for ballistics. On the counter is the Tupperware container holding the various items dug up with the victim, which will soon be delivered to the evidence lab or, in the case of the pot, to narcotics. As Bradley packs and labels the clothes, slipping each into a separate bag, O'Hara looks them over again and continues the effort she began in the garden to make sense of them. Several items are currency, or a form of it—the $20 bill, the pesos and yen, the old subway token, maybe even the marble and the fake pearl. The knife, the roach clip, and the titty lighter are, loosely speaking, tools, and the booze, weed, and CD are entertainment, the makings of a party. Maybe the movie stub falls into that multimedia group as well, or maybe it's a bit of trash that just happened to end up in the vicinity. The tiny bag of weed bears the initials "GMS" in small, discreet script, like a monogram on the inside of a pricey wallet.

The clothes packed and labeled, Bradley sits down for the first time that O'Hara can recall in a nearly twenty-four-hour day and reviews his notes and sketches from the site. "We'll know more in a day or two," he says, "after the dental X-rays and the DNA sample come back, but here are some broad strokes. The date of the movie ticket was 6/11/07, which means that the body could not have been buried in the garden before that. That's a little over two months ago, and the level of decomposition is well beyond what you would expect from a body that had been buried for that amount of time. That suggests that the body spent a significant interval exposed aboveground before it was buried. But the most glaring thing," says Bradley after a pause, "is the manner in which the corpse has been handled. I'm sure you noticed this as well, but this is not the case of a body being dumped in a hastily dug hole. On the contrary, the body was carefully and respectfully laid out. The body was placed flat on its back, arms at his side, and the grave was meticulously dug. The length and width are consistent to within a quarter-inch. Then there's the condition of the shirts. Since there are no bullet holes or blood, and only slight evidence of remains, these can't be the clothes the victim was wearing when he died. That means that the body was prepared and dressed for burial, and considering that at that time there would still have been decomposing flesh on the bones, that would have been a horrendous job. The stench alone would make you retch. The point I'm trying to make is that this boy—and based on his clothes, I'm assuming for now that it's a male, approximately ten years old—was given a decent burial, or at least an attempt at one. A considerable effort was made to send him off with a sense of ceremony."

CHAPTER 13

NO MATTER WHAT gets put in the ground or dug out of it, big picture, nothing changes. The rear of the ME's office looks straight out at the FDR Drive, East River, and Queens. At 7:30 a.m., the sun, with its dumb-fuck optimism, has risen again, and people are going to work, because the FDR southbound is bumper-to-bumper. O'Hara walks around the building to First, buys a buttered roll from a sidewalk cart, and eats it as she leans against the hood of her car.

Half an hour later, moments after it opened for business, O'Hara is back on her stool at Milano's, and for a second it feels as if she never left. On her left and right, she is flanked by the same even more punctual regulars, and from the wall-mounted TV another vintage black-and-white seeps into the room. The only thing separating her from Groundhog Day is that the pretty brown-haired barkeep has changed classic metal allegiances, or at least her T-shirt. Instead of AC/DC, it's Kiss.

O'Hara's NYPD notepad is in her bag, but for reasons of propriety and self-preservation, she leaves it there, and when the bartender delivers her grapefruit juice and vodka, O'Hara asks to borrow the yellow pad beside the dictionary. Standing between O'Hara and sleep is not only the lingering effect of half a dozen cups of bad coffee but the quantity of still-unprocessed evidence unearthed from the garden, then added to in the fluorescence of the morgue. For the next twenty minutes she filters it through her exhausted brain like the mesh filtered the dirt at the site, and although she doesn't make a mark on the pad, the sight of her pen lying across the long, empty page is as calming as her drink. O'Hara smiles at her memory of Bradley's response when Kelso tried to hustle him along. *Excavating is a destructive process. You only have one chance to do it right.* Although strictly speaking, the analogy doesn't apply to police work, and she may have more than one chance to get it right, a composed and thoughtful start could avoid unnecessary missteps and save her a lot of time. Finally, almost reluctantly, she makes the first blemish on the page—a capital *V* and, a couple sips later, *ictim*. Beneath it, she lists what she knows so far:

Caucasian, presumably male, approximately ten years old
Hair color: blond, nearly white
Height: 4-foot-7

Another sip produces a second heading—"Burial Artifacts." She divides them into the three categories she observed at the morgue. Under "Currency" she lists:

$20 bill
5-peso coin
25-yen coin
1 subway token—obsolete
1 pearl
1 marble

Under "Tools" she lists:

1 lighter—female torso
1 roach clip
1 Swiss Army knife

Under "Entertainment" she lists:

1 pint of Ballantine whiskey, unopened
1 small bag of weed, sealed
1 audio CD—Coldplay, titled "X&Y"

As O'Hara reviews her work, she considers adding Kelso to the list under "Tools" but decides it's bad form to kick a man when he's down, particularly when you're the one who put him there. Now O'Hara creates a fourth heading—"Clothes"—and beneath it writes:

1 baseball cap, New York Yankees

Unlike most New Yorkers, and cops in particular, O'Hara roots for the underdog. Instead of the Yankees, she pulls for the Mets. Instead of the Giants, she roots for the Jets; instead of the Beatles, the Stones. Her exboyfriend, the medical examiner Leibowitz, another Mets fan, said pulling for Steinbrenner's Yankees would be like going to Vegas and rooting for the house. Continuing the list of clothes, O'Hara writes:

1 dress shirt—blue with yellow stripes
1 T-shirt, "The Germs"—clean

O'Hara looks up from her list at the bartender in her long-sleeved Kiss concert tee and wonders if at this point in the history of civilization, it is possible to infer anything about a person from the name of the band emblazoned on her chest. To do so, you'd need to know the exact degree of irony with which the garment is being worn, and to know that, you'd have to interview the wearer. O'Hara doesn't doubt the barkeep likes Kiss. How could anyone not like Kiss? At the same time, it's worn with a bit of a wink. T-shirts for AC/DC, Kiss, and Def Leppard are heavy metal ironic, just as T-shirts for the Stones, Zeppelin, and the Beatles are rock royalty ironic. The Strokes are prematurely obsolete ironic, the Wings and Ted Nugent b-list ironic or, if you're a contrarian, underrated a-list ironic. The only thing you can know for sure is that the T-shirt is no longer just about the band, because at this point, no one is willing to give it up blindly to anyone, not Mick or Keith, and certainly not Gene Simmons.

The only exception might be a band so obscure no one's heard of it. O'Hara hasn't heard of the Germs, so maybe they fall into that last category, but who knows? O'Hara takes a sip and adds:

1 pair of jeans
1 pair of sneakers—Converse high-tops, white
(No socks, no underwear)

As O'Hara ponders her various lists, she gets a call on her cell, and for the breach in early-morning Milano's etiquette, a dirty look from the female on her left. "I just learned something else about the victim," says Bradley. "I want to tell you now because it could be helpful in making an ID. When I cleaned up the bones, there was a major difference between the right and left femurs. The left is bowed and much thicker, the result of a fracture that was never set. After it healed, the victim's left leg was a quarter-inch shorter than his right, which is a lot. It would have given him a noticeable limp."

When Bradley hangs up, O'Hara adds "Noticeable limp" to the small list under "Victim." The new piece, which O'Hara shares with Jandorek via text, reinforces something that has already struck O'Hara, which is the disconnect between the caring and the not-caring, the regard and the disregard. On one hand you have a ten-year-old boy in a shallow grave in a community garden with a bullet in his shoulder and a broken leg that was never set. On the other, you have an exactly measured, well-dug grave, a carefully laid-out body that's been re-dressed for burial, and a motley collection of trinkets and refreshments that may have been parting gifts. For a moment, because it makes her feel better, O'Hara focuses on the caring part—on the evidence that at least somebody gave a shit about this kid. In that context, she actually takes comfort in the whiskey and the weed tossed in with the body, because it suggests that despite the brevity of his life and the violence and neglect, the kid managed to make some friends and maybe even have some good times, which is about all anyone can hope for. Suddenly she is overwhelmed with admiration for this plucky urchin with his Yankees cap and his Ratso Rizzo limp and his impish smirk he never surrendered, not even in the grave. It lets her think of a young murdered boy as a kind of survivor, but at the same time, the kid's resilience breaks her heart all the more. The suffering of children is the part of the job that fucks up O'Hara, and everyone else, the most, and she is crawling off to the saddest, bleakest corner of her mind when the bartender appears in front of her.

"Need another?" she asks.

"How'd you guess? But I'm going to resist. By the way, I'm Darlene."

"Holly," says the barkeep.

If I don't come up with something to say, thinks O'Hara, I'm going to start crying, and that's even worse form than talking on your cell.

"Holly, you ever hear of a band called the Germs?"

"Of course. L.A.'s first punk band. Produced by Joan Jett. Their lead singer was Darby Crash, who unfortunately killed himself."

"So the Germs were pretty good?"

"I don't know about that, but they were important."

"How about Coldplay, what you do you think of them?"

"I think they suck."

"And how about this new outfit called the Flat Screens? Ever hear of them?"

"No. Any good?"

"Amazing."

The barkeep has given O'Hara a musical disconnect to go with all the others. Whatever you think about the Germs or Coldplay, they're not compatible. They don't belong on the same playlist, let alone the same shallow, well-dug grave.

"In the spirit of full disclosure," says O'Hara, "I should probably mention that the lead singer of the Flat Screens is my son."

"You don't look old enough to have a son who is the lead singer of a band."

"I appreciate that, although in my case, that's not much of a compliment. I was fifteen when I had him."

"I used to be in bands myself," says Holly. "Lots of them."

"Any I might have heard of?"

"I don't know. Space Mice, Paper Boat, Spungent."

"You were in Spungent? I saw them twice. The last time at Spiral in '97. It was a great show. What instrument you play?"

"Guitar."

"Really?" says O'Hara, and as she studies Holly's face, tries to square it with her decade-old memories.

"Yeah, but in the spirit of full disclosure, I should probably mention that I looked a lot different, and played under a different name."

"Oh, yeah? What was your nom de rock?"

"Richard."

"No shit? Well, thanks for sharing. Now that I know you're a rocker, it puts you in a whole new light."

CHAPTER 14

U'HARA WALKS BRUNO, grabs a few hours of sleep, and returns to the ME's office in the early evening. One look at Bradley's eyes, and she knows he never left. His pupils are the size of nickels.

"Jesus Christ," says O'Hara. "What are you on?"

"Adderall," says Bradley, "same thing that got me out of Davenport, Iowa, and into Harvard. Makes me feel young."

"You started taking that shit in high school?"

"Best thing I ever did. In two months, I went from fuckup to National Merit scholar. I didn't need more attention, a role model, or a good talking-to. I just needed a little support from big pharma. Let me show you a couple things before it wears off."

O'Hara follows Bradley to a counter where the dental X-rays are illuminated by a light box. "I was about a year off," says Bradley. "Your first molars come in about six, and you can see he's already got those. He's also got some of the second—the crowns—and the roots are beginning to form, but they are usually all the way in by ten, so this puts him closer to nine.

"The X-rays show something else that's consistent with the unset fracture in his leg. See the horizontal lines across his front teeth? If you tilt the X-ray, you may see it more clearly. Each of those lines, which is a form of dysplasia, was left on the teeth after a serious illness or high fever. The last time I saw lines like that was just after I left grad school. The state of Tennessee hired me to relocate an Indian burial ground to make way for an interstate. Because they didn't have inoculations or antibiotics, almost every Indian who reached adulthood had survived multiple illnesses. These lines would show up in their dental X-rays again and again."

Maybe she wasn't wrong, thinks O'Hara, to see the boy as a survivor. "Does that mean he was abused?"

"I don't think so. With chronic abuse you get malnutrition and retarded development and growth rates. I don't see that, but I don't think he got even routine medical attention. And there's one other thing," says Bradley, turning from the X-rays to the table where the skeleton is laid out. "When I cleaned these up, I found these small brown oval shells. They're maggot casings, which had to have been left by insects before the body was buried, because they wouldn't have had access to it afterward. Before the body was buried, it had to have been lying aboveground for some time, which also explains the advanced state of decomposition. You see this kind of insect activity in the spring, so I would estimate that the body was buried in late spring, early summer, around the date of that movie ticket." Bradley rips open a bag of peanuts and throws a handful into his mouth. His dilated eyes go blank as his jaw reduces the nuts to powder.

Among the lesser-known side effects of Adderall, thinks O'Hara, is that it turns you into a squirrel.

"Anything else?"

"Yeah. After I cleaned the bones, I took a closer look at the hole in the scapula, where the bullet had been lodged." Bradley brings O'Hara to the other end of the table and points at the indentation in the brownish shoulder blade. Then he picks up a new .22-caliber bullet—the original has already been sent to the lab—and shows, when he tilts the bullet at a slightly upward angle, how neatly the tip fits into the depression. "When I saw that the bullet hit the shoulder at this angle," says Bradley, "I looked to see if it hit anything else first, and found defects on the third and eighth ribs consistent with a glancing impact with a small sphere. The bullet hit here and here and then finally was stopped by the shoulder. I had a medical examiner come by and take a look. She thought the bullet would probably have pierced a part of the lung. Depending where, it could have killed him quickly, or he could have hung for days."

"You're saying the bullet was traveling upward?"

"Yeah. Kind of surprising, considering the victim was four-foot-seven."

"The bullet couldn't have ricocheted?" asks O'Hara.

"I don't think so. The shell would have been far more damaged if it had hit something hard enough to reverse its direction."

"I guess the city doesn't test you for stimulants," says O'Hara with undisguised jealousy.

"There's only one forensic anthropologist, Darlene—me. When there's only one of somebody, they don't test them for Bo Diddley."

CHAPTER 15

O'HARA GAZES THROUGH her filthy windshield. Twelve hours before, the sun was in her eyes and the morning in her throat. Now the sun is behind her, warming neck and shoulders, and it's done something even David Blaine can't do. It's made the East River worth looking at. O'Hara rolls down the window and calls Jandorek at the precinct. "How's Kelso bearing up?"

"He's pissed. Thinks you conned him into digging that grave."

"It's not like I did it on purpose."

"No," says Jandorek. "But it's not like you give a shit either."

"True."

"Kelso's put together a little task force. He's got me handling Missing Persons and ACS, and Ferguson and Hernandez canvassing the schools. So far not a fucking thing. Which is weird. A little blond-haired kid with a limp, you'd think at some point someone would have called Children's Services on the parents. Right?"

"How long until he goes public?"

"Not long. A couple days, maybe less. Here's what I can't get my head around, Dar. If it's the parents, what kind of parent buries a nine-year-old with a roach clip, a tittie lighter, a pint of whiskey, and a bag of pot? And if it's not the parents, but some bad-seed older kids he fell in with, why didn't the parents report him missing?"

"Maybe because they're very bad parents," says O'Hara. "Speaking of which, the kid had lines on his teeth called dysplasia. According to Bradley every one of those lines was left by a serious illness or very high fever. Bradley used to see that in the remains of American Indians, or other people who didn't have access to modern medicine."

"Maybe," says Jandorek, "we're looking for a Christian Scientist or Jehovah's Witness. My fucking favorites. Or some crazy cult motherfuckers."

"Or someone living off the grid," says O'Hara, "but this isn't the Ozarks. It's the East Village."

"If you ask me," says Jandorek, "that garden has a little Ozarks in it."

One last look at the softening sky, and O'Hara heads downtown. She ignores a dozen beckoning bars and walks past the garden, whose gate is secured by a padlock and a patrol car. When O'Hara gets to Henderson's place, he and Paulette are on lawn chairs on the small recessed stoop three steps below the sidewalk. Paulette wears a pretty summer dress. Gus is rocking his signature ensemble: wifebeater, boxers, tube socks, and lace-ups.

"You got yourself a nice spot," says O'Hara.

"If you like ankles," says Henderson with a smile, "And I do."

Henderson seems pretty lucid, thinks O'Hara. Maybe she's caught him on one of his good days. "So, Gus, we dug up that spot under the willow tree. The one you told us about."

"I didn't tell you about a tree."

"Paulette said you told her."

"Do I look like a Paulette?"

"She's Paulette, Gus, and I'm talking to both of you. You remember that photograph of the tree you said I could take?"

"Why, you sold it?"

"Gus, we took a look under that tree, but we didn't find a large black man."

"Disappointed?" says Williamson.

O'Hara ignores that and turns to Henderson. "That got me to thinking, Gus—remember your old running mate, Charlie Faulk? Whatever happened to him?"

"He killed himself," says Gus. "Long time ago."

"That's sad. Do you mind me asking how he did it?"

"He took the train out to Rockaway and walked into the ocean. Told me he was going to do it."

"His mother said that you told her he jumped off the Staten Island Ferry. Which is it, Gus—Rockaway Beach or the Staten Island Ferry?"

"What difference does it make? Before he left, he gave me his record collection. He had some great vinyl—Rollins, Monk, Clark Terry."

"Still have them?"

"Sold 'em that day. Got high for a week. Those were some good times."

"Weren't you mad at him for rolling over on you on that robbery?"

"Why? I would've done the same thing."

CHAPTER 16

BY THE NEXT day, the investigation has been broken down into half a dozen smaller ones. O'Hara and Jandorek spend the morning checking in with each, greasing the wheels and nudging them along.

The .22-caliber bullet that fell out of the victim's shoulder is in the ballistics lab in Queens. Once the tests are completed, the results will be transmitted to every city, state, and county police department in the country to see if the same weapon was used in the commission of other crimes, although, considering its modest stopping power, that seems unlikely.

The little bag of weed, stamped "GMS," is being tested by narcotics, and evidence is running various tests on the artifacts and clothes, looking among other things for hair, fiber, or DNA that might belong to someone other than the victim. To ascertain that, they first need the results on the DNA of the victim, and in the late morning O'Hara gets a text from Bradley, saying the tests, based on a tiny fragment of shaved-off bone, have been completed and confirm that the victim is a Caucasian male.

Also ongoing is a canvass of city grammar schools. Ferguson, Hernandez, and detectives enlisted from other precincts are visiting every grammar school in Manhattan, Brooklyn, and the Bronx, interviewing administrators, going through enrollment lists and old yearbooks, inquiring about a blond-haired kid with a limp in third, fourth, or fifth grade who abruptly stopped showing up or whose parents notified the school that they were moving out of the district. By the middle of the day, they haven't turned up anything. Neither has Missing Persons or ACS, the Agency for Children's Services. The only thing close to a lead is something that turned up on a national database for missing children. In 2003 in a part of Oakland called Alameda, the local children's services agency received several reports of a boy about five, with long blond hair and a limp, left alone in his backyard for hours at a time. When social workers attempted to contact the parents, the family left town.

To escape Kelso's glare, O'Hara heads back to Thirtieth and First Avenue and checks in with Ken Ashworth. Ashworth, who is rotund and has a slight stutter, runs the evidence lab, which is housed on the third floor of the ME's office. "I was about to give you a call," he says.

Every article of clothing excavated from the grave hangs neatly from a wheeled garment rack at the center of the room, but Ashworth brings her to the far corner, where a crumpled wad of paper is drying under a heat lamp. "I'll break down the clothing in a second. First, I want to show you what we found in the pocket of the kid's jeans. A lot had disintegrated, but I was able to tease apart a couple bits." Ashworth hands O'Hara a magnifying lens and points his tweezers at a piece of paper the size of a postage stamp. In the middle of a dense graph, she makes out:

" . . . AN 665, JUNE 2007, PUBLISHED BY DC COMICS, 1700 BROADWAY, NY 10019." As O'Hara pores over the minuscule typeface, Ashworth makes a noise she takes for his stutter—*"nah nah nah nah nah nah . . ."* Then, she realizes he's singing, but doesn't know what till he reaches the musical punch line: "BATMAN! It's a comic book, Dar, *Batman* number 665, published in June 2007, the same month as the ticket stub."

In addition to the intoxicants and shitty tunes, thinks O'Hara, the kid was sent off with a little reading material. It was like he was taking a trip on Amtrak.

"Any way of knowing where the comic was sold?"

"Not really. *Batman* is mass-market. They print about a hundred thousand copies per issue. You could buy one anywhere from a newsstand to a CVS."

"The clothes?"

"From all over the place," says Ashworth, and pulls a small notebook from his shirt pocket. "The shirt is Gant, manufactured in '74, originally sold to department stores in the Southwest; the jeans are Gap circa '95, sold in California; the T-shirt is a Fruit of the Loom blank from the eighties, which was sold to a classic rock apparel company, who then added 'The Germs.' Although the clothes weren't new, they were clean, and had been washed before they were put on the victim. Because of that and because they come from such a variety of regions, I'm pretty sure that whoever bought them purchased them together at some vintage store, which unfortunately could be anywhere, since these shops are all over the place. A lot of these places buy the clothes by the pound. They don't even know what's in their own inventories."

CHAPTER 17

AT 8:40 P.M., Casey Fagerland sits down with O'Hara and Jandorek at the only table in homicide that fits three. "How can you work here?" asks Fagerland. "There are no windows."

"We're detectives," says Jandorek. "Natural light gives us hives."

Fagerland is a large woman in her mid-forties with straight brown hair and a pleasant, open face. She is the president of the Community Garden at Sixth Street and Avenue B. When O'Hara contacted her, she told her that they were working on a missing person case involving a member of the garden.

"Casey, you bring a list?"

"Three," says Fagerland. "I made copies. But I got to warn you, it's long. There are somewhere between eighty-seven and a hundred and twenty active plots right now, and most are shared. Every name should be on here, but I can't swear that every address, e-mail, and phone number is up-to-date."

"How many names?" asks Jandorek.

"Over two hundred."

"Jesus. And they all got keys?"

"'Fraid so."

"What kind of people we talking here?" asks Jandorek. "I've seen the garden. It's pretty funky."

"Democracy is messy," says Fagerland. "You got two hundred people sharing a quarter of a square block, and every one of them gets a vote."

"Based on the gate," says O'Hara, "I assume the garden has been around since '83."

"That's right—twenty-four years. Let me give you some history. Originally that part of the city was a salt marsh, an arm of the East River. The only inhabitants were birds. The first tenements went up in 1845."

"Case," says Jandorek gently, "we're going to need it condensed. We don't have time for the full Rick Burns."

"Fast forward to the 1980s," says Fagerland, "a very shaky period in New York real estate. Like now, but much worse. A quarter of the buildings in the East Village, the landlords stopped paying their mortgages and taxes and walked away. At Sixth and B were five buildings and a parking garage, all abandoned, and after the junkies took over and turned them into a shooting gallery, the city tore them down."

So that's Henderson's connection, thinks O'Hara.

"Suddenly, you've got seventeen thousand empty square feet. People walking by would throw garbage over the fence. Around this time, a hippie chick named Joanie, who is still a member, noticed seeds sprouting from the garbage. She climbed over the fence, laid out a circle of stones, and created the first garden."

Like *Spinal Tap*, thinks O'Hara, minus the smoke machines.

"This was the era of East Village radicals," continues Fagerland, "squatters and homesteaders. People were taking over buildings, fixing them up. They became the first members of the garden, and though most got priced out of the neighborhood, they still make up the core. To give you an idea, the annual dues for a plot is twelve dollars a year. At Starbucks, that's two Frappuccinos."

"I'll take the Frappuccinos," says Jandorek.

"That's one kind of person we're interested in," says O'Hara. "A little off the grid, homesteaders, homeschoolers."

"I can give you names," Fagerland, "half a dozen come to mind—but they're older. Their kids are grown. The ones with kids now, are bankers and lawyers. They send their kids to private schools."

"What's the attraction of the garden for them?" asks Jandorek.

"Community has become trendy. At least in the East Village. Maybe they think it will help get their kids into college. For all I know they're right."

O'Hara scans the list and stops at "Malmströmer." There are four of them—Lars, Marjetta, Inga, and Christina.

"I met Christina Malmströmer at the garden," says O'Hara. "She only mentioned her father."

"Her mother, Marjetta, died in '96. Breast cancer. It was awful. Lars was left with two teenage girls. The older, Inga, was about seventeen; Christina, fourteen. Inga, who looked like a model, started hanging out all night, smoking pot, etcetera, and the old man didn't handle it well. Maybe he threw her out of the house, or maybe she ended up running away, but as far as I know, she hasn't had contact with the family since."

"How about the old man?" asks O'Hara.

"Very tall, very handsome, very Scandinavian. Came here in his teens as a carpenter's apprentice and did well. Owns a hardware store and a couple buildings on Sixth Street he bought for nothing when they were giving them away. He lives on the top floor of one of them, where he grows some of his own food. He keeps an eye on Christina with his binoculars."

O'Hara puts a mark next to Lars.

"The Malmströmers," asks O'Hara. "Are they all blond?" At the garden, Christina's hair had been pulled back and stuffed under a large sun hat.

"Lars has been gray as long as I've known him. Marjetta and Inga were blond. Christina has brown hair."

"You're quite the authority on Lars and his brood," says Jandorek.

"I dated him for about ten minutes, after his wife died, when all this was going on. The single dad raising the kids alone, I've always been a sucker for that one. And I felt bad for the girls, particularly Christina. Now her father is hyperprotective, but then—with the illness of her mother and the drama with her sister, and her father working day and night to keep his business afloat—she was lost in the shuffle. Christina used to be such a vibrant girl. She's never really been the same."

"So what happened?" asks Jandorek. "I mean with you and the big Swede?"

"Too Nordic for me. I think of myself as a warm person, but I couldn't thaw him."

"You know anything about his life since?"

"He never remarried. He spends a lot of time in his basement workshop. One day I got it into my head to visit him there. It was weird—like I walked in on him with another woman—but I'm sure he thinks I'm a weirdo too."

"Any people not on this list with keys?" asks O'Hara. "Maybe off-the-grid types?"

"We hired a guy to trim the trees. He was an itinerant worker. I guess you could say he lived off the grid. He did some work on the willow itself, shoring it up."

"When?"

"Three years ago."

Too long, thinks O'Hara. Doesn't fit the time frame. "How about the shows on weekends?" she asks, recalling the flyers taped to the trees. "What kind of performers do you get?"

"Bad ones mostly. Folksingers, stand-ups, puppeteers, poets, spoken word. A circus troupe performs every year called Circus Amok. They're actually very good, run by a woman named Jennifer Miller, who happens to have a beard."

"She also happen to have a key?"

"Probably. I've seen her in the evenings now and then, smoking a joint."

"What's her circus like?" asks Jandorek.

"It's for kids mainly. But it's a queer circus—every one in the company is gay or transsexual, and everything is turned on its head. The strongman is a big butch dyke. While balancing on the rope, the slackliner changes out of his pants into a dress and heels. And the MC is Jennifer with her black beard. She comes out juggling on her unicycle and shouts, "What the fuck! It's Circus Amok!""

"You call that a kid circus?" says Jandorek.

"Kids love it—they have a treasure hunt where kids dig up little bits of foreign money."

"What kind of money?"

"Lira, yen, pesos. It changes every year."

"Any of the performers have children?" asks O'Hara.

"Not sure. Possibly."

"This Miller," asks Jandorek. "She has a real beard?"

"Like the old-time freak shows," says Fagerland. "In fact, she performs in a sideshow on Coney Island."

"Any other nutjobs and deviants?"

"We had to ask one member to stop turning tricks in the garden. It's never easy to get people to behave."

When Fagerland leaves, O'Hara and Jandorek stay put under the buzzing fluorescent bulb. "Lars," says Jandorek, "a broken-down junkie, and a broad with a beard."

"The bearded lady is pretty interesting," says O'Hara.

"Because she has a beard?"

"A woman with a beard is interesting, no question. But I was thinking about the grave. With all those different kinds of money and trinkets tossed in, it seemed like a group effort, everyone contributing something different."

"A potluck funeral," says Jandorek.

"An off-kilter circus troupe fits that pretty well. And a kid growing up in one might not have time to go to school, which could explain why there's no trace of the kid in the system."

"I can see that," says Jandorek. "And you got the yen and pesos from the treasure hunt—but I like Lars. He's big, he's weird, and he's got a family of blonds, one of whom is already missing. Bradley told you, that grave was laid out and dug like a jewel box, and this guy was a carpenter."

"Jesus was a carpenter," says O'Hara.

"So was Karen till she lost her appetite. One other point in Lars's favor. There are a hundred and ten plots in that fucking garden, and his family just happens to have the one next to where the kid was buried. What are the odds of that?"

"One out of a hundred and ten."

"You sure you're not autistic?"

"How about I head to Coney Island, and you see what you can learn about the Swedish Family Malmströmer."

"Works for me. Speaking of which, I thought Fagerland was kind of cute."

"I noticed."

CHAPTER 18

O'HARA PARKS ON Neptune and follows the croak of the boardwalk talker until she stands on the last corner of the steaming metropolis—Twelfth Street and Surf Avenue, Coney Island, Brooklyn. Across the street is Sideshows by the Seashore, which, according to the ballyhoo, is the last permanently situated ten-in-one freak show still ripping tickets in America. O'Hara hands $3 to a tattooed cashier and steps into a dark box. Despite its name, there's no sea breeze here, just stale sweat, a raw plywood stage and steel bleachers. Beside the stage is a dressing room, and from the edge of the door light leaks onto an aquarium containing a plastic model of a reptile with a human head. Scrawled above it on the wall is the question "What is it?" as if perhaps it is something other than a piece of plastic. At 11:20 p.m. on a Sunday, the hipsters and tourists have long since fled the boardwalk, and the audience skews heavily Puerto Rican, and many seem caught in the late weekend purgatory between drunk and hungover. The show runs nonstop in a lethargic loop, and the first act O'Hara catches is the third on the bill. He is Koko, advertised as a three-foot-seven-inch dwarf, and as he struts onstage, O'Hara thinks of the upward-trajectory bullet that killed the boy. For what must be the thirtieth time that day,

Koko whips himself into a frenzy. With vigorous thrusts of his pelvis and forearm, he recounts the night he caught his wife Evangeline in the arms of another man and stabbed them both.

Frank Hartman, aka the Human Blockhead, takes the stage next. He drops an awl down one nostril, then swallows a sixteen-inch sword— "down the hatch without a scratch." According to the flyer, Miller, working under the name Xenobia, is on deck, but instead a very familiar-looking dwarf returns to the proscenium. Now dressed in the harlequin suit of a court jester, he introduces himself as "Roland the Crappy Juggler." Dwarfs shouldn't wear patterns, thinks O'Hara. It makes them look short.

The crowd, already hot and restless, turns cranky. Having dropped $3, they were counting on something genuinely freaky, and Roland ain't getting any shorter. They greet him with boos and balled-up programs turned into projectiles. "Hey, Koko," someone yells. "I fucked your wife too." And when the dwarf pirouettes, drops his pantaloons, and invites the heckler to kiss his ass, O'Hara takes it as her cue to end her evening at the theater.

Outside, leaning rakishly against the rail of the boardwalk, is a thin young man. He wears a straw boater and jeans rolled up to expose a couple inches of skin above his ankles. He must be the impresario because he is pitching the rewards of his stage to a sexy double amputee.

"The sideshow," he tells the girl, straight-faced, "will help you find a new narrative and at the same time help you get in touch with the roots of the iconography you're already being viewed in relation to."

"Pardon the interruption," says O'Hara, "but what happened to Xenobia?"

"I fired her."

"Why the hell you do that?"

"She had an attitude problem."

"Or maybe she found a new narrative," says O'Hara.

"Can I help you with something?" Before O'Hara leaves, she extracts Miller's address from the postmodern pimp, and on her way to her car, she gets a call from Jandorek.

"A couple tidbits on Malmströmer," he says. "The older daughter
Inga, who would now be twenty-eight, has never been arrested. So how
much trouble could she have gotten into? And, he didn't report her missing until '99, which according to the report was more than three years
after she ran away."

"What are you saying?"

"Not sure. But it's weird. He's so obsessed with one daughter he won't
let her out of his sight, and another daughter he doesn't report missing
until she's an adult. It doesn't add up."

O'Hara hasn't spent much time in South Williamsburg. Twenty minutes and a couple wrong turns later, she pulls onto South Kent, a street so
treeless, she shudders at the thought of Bruno scouring the vista in vain
for something worth pissing on. She finds the building and rides a service
elevator floored with wooden planks that look like they were ripped from
the submerged portion of a wharf. O'Hara considers her privileged access
to fringe New York one of the perks of her job, and has never had a boring
conversation with a drag queen or trannie. But O'Hara has never encountered anyone like the figure who meets her at the elevator in a black slip,
holding a bowl of Cheerios. O'Hara thinks of the question—*What is it?*—
scribbled on the wall in Coney Island, but only for an instant, because the
person in front of her has the unmistakably soft features and smile of a
woman. Despite the full black beard and arms and legs as hirsute as a
Hobbit, Miller is a fem. She's a girly girl.

"I'm Darlene O'Hara, NYPD. You must be Jennifer Miller."

"How'd you guess?"

O'Hara follows Miller into a loft whose rawness is of a piece with the
elevator. The decor is early millennium circus. Paper masks of lions and
bears share space with stilts and unicycles, a tuba and an accordion. Overhead is a tightrope, and against one wall is the yellow-green bike O'Hara
saw bolted to the gate that first night. In the middle of the room, enough
equipment has been pushed aside to create a sitting area, and O'Hara
accepts the offer of a stuffed chair.

"I'm working on a missing person case related to the community garden at Sixth and B. Casey Fagerland said Circus Amok has performed there many times. She also thought that she had given you a key."

"I returned it." Miller slurps her Cheerios and studies O'Hara with the most watchful eyes O'Hara has ever seen. They are barely less riveting than her other striking feature.

"Interesting," says O'Hara.

"Why?"

"A couple nights ago I saw that bike outside the gate. I'm pretty sure I saw you sitting inside."

"You're right," says Miller, holding up a fat key chain. "I still have it. For me, a place where I can sit outside and be left alone is a big deal." Miller's eyes fill with sadness. "Does Casey want the key back?"

"She didn't say that. She did say that Circus Amok is great."

"We practice hard."

"She mentioned a treasure hunt for foreign coins."

"Loose change my friends bring back from mysterious distant lands. Nothing worth more than half a cent. I'm too poor to give away real money."

"How do kids react to you?"

"You mean, how do they react to my beard?"

"Yeah."

"They gawk. They ask questions. They're curious. They want to touch it. But unlike adults, it doesn't make them want to beat me up."

"I went to Coney Island tonight to see your show. That line above the aquarium—'What is it?' Do you know who wrote that?"

"I don't know who scribbled it on the wall. Probably the asshole who runs the place. But P. T. Barnum wrote it originally."

"The guy who said a sucker is born every day?"

"He's known for that, although it's not clear he ever said it. Either way, he was a genius."

On a corner table is a framed picture of a man with Miller's eyes and beard. "Your father?"

"No, that's my mother. Just kidding. He died a couple years ago. He was head of the philosophy department at Mount Holyoke."

"No shit."

"My mother," says Miller, pointing at another picture, "died even younger. She taught at Teachers College. A couple brainiac do-gooders."

Clearly Miller is smart too and O'Hara is perplexed. Why grow and keep a beard, when getting rid of it would have been so easy and keeping it turned her into a sideshow freak? Although she's not angry at her, like those adults Miller describes, she feels the frustration of a parent dealing with a stubborn kid. Why did you do this with your life? But then again, why does anyone do anything foolhardy or brave? Why did Axl drop out of school and form a band?

"If a kid comes to your show and says he wants to run away to the circus, what do you say?"

"Whaddaya got for me, kid? Can you juggle? Eat fire? Ride a unicycle? Make people laugh? What's your act?"

"So why'd you do it?" asks O'Hara.

"I didn't. I had nothing to do with whatever happened in the garden."

"I know," says O'Hara. "I mean, why'd you grow the beard?"

"Here's the short version, and pretty much true. When that first hair sprouted, and in the beginning there was only one, I was a teenager, and just coming out as a lesbian. I was going to pluck it, I came this close, but I didn't want to bow down. A second hair appeared, then a third. I didn't pluck those either, and I saw, from how disturbed people were getting, that I'd stumbled on something important. Since then, I've thought of shaving it a thousand times, but by now my beard and me are so intertwined, I'm not sure who I'd be without it."

"You'd be Jennifer."

"What if that's not enough anymore?"

CHAPTER 19

THE CUP HOLDER of the '94 Jetta is no match for a large '07 Dunkin' Donuts iced coffee. O'Hara holds her doughnut in one hand, the thermos size iced coffee in the other, and when her ringtone intrudes, she stuffs the doughnut in her face and flips open the phone. It's Grimitz in narcotics.

"Darlene, we got the results on the cannabis. It's the strongest we've ever tested. Hydroponic. Grown in custom greenhouses by stoner PhDs, and very pricey. Not the stinkweed you associate with kids. . . . Darlene, you there?"

"Yeah. . . . How about the initials—'GMS'—ever come across them?"

"No. NYPD doesn't devote a lot of narcotic dollars on designer weed maybe because the people involved rarely kill each other. But it reminds me of something. Last summer, a teenage kid rolls into the ER at Beth Israel on his skateboard. A nurse, who I was dating at the time, asks what's wrong. He tells her he's flipping out. She asks on what, he says weed. Over the next two days five other kids wander into the ER with the same story, and according to the nurse, who I'm no longer dating because she turned out to be a pain-med junkie herself, they all know each other from Tompkins Square, again not the type you associate with fifteen-hundred-dollar-an-ounce pot. I guess they're not used to it either, which is why they ended up in the ER. I never thought about it till now, but it could be GMS."

Instead of heading to the precinct, O'Hara texts Jandorek and drives to the East Village, where she parks on C and enters the park at Ninth. Although another scorcher is forecast, the park still retains a bit of its overnight freshness. A couple old-timers are getting in their handball game early, a young kid practices foul shots, and the local muscleheads have turned the jungle gym into something between a prison yard and an Equinox. But the real jocks are in the dog run. As O'Hara walks by, a German shorthaired pointer, all chest, hindquarters, and lolling tongue, bounds back and forth over the five-foot fence as if on a pogo stick, his owner barely looking up from his *Times* to toss the slobbery ball.

The skateboarders have been allotted the northwest corner of the park, a generous-sized chunk that looks out on the small-scale commerce of Avenue A and the elegant town houses on East Tenth Street. In this quadrant, everything in sight is scuffed—the cement, the wooden benches, the garbage cans, even the bark of the trees. As O'Hara takes a seat on a scarred bench in the corner, she hopes she's not going to have to pull a sliver out of her ass. Half a dozen skaters, who have risen early to beat the heat, work the grinding pole in the center of the playground. Some kids pull off their tricks with practiced nonchalance. The less athletic labor at them. Either way, there is something heartrending about how earnestly they apply themselves to perfecting the same small bag of tricks.

The sounds and movements unfold with a hypnotic rhythm. First the push and glide, and then, after a quick tug at the back of the baggy jeans, the crouch and jump. Miraculously, the board levitates with the sneakers and slides along the top of the pole, the skilled ones carrying enough speed so that when they drop off the far end, there is enough momentum to complete a turn back to the starting point. A tall, skinny skater stands out for his speed and lift and stripped-down style, his every gesture pared to the nub. When he takes a break, the others crowd around him in the shade, and O'Hara edges closer. After a couple minutes, an aromatic cloud wafts her way. O'Hara glances at her watch—8:03 a.m.—and she can't help but notice it's the time of her last two drinks at Milano's.

"Smells good," says O'Hara.

"Tastes good too," says the tall skater. He has thick greasy hair and acne and looks even more emaciated off his board. Beside him sits a short, handsome kid with a clean white T-shirt and a beard. He looks likes Springsteen on the cover of *Born to Run*.

"It's not by any chance that hydro I heard about last year?"

"Out of our price range," says the tall kid. "Besides, that shit's almost too strong."

"I've been looking for some forever. Want to surprise my boyfriend."

"Boyfriend?" says the skater, with an electric grin that eclipses his acne. "What a way to start a conversation."

"Did I say boyfriend?" asks O'Hara. "I meant my cousin Stanley. My mentally and physically challenged cousin Stanley."

"Should you be giving hydro to a retard?"

"Probably not," concedes O'Hara.

"Don't mean to interrupt," says Springsteen, "but who the fuck are you? And how do we know you're not a cop?"

There are three ways a patrolman gets promoted to detective. The most dependable, of course, is nepotism, having a hook or rabbi, an uncle who's a captain, a father who's a lieutenant. Another is by earning a reputation as an active cop, which O'Hara did, fresh out of the academy, in an anticrime unit in Times Square. The third route goes through narcotics, doing buy-and-busts undercover, which is by far the most dangerous and colorful. O'Hara has heard all the stories, particular about Jerry Reinsdorf, a detective who now works with her in homicide. Reinsdorf was legendary for his ability to channel a strung-out junkie from Jersey. He'd lie in the middle of a puddle in Washington Square and start bawling like a toddler, or pull out his dick and examine it with scientific detachment, as if he'd never seen anything like it before. His shameless performances invariably led to a score and a collar and made the unmarked van, parked nearby, rock with laughter. The stories confirmed something O'Hara has long understood. Half of being a good cop is being a good cop. The second part is making other cops laugh. O'Hara has also heard about the less gifted, like Doris for example, who was so unconvincing that the guys said she couldn't get the blind Pakistani at the corner newsstand to sell her a *Post*. "Hey, Doris, while you're out there, could you pick me up a coffee? On second thought, don't bother—they probably won't sell it to you."

So who is O'Hara going to be, she wonders, Jerry or Doris?

"Do I look like a cop?" asks O'Hara.

"Ah . . . as a matter of fact," says the tall kid.

"Let's see," says his watchful sidekick, as if working from a list. "Uncool jeans—check. Uncool hair—check. Uncool shoes—big, fat check."

"That was harsh," says O'Hara. "How about these sunglasses? Don't tell me they're not cool, 'cause I paid seven bucks for them. As for the shoes, I'm a bartender. I'm on my feet all day."

"Then take a hit and prove us wrong," says little Springsteen. "We all make mistakes."

"I can't show up reeking of pot. It's like advertising for the other side."

"Where do you work that opens this early?"

"Homicide."

"Seriously."

"Milano's on Houston."

"Take a hit," says the shorter one. "Or take a hike. This isn't a spectator sport."

"Twist my arm," says O'Hara and slides over. "Darlene," she says. "Friends call me Dar."

"Ben," says the tall kid. "And this small bucket of filth is Jamie." He treats himself to a lungful, then passes the pipe. She takes a long hit and collapses into violent coughing that lasts for minutes and provokes a fair amount of hilarity. Unlike firemen, cops are subject to random testing. When she finally stops coughing, the sky sparkles in a way it hasn't for fifteen years.

"So you want to know the way to Grandmother's house?" asks Ben.

"Grandma?"

"Grandma, as in hydro dealer. Remember, for Stanley? Your handicapped cousin."

"Yeah, I do."

"Then follow me," says Ben. He drops his board at his feet and stands on it. "It's around the corner."

O'Hara follows him west past the boutiquey shops on Ninth Street—an antique store called Upper Rust, a vintage place called Magic Fingers, a couple hair salons and tiny bars. Every twenty feet or so, Ben busts an understated bit of skateboard suaveness that makes her smile.

"That was nice, Ben."

"Thanks, Dar." Covering ground on foot is a lot harder than on the board. Even in her telltale clodhoppers, O'Hara struggles to keep up. At Third, she runs into Duane Reade to withdraw $500 from an ATM and try to collect her thoughts.

"What took you so long?" asks Ben. "It's been like ten minutes."

"No way."

"Yes way."

At Fourth Avenue, Ben turns north. A block and a half later he stops in front of a postwar building on the east side of the street. The lobby, which has a funky deco facade, is two steps down.

"I've always liked this building," says O'Hara.

"You're about to like it more. There's a doorman. Tell him you're here to see Dr. Kurlander. When you get upstairs, just say you're a pal of Ben's. And good luck with Stanley."

O'Hara glances in the direction of the lobby. When she turns back to thank her guide, he's halfway down the block, one hand raised in farewell. O'Hara retreats to the bodega on the south corner, and buys a Red Bull. When it's done, she deems herself straight enough to proceed.

"Dr. Kurlander," O'Hara tells the doorman. At seven, the elevator opens on a frosted glass door. Etched in white letters is "East Village Women. Ob-Gyn Associates, LLP, Dr. Elizabeth Kurlander & Dr. Ellie Weisenberg." Rather than hook her up, Ben has referred her to a gynecologist, which answers her question. O'Hara is Doris.

CHAPTER 20

"I HOPE WHAT I'm smelling is secondhand," says Jandorek.

"It is. The skaters were hitting the pipe at eight a.m."

"They better have been hitting it alone. The last thing you need is another vice."

O'Hara and Jandorek are parked in front Lion's Hardware, a freestanding brick building on B and First, across from a large mural dedicated to John Lennon. It's the only facade on the block unblemished by graffiti, and when O'Hara gets a good look at the man behind the counter, she understands why. Malmströmer is at least six-seven and solid, with the severe countenance of a man from a harsher time and place, not the sort likely to see the upside of having some asshole's initials on his store. After a super with a boil on the back of his neck picks up his preordered faucet, O'Hara and Jandorek follow Malmströmer to the office in the back.

"Mr. Malmströmer," says Jandorek, "as you might have heard, we're investigating the disappearance of a young boy whose family may have been members of the community garden."

"I hadn't. And I doubt I'll be of much help. I'm never there. Christina has the plot now, and from what I can tell she's doing a very good job with it."

"How do you know, if you're never there?" asks O'Hara.

"I live around the corner from the community garden. From my own garden on the roof, I have a pretty good view of her plot."

"I met your daughter last week," says O'Hara. "She's lovely."

"Christina's my angel," says Malmströmer.

"We heard you watch your daughter with binoculars," says Jandorek.

"Casey should mind her own business."

"Or maybe you should mind yours, Mr. Malmströmer. I doubt a twenty-five-year-old woman appreciates being kept under surveillance by her father." Malmströmer's eyes flicker with indignation. He glances at Jandorek, holds the stare for a beat, then looks down at his own enormous hands, as if admonishing them not to do anything rash. "I have a garden, and Christina has a garden, and it so happens that when I am working on mine, I can see her working on hers. . . . Excuse me." A young clerk stands outside the office. "Do we have any more rat traps in the basement? A customer wants a hundred."

"Tell him we can have them tomorrow. But take a deposit."

"I hear you have quite a garden yourself," says Jandorek.

"Casey again?"

"What do you do with all the stuff you grow, Mr. Malmströmer?" asks O'Hara.

"You want me to account for my vegetables?"

"Your daughter has her own garden. You live alone. That's a lot of produce. What do you do with it?"

"I eat some. And give the rest to the Bowery Mission. They seem to appreciate it. Is there anything else I can do for you, detectives?"

"I understand you have an older daughter," says Jandorek.

"I'm afraid I lost Inga to the streets."

"What was she doing that was so awful? There's no record of an arrest."

"Taking drugs, lying about it, and disobeying me."

"Eighty percent of the kids in New York do that. Why'd you wait three years to file a missing person report?"

"I thought that if I was patient, she would just walk in the door one day. I still hope that will happen."

CHAPTER 21

AT 3:05 A.M. O'Hara and Jandorek visit Malmströmer again, this time in his home at 538 East Sixth Street. The rooster on the roof crows like a Doberman and Malmotrömer, a tired man in a bathrobe, is shown the freshly signed warrant.

"You have a permit for livestock?" says Jandorek.

"You came in the middle of the night for that?"

"No. We came to search your apartment and basement. The warrant is good for both. Let's start at the bottom." They drag him down seven flights and wait for him to open the steel padlock below a large KEEP OUT sign. Inside is a well-appointed workshop, lined with band- and jigsaws, a planer and a lathe.

"We hear you spend a lot of time down here, Mr. Malmströmer. What do you do?"

"Make things."

"What sort of things?"

"Anything I want to."

With a tip of his finger, Jandorek nudges an expensive drill just far enough over the edge of his worktable so that it falls onto the cement floor. They step over it and walk to the far end of the shop, where a small dresser, recently stained, is drying. Although the scale is Lilliputian, the detail and design are exquisite. "Why so small?" asks O'Hara.

"It takes up less space."

"And you'll give it away, like your tomatoes?"

Malmströmer doesn't reply.

"Who'd you make it for, Mr. Malmströmer?"

"I made it for myself."

"I thought you were going to say it's for your grandchild," says Jandorek. "But you don't have any, do you? Because you threw your own daughter into the street for smoking a joint or holding hands. And your other daughter hates you because you spy on her with binoculars."

"She doesn't hate me."

In the corner of the room is a half door, also steel, fortified and padlocked.

"What's back there?"

"Nothing much."

"Open it," says Jandorek, and it occurs to O'Hara that her partner's hard-on for Malmströmer may be related to his hard-on for Fagerland. Malmströmer takes out his keys. With his hands shaking, he struggles to separate the right one from the ring and slide it into the lock. Finally he undoes the bolt and pushes open the door. It takes several seconds for a flickering light to come all the way on. When it does, they see a low-ceilinged room crammed with wooden miniatures as beautifully crafted as the dresser. Among the furnishings are a bunk bed, a desk, and a rocking chair. There's also a pair of hand-crafted hockey sticks, a scooter, and a small perfectly proportioned dark green canoe with a white pinstripe.

"I thought you said you didn't have grandchildren."

"I don't."

"So why all this?" asks Jandorek.

"I drove Inga away, but it's not too late for Christina. She could still have a family."

O'Hara stares back into the crawl space. The old world pieces seem too small to contain all the anguish and love that has been instilled in them.

CHAPTER 22

O'HARA SITS AT her desk and tries not to flinch every time Kelso walks by. If their roles were reversed, O'Hara would be just as pissed. A week after they brought the kid out of the ground, they still don't even have an ID, and her only suspect, Henderson, is both incompetent and incontinent. Even though Gus got the body wrong, he got the burial spot right, so there has to be a connection, but the thought of returning to his malodorous apartment is no more appealing than sparking up another adult chat with Kelso.

"Any ideas?" O'Hara asks Jandorek.

"I was thinking a nice piece of fish."

"I mean the homicide."

"This afternoon Kelso's giving it to the media in time for the evening news. We got so little, he has no choice." Jandorek adjusts his voice downward to the basso profundo of a TV newsreader. *"An idyllic East Village garden has become the scene of a grisly discovery . . ."*

"Idyllic my ass."

"You need the contrast, Dar—the idyllic and the grisly—otherwise it doesn't sing. In any case, a towheaded Yankees fan with a limp, someone's going to pick up the phone. In fact too many people will pick up the phone, and ninety-nine percent of it will be useless. The rest will be atrocious. It always is when you set up a hotline for a murdered kid. The shit you hear . . ."

They are interrupted by a call to O'Hara from the desk sergeant.

"I got a Ben and a Jamie here to see you."

When O'Hara is slow to respond, the sergeant adds some memory-jogging detail. "Long hair, about eighteen, skateboards. They claim they're pals of yours."

"That's an exaggeration," says O'Hara. "They don't by any chance reek of pot?"

"I don't think they'd roll into a police station if they did."

"Don't be so sure."

"You want me to bring them up?"

"Absolutely not. I'll be right down."

Rather than wait for the elevator, O'Hara and Jandorek take the back stairs to the lobby and hustle the visitors outside to the sidewalk. "I guess you really are in homicide," says Ben.

"That's what I tried to tell you."

"Bullshit you did," says Jamie.

"Listen," says Jandorek. "I don't know what the fuck this is about, but if you came here to cause trouble, you picked the worst place on the planet to do it. And you didn't pick a good time either."

"That's not why we're here," says Jamie.

"I'm glad that's settled. Why are you here?"

"About a friend of ours," says Ben, "a little kid, who we haven't seen in months. We're worried about him. We'd been thinking about what to do for a while, but we couldn't get it together to go to the police. Then yesterday, we met Darlene in the park, and even though we had a little fun with her, we decided she's basically good people."

"So we went to look for you," says Jamie, picking up the thread and now addressing O'Hara. "We started at the Nine, but they weren't very helpful. Then we tried the Seven, and they sent us here. We thought, Damn, homicide, pretty good for a sto—"

"Jamie," says O'Hara, cutting him off. "Tell us about your friend. What's his name?"

"We don't know his real name. He didn't tell us. We called him Hercules." Jesus Christ, thinks O'Hara, her hopes sinking again.

"We called him that as a joke," says Ben. "Because he was so skinny. He was this little guy, about eight, nine, who hung around the skateboard park the last year or so, and he was such a cheeky little gink, we sort of adopted him and made him our mascot."

"What color hair?"

"Blond."

"Dark blond or light blond?"

"Almost white, like a little surfer. And he had a slight limp from when he broke his leg. I guess it never healed right."

"Why wasn't he at school?"

"Good question. I asked him once. He said he was homeschooled, not that I believed him, because he was never at home either. I guess I should have gotten on his case about it, but it's not like he was the only one of us who should have been at school. And maybe he was homeschooled. He could read okay."

"How do you know that?" asks O'Hara.

"He read comics," says Jamie.

"Oh, yeah. Which ones?"

"*Superman, X-Men, Destroyer*. But more than anything *Superman*."

"Not *Batman*?"

"Never saw him reading that."

"Me neither," says Ben.

"Let's get out of the heat," says Jandorek, pointing at a filthy Impala parked ten feet away. "It's a piece of shit, but the AC works." He unlocks the door, and they climb in—Jandorek and O'Hara in front, Ben and Jamie in back.

"Here we are," says Jandorek, "a perfect family."

"All we need is Herc," says Ben.

O'Hara looks away as Jandorek starts the car and cranks the air. He opens the glove compartment, takes out two notebooks, and gives one to O'Hara.

"You know where he lived?" asks O'Hara, twisting toward the rear. "Who his parents were?"

"No," says Ben. "He just tagged along with us at the park. He didn't want to talk about his life. It was obviously something not so wonderful— maybe a foster home. I should have asked more. Gotten involved, like you say, but I didn't." He looks nothing like the arrogant brat from yesterday. He looks like he's going to cry.

"You're here now, right?" says O'Hara. "You're doing the right thing now. That's what counts."

"We waited too long."

"You never saw him with anyone?" asks Jandorek.

"Every once in a while someone would come to the park, looking for him," says Jamie, "but they didn't seem like his mother or father. Didn't look like it, or act like it."

"He was never glad to see them," says Ben, "but he left with them anyway, like he had no choice. He'd disappear for a couple days, or a week or even a month, and then one morning he'd roll into the park and every- thing would be back to normal."

"You ever ask where he went?"

"Once. All he said was he went on a trip."

"I need you to describe the people who picked him up," says O'Hara. "Take your time and try to remember. It's very important. Anything you remember at all."

"The thing is, it was never the same person," says Jamie. "I remember a guy, a little guy. Kind of low-key. Herc actually seemed to like him okay. And a woman who was quite unattractive, and another that was borderline hot—big tits, big hair. Kind of sexy."

"The woman who was unattractive," asks Jandorek, "you remember what about her was unattractive?"

"Her face, I guess."

"When he came back," asks O'Hara, "from being gone, did he look different? Act different? Were there any bruises on him? Any indication like he'd been roughed up or treated badly?"

"Not really. To be honest, he got more banged up with us in the park, falling off his board."

"When he came back," says Jamie, remembering something, "he'd have a little money. He'd buy pizza for everyone. Or buy two comics instead of one. The money never lasted long."

"No idea where he lived?"

"I assumed it was in the neighborhood," says Ben. "When he left the park, he was usually walking south."

"Tell us about him," says O'Hara. "What did he like to do other than read comics?"

"He was a good kid. He was very smart. Good company. He didn't feel sorry for himself about anything. He cheered us up."

"Was he a skateboarder?"

"Absolutely. He kept his left leg, the shorter one, on the board and pushed with his right. It worked pretty well. He already knew how to ride when we met him. He said he lived in California for a couple years, so he must have started there. He was starting to carve out a nice little style. Some people called him Ben Two. After me, I guess."

"Did he smoke pot with you?"

"Maybe yeah, sometimes. But we wouldn't let him do it much."

"The kid was nine years old, and you're giving him pot?" says O'Hara.

"We all smoked at that age," says Ben, disconsolate again. "When you have your first beer? I bet it was younger."

O'Hara doesn't have to do the math to know he's right.

"What kind of music did he listen to?" asks O'Hara.

"He liked the stuff we did—thrash metal, punk metal, hardcore.

Bands like Turnpike Wrecks, Last Call Brawl, Murphy's Law."

When O'Hara asks if Hercules liked Coldplay, Jamie winces. "Herc didn't listen to pussy music."

"How about a picture?" asks Jandorek. "Do either of you have pictures of him on your phone?"

"No," says Jamie, "but we know a place where there's a huge picture of Herc. About the size of the windshield."

"Seriously?"

"Yeah. In Chelsea."

CHAPTER 23

"BUCKLE UP, KIDS," says Jandorek. "You too, dear."

To a sound track of siren and screeching tires, Jandorek hustles the Impala crosstown, where the trip ends on Twenty-Second just west of Tenth, two wheels on the curb. Ben and Jamie lead them into a three-story tenement. One flight up, they enter a pristine space with track lighting and beautiful plank floors. Stenciled directly on a whitewashed wall, is "Freek Staps / 1954–2006." Even as O'Hara digests the odd foreign name and the fact that he is no longer alive, she is struck by the scent. Then she remembers where she's smelled it before. The Prada store in SoHo, where she and K arrested a clerk on a domestic dispute. That place had the same bouquet—the smell of money.

"Freek was Dutch," says Jamie, referring to the wall, "but he was in Berlin when he OD'd." While the luxe interior and aroma suggest high-end retail, the subjects of the black-and-white pictures on the wall are dead-end kids. O'Hara recognizes East River Park and Tompkins Square, and one shot was taken ten feet from where she, Ben, and Jamie were sitting the day before. Boys and girls in their early to mid-teens are photographed on benches, in diners, and in subway cars, but mostly they're partying in a barely furnished unsupervised space. They share forty-ounce bottles of malt liquor and pass joints, and to an unseemly degree, the revelers are beautiful and semi-naked. The boys are shirtless, the girls in panties and bras, and while the precocity is intended to shock—one kid who looks no more than fourteen sits on a toilet, shooting up—it doesn't take a PhD in bullshit to know that the photographs are as staged as a fashion ad, kiddie porn masquerading as social commentary.

In addition to the four of them, there are two middle-aged couples in the gallery. They take in the work in an awed hush, as if the stained planks are sacred ground. Ben and Jamie lead O'Hara into the gallery's second room and position her in front of the show's largest image, centered on an empty wall. "That's Herc," says Ben, and nods toward a shirtless boy, whose long blond hair spills out from under a Detroit Tigers baseball cap. A girl, also blond, not much older, wearing only panties, stands beside him, but Herc, who is sucking the last bit out of a fingertip-burning joint and stares directly into the camera, is the focus. Since Staps died in '06, Herc couldn't have been more than eight when the picture was taken, and with his pale skin stretched tight over his belly and ribs, he is little-boy skinny. But you can see why the photographer and gallery gave him top billing, and why his friends gave him the name Herc. Small and skinny as he is, the kid is all bravado. He acts as if getting semi-naked with a little blond beauty is no big thing. Hell, it happens every day. An eight-year-old James Cagney couldn't have pulled off a cheekier performance, and his grin is penetrating, as if asking Staps, "This is what you wanted, right?"

"When was the party?" O'Hara asks Ben.

"Last summer. It was in an empty loft on Bowery they couldn't sell. Somehow Freek got ahold of the keys from a broker. He invited all these kids, stocked the cabinets with booze, and had all this killer pot lying around. While everyone got fucked up, he walked around with an assistant and took pictures. We got invited after one of his talent scouts spotted us skating in the park, but it was obvious he was only interested in Herc. We were too old."

"He ever touch any of you?" asks Jandorek.

"No, he just liked to watch," says Ben. "And take pictures."

"And sell them," says Jamie, pointing at the red dot under the name of the picture, titled *boy / girl*. "The same talent scouts who invited us to the party invited us to the opening last month. They told us not to get dressed up. They wanted us to look street. It was creepy. While I was there, I checked out the price list. The cheapest picture was twenty-five thousand dollars. For Herc and the girl, they were asking eighty grand." The snotty discretion about the prices reminds O'Hara of the Prada store too. Out of morbid curiosity, she had wanted to find out the price of a cashmere coat. She had to sort through five different tags before she finally found it in tiny numbers—$4,200.

"At least we got a picture now," says Jandorek.

"What I would like to do is take this one, fucking rip it off the wall, and leave, but I figure you're in enough hot water already, just by association."

"Don't worry about me, Dar. I can take care of myself. Whatever you want to do is jakes by me."

O'Hara smiles for the first time in a couple days. Instead of grabbing the photo, O'Hara walks back to the front of the gallery. Behind a partition is an enamel table lined with large-format coffee-table art books, including a lavishly bound catalogue of the show: *Freek Staps / 1954–2006*.

"Freek was an amazing artist," says a stylish woman in a very short dress.

"An amazing asshole," says O'Hara, and puts two of the catalogues under her arm.

"Excuse me, those are two hundred and fifty dollars each."

"Go fuck yourself," says O'Hara, and the four of them leave.

CHAPTER 24

O'HARA NURSES A beer and seethes. As far as she is concerned, the $250 coffee-table book, with its thick stock, lavish jacket, and fawning commentary, is more offensive than rank porn. At least porn is up-front. That this piece of crap is even in her home, and that she is looking at it on the same couch where Axl and Bruno do some of their best napping, disturbs her. As best she can, she avoids thinking about Ben's face. After they left the show, O'Hara had to tell Ben and Jamie that Herc was dead. Since the story was going to be on television in hours, and the papers the next morning, they deserved to hear it from her. Ben took it as hard as a sibling and blamed himself, and his crumpling face was one of the saddest she'd seen since she became a cop. O'Hara studies the catalogue, and learns as much as she can from it about the charismatic subject of its most expensive photograph. When she looks at the Tigers cap, she remembers the Yankees atop his skull in the garden and how even in the grave he seemed to be smiling. The hat shows that the grave was also a phony tableau: whoever staged it kept getting the details wrong. For starters, he wasn't a Yankees fan. He probably wasn't a baseball fan at all, but if he was going to be buried in a baseball cap, he would have wanted it to be a Tigers hat, not a Yankees cap, for Christ's sake. Same thing with the *Batman* comic and the Coldplay CD. Whoever dressed the kid and threw in the gifts didn't know him that well.

On the other hand, Herc did like comics, and he did like music, and he did wear baseball caps, so whoever it was hadn't got it completely wrong either. They got it half right. What kind of people get those things half right? It's not your friends. Your friends, God bless them, know exactly what you like to wear and smoke and drink and listen to. The people who get those things wrong, or half wrong or half right, however you want to put it, are your fucking family, so maybe the kid had a family after all. As O'Hara thinks about the semi-ignorance, semi-loneliness of families, and sinks deeper into her funk, her cell rings, and it's an area code she doesn't recognize.

"Is this Darlene O'Hara?"

"Who are you?"

"Connie Wawrinka, a detective with the Sarasota Police Department."

O'Hara panics, fearing that something has happened to Axl. She reminds herself that she talked to him a couple nights ago and he didn't mention anything about Florida. Of course maybe he wouldn't. She's just the kid's mother, and not a particularly good one. "We got a match," says Wawrinka.

"A match?"

"From ballistics." O'Hara realizes Wawrinka is talking about the ballistic report on the .22-caliber bullet. NYPD sent it to every police department in the country. "Six months ago," says Wawrinka, "we pulled the same kind of bullet, shot by the same weapon, out of the brain of an eighty-seven-year-old resident of Longboat Key named Benjamin Levin."

"What happened?" asks O'Hara.

"He put the barrel of the rifle in his mouth and shot himself."

PART II

INSTEAD OF A shot from a starter's pistol, there's the *bing* made by a microwave when the soup is warm. O'Hara pushes from her seat in the second-to-last row and with two hundred compressed, vaguely nauseated travelers plods toward the exit. She presses through the malodorous air of coach and the still-warm party debris of business and does that little perp walk past the chipper smiles of the flight crew. When she steps into the rubber hose that connects the plane to the terminal, the crappy seal offers the first inkling of Florida heat.

Inside the terminal, O'Hara washes her face and buys a bottle of water, then lets the conveyor sweep her past a Starbucks and TGIF. After a glossy billboard for Accenture, which features the magisterial focus of Tiger Woods, come local ads for Barnacle Bill's Seafood, and the Varicose Vein Center of Sarasota, where you can "walk away from varicose veins." Ahead, at the end of the walkway, an elderly couple, who O'Hara suspects have been waiting without a hint of impatience for hours, extend a frail, blissed-out welcome to their grandchildren, and behind them, in the floor-to-ceiling aquarium, a baby hammerhead makes tight angry circles, his dead eyes assessing the meat parade.

O'Hara dodges the family reunion and hungry shark and takes the

escalator to ground transportation. On the way down, she passes a monu-
mental bronze of Hernando de Soto, and learns that the Spanish explorer
arrived on the Gulf Coast around 1540. Till now the only celebrity O'Hara
associates with Sarasota is Pee-wee Herman, but she appreciates that
Pee-wee might not be the way the chamber of commerce would choose
to welcome visitors.

When O'Hara steps outside, a rosy smudge is all that's left of the day,
but even at 9:00 the thick swamp air paws at her, and in the time it takes to
walk through the lot to her rental, the back of her shirt is soaked through.
She's booked a room at a Marriott but is in no rush to get there and too
out of her element to look for trouble. Instead, she decides to take a little
drive, roll the windows down, and become a tourist of humidity.

The airport labyrinth spits her out at the entrance to the Tamiami Trail,
Route 45, the main drag into Sarasota. Idling in front of her is a rusted
pickup. "When I get old I'm moving up north and driving slow," reads the
bumper sticker. Across the street is the John Ringling Museum, a huge
marble edifice bequeathed to the state of Florida by the circus impresario.
Ringling was the partner of P. T. Barnum, whose words were scrawled on
the wall in Coney Island, and she shakes her head at the divide between
this palazzo and that sweaty box on the boardwalk. O'Hara heads east and
the neighborhood takes a dive. Two-story cinder block lines the road on
both sides—the Cadillac Motel, the Flamingo Inn, a cocktail lounge called
Memories. Sprouting among the vacancy signs are billboards for Mom's
Bail Bonds, Justice.com, and Credit Repair. Others don't even have ads,
just LEASE ME and a phone number, and the combination of heat and squalor
feels third-world. A shirtless boy pedals his bike through an empty parking lot. He's probably just trying to stir up some breeze and feel the air on
his skin, she thinks, but even at forty miles per hour, the air barely moves.

As O'Hara takes in the local color, she returns to the questions she
brought with her from New York. What does it mean that the same weapon
that killed a nine-year-old street urchin from the East Village ended the
life of an eighty-seven-year-old retiree from Teaneck, New Jersey? What

connects the young and old bodies a thousand miles apart? As soon as the NYPD got the ballistics match, they sent the boy's DNA down to Florida to determine if the two were related, but it bounced back negative. At the moment the only thing that connects them, at least roughly, is the timing. The old man died a little over six months ago, on March 3, and based on the deterioration of the boy's body at two sites, the first exposed, the second buried, and the maggot casings in the skeleton, that's about the same time frame Bradley came up with for the boy's death.

A marquee reads ADULT MOVIES, XXX VIDEO CLUB, and behind it is a minimal white structure whose bleakness is only exceeded by the imagined bleakness inside. Is this where they busted Pee-wee? O'Hara read somewhere that he was watching a titty movie called *Nancy Nurse*, because that unfortunate detail is still lodged in her brain. Was it really necessary to nab Pee-wee for that? Of course they didn't realize who he was till after, but maybe, thinks O'Hara, certain less annoying celebrities should be immune from arrest for trifling but embarrassing misdemeanors, not for their benefit as much as for everyone else's.

The blight of the Tamiami Trail moderates, and the reflecting glass of downtown reassures motorists that they'll soon be safe and sound in the land of money. O'Hara turns away from the business district and climbs a graceful bridge over the harbor. To her left is the Gulf of Mexico and to her right the intercoastal waterway; below her, sleek powerboats bob at the private docks of the waterfront mansions. At the apex of the bridge, O'Hara catches little filaments of light in her peripheral vision and sees that they are fishing lines, connected to dark-skinned men in T-shirts and shorts, trying to pull some free protein from the harbor.

A short distance beyond the bridge, O'Hara slows for a shopping roundabout and through her open windows hears the tinkling of a piano set up outside a restaurant. O'Hara recognizes the melody but can't quite name the song. A white-haired couple window-shop—the woman in heels and a dress, the man in slacks and white patent leather shoes—and despite the heat, hold hands. Halfway round the circle, O'Hara sees signs to Longboat Key, which she remembers from her conversation with the Sarasota detective Connie Wawrinka as the address of Benjamin Levin.

O'Hara crosses a second bridge and gets another view of the Gulf, this time under a crescent moon, before picking up the flat, straight road that bisects the narrow key with its golf courses, tennis courts, and elegant twenty-story condos. For a penultimate stop you probably can't ask for much more—although there are "Units for Sale" signs at every gated entrance—and O'Hara enjoys the moneyed hush until the sight of a grocery store called Publix reminds her of her eight-pretzel dinner.

There are only seven minutes till closing, and the parking lot's empty. In New York she'd be banging on the glass, pointing at her watch. Here, as she steps through the sliding doors, she is approached by a smiling man in black slacks and a lime green shirt. He says "Welcome to Publix" and seems to mean it, and in the few minutes it takes for O'Hara to grab a six-pack of Amstel and get a turkey sandwich at the deli counter, two employees ask if there's anything they can do to help. And they're not giving her the bum's rush. Did she die in a plane crash, or has she stepped into an alternate universe?

At checkout, it's more of the same. Did she find everything she needed? Has she had a nice evening? Why is everyone acting so fucking nice? Is it the heat, the sun, the dire economy? Is business so bad that every customer is appreciated, no matter when they straggle in? And yet despite that, the visit ends on a disquieting note. After O'Hara has paid and collected her change, her mostly liquid supper is bagged by a man wearing large plastic glasses and a loose-fitting apron. As his sinewy arms and translucent skin register in her brain, she realizes that the man working at minimum wage in his golden years is not a day less than eighty. He hands her the bag with a lovely smile and says, "Have a great night."

CHAPTER 26

"NOT MUCH BLOOD," says O'Hara. She entertained hopes of a modern glassy structure streaming with tropical light à la *Dexter*. And maybe a nice view of palm trees and water and a buff Latin cop or two. Instead, she finds herself in a windowless room filthy enough to be back in the 7, studying a dozen eight-by-tens of an elderly Jewish man on his bathroom tiles. The photos, taken in the early afternoon of March 3 in Unit 306 of a Longboat Key condominium called Banyan Bay, offer a pretty fair idea of the final moments of Benjamin Levin, a retired eighty-seven-year-old manufacturer of cosmetic gloves for women.

"That's what you get for using a rabbit gun," says Connie Wawrinka, the Sarasota detective O'Hara talked to on the phone a couple nights before. "It's not like he blew his brains out. The twenty-two-caliber bullet never left his skull. Didn't even reach it."

The first row of photos shows, from various angles and distances, Levin on his bathroom floor, his tennis shorts and shirt slightly darker than the white tiles. The only inkling of how he came to be there is the dried trickle that connects his nostrils to his upper lip and the dark stain no bigger than a tablespoon ballooning from his thin mouth like comic-strip dialogue. Despite his age, his hirsute limbs are still wiry, and O'Hara wonders if Leibowitz will look this lithe at the end. Jews age well, she thinks. Then again, considering the knee-jerk litany of nos and toos—no drinking, no smoking, too late, too spicy, no this, too that—it's not much of a payout.

"Take a look at this one," says Wawrinka, and points to a picture of Levin's bedroom in the next row. To the left is the victim's neatly made bed with a dark rectangular shape on top of it. To the right, just outside the bathroom door, are the rubber soles of Levin's tennis sneakers. In between, leaning against the night table, is the antique wooden rifle Levin used to end his life. "Even after firing a bullet into his brain, he was able to prop the gun against the nightstand and get almost all the way into the bathroom."

"He didn't want to leave a mess," says O'Hara. Just like Leibowitz, she thinks, and longs for him in a way she hasn't for weeks.

"EMS said the body was still warm. The poor fuck took ten minutes to die. He's lucky he died, period." O'Hara looks up from the picture at the six-foot Wawrinka. Although she reminds herself not to stare, she holds her gaze a beat too long or reveals something nonplussed in her expression, because Wawrinka smiles and says, "Hawaiian mom, Polish dad."

That's funny, thinks O'Hara, but is it a joke? Like a lot of things about Wawrinka, O'Hara isn't quite sure. Wawrinka's disclosure of her mutt ancestry explains the almond eyes in the fleshy East European face, but it hardly decodes the spectacle of Wawrinka's striking androgyny. NYPD is thick with butch gay females. It goes with the territory, but what Wawrinka is doing with her button-down oxford shirt, jeans, and old-school Pumas is more charismatic and stylish, more like cross-dressing. With her thick jet-black hair and short bangs carved like sideburns, she resembles a Polish-Asian Elvis. "Is that a book?" asks O'Hara, referring to the dark shape on the bedspread.

"A framed photograph," says Wawrinka, "of his grandson. Apparently, before he shot himself, he took it off the night table, looked at it one last time, then left it facedown on the bed."

"How about that dark shape on the floor just under the bed?"

"Don't remember exactly—a hanger maybe, or the edge of a shoe."

"At the time, nothing struck you as hinky?"

"No. Just a lonely old widower who decided he'd had enough. Now we know the same gun also killed the boy, we start from scratch, no question. But like I said, at the time, we didn't see a single thing that didn't support a straightforward suicide."

As striking as Wawrinka's rockabilly swagger is her lack of attitude. A homicide detective from NYC waltzes in and informs the locals they got their heads up their asses, you expect nothing but pushback and a fuck-you smile, but Wawrinka isn't playing it like that. Not at all. O'Hara gets more bullshit on a daily basis from her own sergeant.

"So let me ask you something, Connie, you ever do karaoke?"

"Of course," says Wawrinka. Like O'Hara, she is in her mid-thirties, but with her schoolboy attire seems half a decade younger.

"What do you do—'Heartbreak Hotel,' 'Blue Suede Shoes'?"

"That would be a little too easy, don't you think?" says Wawrinka, running one hand through her mop and curling her upper lip. "No, I do Warwick, 'Walk on By,' or the Carpenters' 'Close to You.' The room goes so quiet you can hear the panties drop."

"That's fucking quiet," says O'Hara, and Wawrinka laughs. "Do me a favor," says O'Hara, "no matter how obvious, take me through everything that said straight suicide. Help get my bearings."

"For starters, you got an eighty-seven-year-old sprawled on his bathroom floor with a bullet in his brain and a rifle by the bed. He's sick—according to the autopsy, advanced melanoma and prostate cancer. He's alone; his wife of sixty-one years—I know, it's sweet—died eight months earlier. And according to his daughter, it wasn't pretty. A stroke, a second stroke, feeding tube, infections from the feeding tube, infections from all the time in the wheelchair. And she died at home, so Levin had a front-row seat. Knew what he had to look forward to. Alone. At a certain point, getting it over with is a pretty good option, and it looked like Levin had gotten there."

"And nothing about the scene looked off?"

"No. I know the killer could have taken a picture off the night table and dropped it facedown on the bed, but the truth is, nothing about the scene felt staged. You stage it, you wipe the gun down and place it in the victim's hand. At the very least, you drop it on the floor beside the body, you don't lean it neatly by the bed. Plus this gun was covered with twenty years of prints. But the main thing was that there was no evidence of anyone else having been in the place. No sign of a break-in, no one else's blood, no sign of struggle, nothing stolen."

O'Hara glances at the autopsy report lying beside the pictures. "You said someone could easily have flipped the picture, given us a little detail to make it look legit, but you don't think someone could have overpowered him, put the gun in his mouth?"

"Possible, but there were no bruises on Levin. No sign of any struggle."

"According to the report, Levin was five-six and a hundred and eighteen pounds. How much of a struggle could he have put up?"

"Maybe he would have gone down, but he would have fought back."

"What makes you so sure?"

"In the last eight months, he was arrested for assault. Twice."

"I thought he was a nice old Jew from Teaneck."

"First incident was at a restaurant called Sweet Tomatoes. Apparently some guy cut the line at the early-bird special," says Wawrinka with a straight face.

"Sweet Tomatoes?"

"A salad bar on Tamiami. Even after seven, it's like eight dollars all-you-can-eat, soup, dessert, everything. And it's good. I have no clue how they make money. Maybe it's a front for the cartel. Those old fucks wolf it down like there's no tomorrow, which is pretty much true. At five o'clock, people are lined up out the door, guys in their patent leather shoes, ladies all dolled up. Except for grandchildren, no one's under seventy."

"What the hell happened?"

"Like I said, some guy cut the line."

"Cut the line at the early-bird special at Sweet Tomatoes?" says O'Hara, as if repeating the words will give them meaning.

"Not a good idea when Benjamin Levin is in the line. He walks up to the guy, who is about a foot taller and seventy pounds heavier, and he tells the guy to go to the back of the line. And he doesn't do it nicely. The guy says something back, and Levin decks him."

"The guy is like a hundred pounds?"

"One punch," says Wawrinka. "Lays the guy out across the croutons and sliced beets. The beets stain the guy's pants, which is half the reason he files charges. I can get you the police report."

O'Hara flashes back to the picture of the kid in the Chelsea gallery with his arm around his girl and smiling up at the camera like it's nothing, and thinks, related or not, the old man and the kid are two of a kind. Little guys with brass stones.

"Okay," says O'Hara, "that's assault number one."

"Three months earlier, same story, different place. This time on a golf course. He's playing with his buddies at Landmark, up near the airport. Instead of the early-bird special, it's the senior off-season discount. These nutjobs out in the midday heat to save a couple dollars. Apparently Levin's foursome isn't moving fast enough, hardly surprising considering it's a hundred eighteen degrees. And someone in the group behind them yells something. Levin drives the golf cart back, asks who's in the big hurry. Finds out it's a fellow named Frank McGraw, and knocks him out cold. In the golf cart, on top of the steering wheel, like Faye Dunaway in *Chinatown*."

"Except there's no horn on a golf cart," says O'Hara. "Not the same without the horn."

"True."

CHAPTER 27

SHAMELESSLY SQUEAKING THE tires, Wawrinka one-hands the Crown Vic through the tight turns of the basement garage. When she guns it at the ramp, the two-ton vehicle shoots onto the sun-blasted street like the Batmobile exiting the Batcave.

"Apparently," says O'Hara, "they still let you burn a little fossil fuel down here. I'm lucky to get a Prius with enough volts to play the radio."

Wawrinka grins beneath reflecting aviators. "This is Florida, Darlene, the state that gave us W."

"Thanks for that."

Wawrinka makes short work of Sarasota's small downtown, and they're soon flying over the bridges O'Hara traveled the night before. The tranquil moonlight has been replaced by a murderous glare, and for O'Hara the lack of visual content is unsettling—all that sky and water and nothing in it but the speck of a bird or the wisp of a boat. In the midday heat, the tennis courts, golf courses, and beaches are deserted, and even the most elegant limestone condos look like little more than a place to pull the shades and hide. Although O'Hara fears she'll find out soon enough, she can't imagine what it would be like with a hangover.

A couple miles past Publix, Wawrinka turns into a relatively modest two-story development called Banyan Bay, and they hustle from the carport to Unit 306. At the door, O'Hara tries to conceal her impatience as Wawrinka fishes for the key.

"Having a little trouble with the heat?"

"Only when I'm outside. Ever get used to it?"

"No."

Wawrinka leads O'Hara past the kitchen into a living room/dining room and hits the lights. "The place looks exactly the same," she says.

"It's six months," says O'Hara. "It hasn't been sold or rented?"

"I guess you haven't been following the Florida real estate market. A couple years ago, a place like this on the Gulf was worth a million. Now it might be worth half that, if you could get someone to buy it, which is unlikely. As far as I know, Levin's daughter hasn't bothered to put it on the market."

"No one's been here in six months?"

"It's not a crime scene. A neighbor might have given in to morbid curiosity and talked the super into giving him a tour. Or maybe some broker has wormed her way in, but it doesn't look like it. Either way, I brought the pictures to compare."

With Wawrinka behind her, O'Hara steps gingerly into the master bedroom, where the last minutes of Levin's life played out. She studies the corner of the bed, where he sat when he presumably shot himself, and the nightstand against which he propped the gun, and takes the same three steps Levin took before he collapsed in the bathroom. When she compares the pictures with the present, she finds the same pale yellow bedspread and the frame still facedown in the middle of it.

In the bathroom, the only visible difference is that the blood has been scoured from the tiles. O'Hara isn't sure if she's more grateful for the unlikely integrity of the crime scene or that Wawrinka thought to call the super to turn on the AC. Without it, the walls would be sweating. When O'Hara flips over the picture with her pen, she sees why Levin might have chosen it for his final glimpse of the world. In the shot, Levin and his brown-haired grandson, who is about the same age as Herc, are stretched out on the same bed, playing cards. Neither is aware that he is being photographed, and they are completely engrossed in their game and at ease with each other. In front of the bed are a dresser and TV stand, on the far side a chaise and a tall halogen reading light. Beyond them, a large window faces the Gulf, and when O'Hara crosses to the far side of the bed and peeks behind the blind, the light bouncing off the sand rebuffs her.

Take your sweet time, she tells herself. All that's waiting is a preheated oven of a car and the four walls of her motel room. With her back to the window, she does a calm scan of the room, ending at the TV stand in the corner. In addition to an outdated, modest-size TV and a DVD player, the shelves are covered with a dozen cans of yellow tennis balls, half of them opened. On the top shelf beside the TV is a remote control, and next to the remote a wooden spoon. "See the wooden spoon on the TV stand?" says O'Hara. "Remember that?"

"No."

"You think it was there six months ago?"

"I don't know, but I don't see why anyone would have brought it in since."

"No cooking going on when you arrived? No sauce simmering on the burner? No boiling pasta?"

"I would have remembered that."

I would fucking well hope so, thinks O'Hara.

"It was eleven in the morning," says Wawrinka with a hint of annoyance. "The guy wasn't cooking spaghetti in his tennis whites."

"So why would he bring a spoon into his bedroom that morning?"

"Maybe he didn't bring it that morning. Maybe he brought it sometime before and forgot about it. Maybe he used it to scratch his back or some other part of his anatomy I'd rather not think about. Maybe he used it to squash a water bug. Maybe he had a hooker come over and spanked her with it."

"A drive-by spanking."

"Yeah, but in that case I don't think he would leave it lying around."

That's true, thinks O'Hara, impressed. Not after using it for something vaguely shameful. In the kitchen, she opens cabinets until she finds the drawer with the cooking utensils. Stuffed inside and crammed together are a big plastic spoon with a hole in it, two different kinds of cheese graters, three spatulas, a Rabbit wine opener, and two more wooden spoons like the one in the bedroom. "So this is where the spoon came from," says O'Hara.

"Looks like it."

"You know the band Spoon?" says O'Hara. "I think they're okay."

"Not bad," says Wawrinka without enthusiasm.

"You're probably right. My son's in a band—the Flat Screens."

"What's his name?"

"Axl. Axl Rose O'Hara."

"Seriously?"

"He swears he forgives me."

O'Hara opens the fridge. It's empty except for a six-pack of Amstel on the bottom shelf.

"It's like a sign from God," says O'Hara. "Want one?"

"It's a little early for me."

"It's actually a little late for me, but we got to drink at least one. I read somewhere it's bad luck not to."

"Where you read that?"

"The New Testament or the Old Testament. One of the two. Besides, it's one-oh-three outside, and cool in here."

"Fine."

They take their beers and the crime scene photos into the shade-drawn living room, where they stretch out on opposing couches. Nice place, thinks O'Hara. No kitschy beach shit or store-bought pictures. A simple place on the beach.

"What made you become a cop?" asks O'Hara.

"I think it was the butch toys—the gun, the holster, the cap, the badge, and best of all, the cars."

One of the more honest answers I've gotten, thinks O'Hara.

"How about you?"

"I had Axl when I was fifteen, and barely finished high school. It's not like the world was knocking down my door."

"And you made homicide, good for you." Wawrinka makes a little salutary gesture with her bottle, and O'Hara sits there embarrassed, surprised as always that anyone might see her as a success.

"At the station, I asked you about everything that said straight suicide. In hindsight, now that we know it wasn't, is there anything that seems off?"

"The gun," says Wawrinka, "particularly that one. It's such a stupid way to kill yourself. He could have ended up in a wheelchair as easy as dying. And the timing. Maybe he had his reasons, but why then? His cancer wasn't so bad that he couldn't play three sets of doubles the day before and win two. Something happened that morning."

O'Hara puts her empty on a *Newsweek* on the corner table beside the couch. As she eyes it wistfully, wishing she hadn't drained it so fast, she notices the answering machine behind it, reaches over, and hits messages. After some static comes a male voice. The speaker is old, but not so old that he can't be pissed off.

"Bun, it's Sol. What'sa matter, you don't return calls anymore? Don't be a schmuck. Give me a call."

"Don't be a schmuck, Bun," mimics Wawrinka. *"Give me a call."*

O'Hara laughs. "That's not bad."

"Work in Florida, you learn how to do an old Jewish guy."

"I believe that."

The other two messages are also from Sol, also exasperated, hocking his old pal to get off his bony ass and call him back. "Sol was worried about him," says O'Hara, thumbing through the crime scene pictures on her lap. "I hope when I stop returning calls, someone gives enough of a shit to get on my case about it."

"Jesus," says Wawrinka. "One light beer, and you get morbid."

O'Hara stops at the picture that shows the gun leaning on the night table and looks at the dark shape in the shadows at the edge of the bed. She gets up and walks into the bedroom. The dark shape in the picture is gone. She steps over to the TV console, grabs the wooden spoon, lays it on the floor in the same spot half under the bed, and studies the picture again. "I'm pretty sure that spoon was the dark shape by the side of the bed."

"Makes sense," says Wawrinka, who has followed her into the bedroom. "EMS would have picked it up and moved it out of the way when they wheeled Levin out."

"And if it was on the floor by his bed, it probably hadn't been there long," says O'Hara. "So why the fuck would Levin have brought a wooden spoon into his bedroom that morning?"

Not ready to face the heat outside, O'Hara returns to her spot on the living room couch, but not before a detour to the kitchen for two more Amstels. If you can't take the heat, she thinks, get into the kitchen.

When O'Hara first walked into the apartment, she noticed a shape perched on the wall above the pass-through from the kitchen to the dining room, and now sees it's a lovely antique angel carved out of wood, with pink chubby cheeks and dimpled cherubic thighs, strategically perched in the corner so that she can look out over the whole room.

"See that angel?" asks O'Hara.

"She's kind of a honey."

"I bet when Levin's wife realized she was dying, she put that angel up in the corner so that she could look out after her husband."

"You could be right. Too bad she did such a half-assed job."

CHAPTER 28

SOL KLINGER IS not one to take unnecessary risks. Although the early-bird special at Sabia's runs a generous hour and a half, from 5:00 to 6:30, he arrives at 4:45. When O'Hara walks in twenty minutes later, she finds him settled in a corner, the only customer in the place, gnawing a breadstick and studying the menu for loopholes.

"To old friends," says O'Hara after the waiter drops off her Amstel.

"To Bunny 'Schoolboy' Levin," says Klinger, "inch for inch, pound for pound, the toughest Jew I've ever known." In his mid-eighties, Klinger still has some hair and some heft and some light in his eyes. Swathed in high-end fabrics, reading glasses dangling from a gold loop attached to a neck chain, he looks prosperous and relaxed in a way that makes the connection between the two obscenely transparent.

"I guess that poor fellow at Sweet Tomatoes didn't stand a chance," says O'Hara.

"I'm not talking about an old fart with a quick temper," says Klinger, waving away whatever O'Hara may have heard with the stub of his breadstick. "I'm talking about a kid who as a junior at South Newark High School beat a leading contender for the lightweight title. The next day, his classmates carried him around the playground on their shoulders. Can you imagine how good that must have felt? I can't, and I've been trying for seventy years."

Klinger reaches into a leather portfolio and drops an ancient publicity shot on the table. "This is from '37," he says, "before they banned religious symbols. Bun was seventeen."

Seventy years ago in a Newark gym, Levin adopts the classic pugilistic crouch. His thickly muscled arms and legs are poised for action, his taped fists ready to fly. But as always, it's the eyes. Levin's are soulful and belligerent and calm to the point of indifference, as if quietly informing his opponent that they can settle this now in the ring or some other time on a street corner, it's all the same to him. Sewn on the leg of his silk trunks is the Star of David, and written in script across a bottom corner of the picture "Bunny 'Schoolboy' Levin," although with his glistening black hair and fearless eyes, Levin looks more like John Garfield than a schoolboy.

Kids grew up faster then, thinks O'Hara. Then she remembers the scene, however contrived, on the wall of the Chelsea gallery, and dismisses the thought as nonsense.

"At seventeen, Bunny already had twelve pro fights. Three at the old Garden, two at Saint Nichols Arena on Sixty-Sixth Street. I know because I saw them all."

"You two been friends since then?"

"Friends? He was the neighborhood hero—'Schoolboy Levin.' I was just Klinger, an actual schoolboy. I tagged along as much as he would tolerate it, and I helped him out. Like most parents, Bunny's didn't approve of the sweet science, even if it helped pay the rent. So I stowed his gear at my place. Our apartment was on the second floor. On his way to a fight, he'd stop below my window and whistle. Then I'd lower his bag down to him in the street."

"Did Bunny ever mention spending time with a young boy from New York, about nine years old, blond hair, a slight limp?"

"I don't think he'd been in New York in years. After the war the GI plan took him to college. Then like all of us, he got married. His wife's family made disposable plastic gloves, the kind women wore at night over moisturizers. He grew the business, moved to the suburbs, and was lucky enough to sell it when it was still worth something. Me, I became a lawyer, did even better. It wasn't until we met again down here that we became more like friends. Equals, almost. The only reference to a kid I can remember had something to do with helping some broad pay for her son's tuition, but I don't recall her being from New York."

"Financially, was Ben okay at that end?"

"He was fine. Ben didn't get excited about money. You saw his place. It would fit in my garage. For him, it was about proving something, making a point. The rappers on my grandsons' CDs, they all sing about 'representing.' That's what Bun was doing too. He represented the corner of East Fifth and Sparrow in South Newark. That's why we all loved him."

"What was your reaction to the news?"

"I was devastated. How do you think I'd feel? And not that I have any right to judge, not knowing all the details, but I was disappointed. In seventy years I'd never seen him back down. It wasn't his style. I don't think he could if he wanted to."

"So you think the suicide was staged?"

"By who?"

When the waiter returns to the table, O'Hara orders a burger, Klinger the salmon. "Could I get a salad with that?" he asks.

"The special doesn't come with a salad, sir. It comes with rice or a potato and the vegetable. Would you like to order a salad?"

"That's okay."

"Come on, Sol," says O'Hara, "order the goddamn salad."

Klinger scowls at O'Hara and turns back to the waiter. "When you get back to the kitchen, if you see some lettuce and a couple tomatoes and maybe a mushroom or two, could you just drop them in a little pile on the plate next to the fish?"

"A little pile?"

"Yeah."

"That sounds a lot like a salad, sir."

"Maybe to you."

The waiter glances at O'Hara in a plea for empathy, but O'Hara looks past him at the empty restaurant. With its long mahogany bar and vintage movie posters, it could be in any city in America except New York.

"At the end," asks O'Hara, "was he still all there? Mentally."

"He was fine. Still did the crossword in ink. It's not like boxing today. Those guys knew how to slip punches. His curse was that he still could fuck."

Why do Jews always find a way to talk about good things like they're bad? What is that about?

"An eighty-seven-year-old widower who can still fuck is just about guaranteed to go out like a schmuck. It would be okay if Bun would content himself with the old widow upstairs, but of course that's not what he has in mind. Who does? He wants someone younger. Believes a young broad could still want him, can't help but believe it, so he ends up paying some stranger's kid's tuition. Which pissed off his own daughter, and I don't blame her."

"You remember anything about this woman?"

"Actually, I think there were two. All I remember is that one had bad skin."

"How did you know that?"

"Bun must have told me. His point, I guess, was that she could actually care for him. She was young, too young for him, but she had her flaws too. Hey, maybe I'm wrong. Maybe she did like him, and I'm just jealous. I've been jealous of him my whole life."

CHAPTER 29

AFTER DINNER, O'HARA and Klinger dawdle under an awning in front of Klinger's enormous pearl gray Lexus.

"I get a new one every three years. That and a colonoscopy."

"Sol, I hope you're good for half a dozen more . . . of each."

"Darlene. It was a pleasure."

It takes Klinger ten minutes to climb in, buckle up, and back out. When his taillights recede, it's all of 5:45, and O'Hara still has way too much daylight to safely navigate. A couple blocks up is a twenty-screen cineplex. Hugging the sides of the buildings for shade, O'Hara walks the three deserted blocks to the ticket window, where she is reminded that a cineplex is a theater showing a long list of movies none of which you want to see. Of the wealth of shitty options, the only time that works is *I Am Legend* at 6:25, but she can't get herself to step up to the glass window and pull the trigger.

Don't be a schmuck, Darlene, she tells herself in her best imitation of Wawrinka doing Klinger. *Buy the frigging ticket, get yourself a nice bottle of pop and a bucket of popcorn, and lay low till the sun goes down.* But as enticing as they are, two dark, sugary, salty refrigerated hours aren't enough to get her to take $11 out of her wallet and hand it over to Will Smith. Not in this lifetime. She'd as soon get mugged.

Next door is a sprawling bar, and when she steps in, she wonders if it's owned by the same guy who owns the Italian place. Rather than old movie posters, the walls are plastered with legendary jocks, not the sweaty battle-tested undergear, which would actually be kind of interesting, but athletes and assorted memorabilia, not that it makes any difference, since it all feels like it was ordered out of the same restaurant/bar decorating catalogue. O'Hara revisits in her mind the wonderful old photograph Klinger showed her of Levin and juxtaposes it with the gallery shot of the still nameless kid. Levin, the poor first-generation immigrant who wandered into a gym and learned to throw and slip punches, would have liked the kid who wandered into Tompkins Square Park and learned to roll a joint and do an ollie. How could he not have? He was an updated version of himself—same balls, same attitude, Street Urchin 2.0. If only the old man had paid tuition for the kid instead of the son of some gold digger, maybe things would have turned out better for both of them.

Unfortunately, nursing a beer is not part of O'Hara's skill set. When her empty hits the coaster, it's 6:15, and the thought of whiling away the evening in generic limbo is less appealing than *I Am Legend*. She remembers the museum by the airport and, on her way to dinner with Klinger, passing a bus stop with an ad for a show there of old-time circus photographs from the turn of the century. She calls the museum from her barstool and learns that on Thursdays, it's open till 8:00.

Twenty minutes later an elderly volunteer hands her a metal pin and a brochure and directs her to the two rooms devoted to the photography of Frederick Whitman Glasier. According to her reading material, Glasier, a failed jeweler, opened a portrait studio in Brockton, Massachusetts, in 1901. Two years later, the Barnum & Bailey Circus came to Brockton, and Glasier spent most of the next thirty years as its semiofficial in-house photographer. "If you ask me," says the woman at the front desk, "he's better than Ansel Adams. And do you know that all his pictures were taken on glass plates, so that they were composed upside down?"

In their heyday, circus companies toured 150 cities and towns a year. A private train pulled into the station, and the whole town watched the animals and performers parade to the fairgrounds, where in six hours sledgehammer-wielding crews put up a canvas big top capable of covering 12,000. In beautiful set shots, Glasier captures the unfolding spectacle, but O'Hara is particularly taken by his portraits, which are displayed with snippets of Barnum's original hyperbole. There are the acrobatic Hugony sisters, "marvels of strength and agility," and the Marvells themselves, contortionists who perform "terpsichorean originalities and odd feats of gyrations with curious and comic episodes." There are the Upside Down Bros., who walked down stairs on their heads, and the iron-jaw acts like the Kimball Twins, who flew through the air suspended by their teeth and performed "daring acts of dental dexterity."

O'Hara can't help but appreciate that none of these gymnasts, contortionists, or aerialists are skinny girls. They've all got asses and tits and thighs proudly presented in skintight outfits that even a century down the road are blatantly erotic. The pictures of these intrepid young women remind O'Hara of her visit to Coney Island and her conversation in Williamsburg with Jennifer Miller, the bearded woman who was once a regular at the sideshow. When O'Hara asked Miller why she grew and kept her beard, she said she didn't want to bow down. In a way that only a teenager can be, she was an impassioned feminist, and just coming out as a lesbian, and didn't see why she should. The cost to Miller of keeping that beard has been biblical. It's pushed her to the margins and made a very smart woman all but unemployable, and maybe she's insane for hanging on to it, but thank God, thinks O'Hara, for young girls with balls. And maybe, thinks O'Hara, that little Coney Island pimp was not entirely full of shit when he was spouting about the value of seeing the iconography against which you will inevitably be judged. Clearly these circus performers were among the first feminists, and if no one is willing to be a freak, nothing ever changes. Without them, for all she knows, there'd still be no females in homicide.

One picture given a prominent spot in the room catches a young aerialist named Maude Banvard as she flies high above the Brockton fairgrounds in 1907. O'Hara sees that fundamentally she's no different from a seventeen-year-old Benjamin Levin stepping into the ring at the smoke-filled St. Nichols Arena in 1937, or Axl Rose O'Hara stepping onstage with the Flat Screens at the Ukrainian Center last week. As Klinger said about his old friend, it wasn't about the money, it was about proving something to their friends and themselves. At some point, all these kids decided that the moments of their lives were worth fighting for, and they weren't dissuaded by the fact that the odds were stacked against them, or that their mothers were worried about them, or that half the world thought they were schmucks for even trying.

O'Hara is still standing transfixed in front of the photo when another old volunteer—this town is full of free old labor, she thinks—taps her on the shoulder and tells her the museum is about to close. On her way out, O'Hara passes through room after room filled with art with a capital "A," including countless old *Madonna and Child*s and even a bona fide Rembrandt and a Rubens. Ringling, figures O'Hara, must have been overcompensating, trying to acquire some class and distance himself from his old cohort Barnum and "The Greatest Show on Earth."

CHAPTER 30

WHEN O'HARA LEAVES the museum, it's still ridiculously early, but she is resigned to call it a night, pick up some beer and take it back to the Marriott, where she can pull the shades and ponder the possible scenarios that would connect a pugilistic prodigy from South Newark and a precocious street urchin from the East Village. O'Hara could get the beer anywhere, of course, but loyalty to her favorite Florida bodega takes her back across the bridges to Longboat Key.

On her second visit to Publix, O'Hara feels like a regular. She shakes loose a shopping cart, and like a dog who knows his route and favorite pissing spots, it tugs her to the happy aisle of beer. Here the choices are more reliable than at the cineplex, and as she gently lowers two six-packs of Amstel into the front of the cart, she notes their resemblance to Park Slope twins.

To prolong her stay, rather than a realistic anticipation of appetites and needs, O'Hara decides to gather ingredients for her next few breakfasts and evening snacks and pushes off into more nutritious regions. At the wall of cereals, O'Hara pulls up beside a tall, stooped man sporting a gray cardigan with suede patches on the elbows. Like O'Hara, he has his eye on the Rice Krispies. "After you," he says.

"No way," says O'Hara. "You were here first."

"I couldn't care less," says the old man. He sounds as if his mouth is full of gravel, and wears horn-rimmed glasses. "I insist."

"Well, okay then."

Based on his lovely lonely chivalry, O'Hara makes him as the surviving half of a once happy couple, the so-called lucky one who fooled the actuaries and dodged the cancers and now gets to fend for himself on the sunny shores of the Gulf of Mexico. O'Hara should slip him Sol's number so they can redeem their coupons and watch each other's backs at Sweet Tomatoes.

"Happy shopping," says O'Hara with a parting smile.

"The same to you, young lady."

Is there a surface as frictionless as well-polished linoleum? When the economy implodes for real, they can turn the old grocery stores into skateboard parks. O'Hara rolls her cart down the wide aisles, sometimes adding items indiscriminately, other times mulling the obscure differences between rival brands as seriously as if she were buying a car. Among other things, she buys reduced-fat milk, whole-wheat English muffins, and aluminum foil. Blue tostada chips, salsa, and a sketch pad. Bananas, blackberries, and five fresh pink Florida grapefruits. And since grapefruits don't cut themselves, she has no choice but to head toward housewares to find a serrated knife. In the course of her circumnavigations, O'Hara makes several sightings of the old man and his cart with its handful of items, always in the smallest quantities available. Whenever their paths cross, O'Hara can see how much the old man values each interaction, however brief. She realizes that his excursion to Publix, for which he dressed so nattily, is a high point of his day.

In the aisle with the kitchen utensils, O'Hara rolls up on an attractive woman wearing a kerchief and ankle-length beach cover-up and her daughter of twelve or thirteen. Something about them, their empty cart and aimless meandering sets off her cop's antennae. Based on the woman's loose-fitting outer garment and location in an aisle lined with relatively costly items, O'Hara guesses shoplifters. Reminding herself that she has her own homicide or homicides to deal with and that a high-tech grocery is more than capable of thwarting them on their own, she pushes the pair out of her mind and rolls past them to the knife display. She purchases the second cheapest of four serrated options, adds a toothbrush, dental floss, and SPF lip balm, and heads for the checkout.

Awaiting her turn, O'Hara scans the other checkout aisles for the gentleman shopper and spots him two aisles to the right. In the penultimate spot in line, he places his blue-and-white box of cereal on the conveyor. As he dips to lift another item from his cart, someone behind him in line touches him on his arm just above the patch, and the old man responds with a smile and then a blush. It's the woman with the kerchief and her daughter.

In an instant, the therapeutic benefit of forty minutes in Publix is erased by rage. Even if their target is her favorite grocery store in the continental United States, which it is, a couple shoplifters can be ignored. But O'Hara isn't going to look the other way while some bitch and her ratty-ass daughter prey on a lovely old man in a cardigan who likes Rice Krispies. Fuck that.

The three get through checkout before her, but O'Hara hustles past them as they slowly exit the sliding glass doors. She reaches her car in time to watch in the rearview as the woman and girl follow the old man across the parking lot and linger as he loads two bags into the trunk of a ten-year-old green Cadillac. After the woman touches the man's arm again, he says something that causes her to erupt with glee and nudge her sullen daughter to do the same. Then, to O'Hara's dismay, the old man opens the back door for the girl and the front one for the mother and walks around to the driver's side. When he backs out of his space, so does she.

Even O'Hara, whose mind gravitates toward worst-case scenarios, didn't see the woman working this fast. She figured the woman would get the old man's phone number and leave in her own car, then O'Hara would get her plates and maybe even follow them back to where she lived. Then she could phone in the information to Wawrinka and let the locals decide on the appropriate level of harassment.

Instead, O'Hara follows them west toward Sarasota. For the first time since she arrived, a drawbridge is up. For the next several minutes, as the sun dips into the Gulf, O'Hara looks through the rear window of the Cadillac and watches the gruesome mime unfolding in the front seat. The woman nods and laughs, and again and again reaches across the space between the seats to touch the man on his arm or shoulder. Maybe she'll overdo it so egregiously that even a lonely old man will see through her, but, considering his trip to Publix is the highlight of his week, what are the chances of that?

O'Hara feels herself teetering out of control. What exactly does she intend to do, and what good will come of it? And what if something goes wrong, as it so easily could? She's already earned a reputation as a loose cannon. Does she think her career would survive a major fuckup a thousand miles outside her jurisdiction?

But watching passively from five feet away is impossible for her. She unclasps her seat belt and reaches for the door. To the extent that she has a plan, this is it: She is going to walk up to the driver's side of the Cadillac, flash her badge, and come up with some pretext to get the old man out of the car. Then, while the woman sweats it out inside, she'll explain to the old man exactly what kind of trash he is dealing with. But as O'Hara opens the door of her car and puts one foot down on the road, the drawbridge begins to drop in front of them, and the driver in the car behind blows his horn and waves his arms in frustration.

O'Hara decides the location is too chaotic. With the horns blowing, the old man won't be able to hear her and is likely to get flustered. Too much can go wrong. O'Hara hops back into the car and follows them into the shopping circle she drove through the evening of her arrival. Partway round the circle, the Cadillac pulls over and parks. The three get out of the car and walk into an old-timey ice cream parlor, where in the front window some poor high school kid dressed in period garb leans over a marble table and kneads fudge.

The place must be empty. In a few minutes the three are on the bench in front—the mother with a pistachio cone and the girl with an elaborate sundae—and O'Hara witnesses another installment of the twisted charade. The woman has never tasted ice cream this good. The old man has to experience it too. She holds out the cone for him to take a taste. And then another. And then she dabs his chin with her napkin. Yet the couples who walk by take no notice. Is it possible that to a passerby, they seem like a father, daughter, and grandchild enjoying a summer night?

Their treat finished, the happy family traipses back to the car. But instead of heading back to Publix, the Cadillac continues north across the harbor into Sarasota. As the night drops completely, she follows them onto the southbound extension of the Tamiami Trail, with its empty retail spaces and bottom-feeder commerce. They pass tattoo parlors and pawnshops and one macabre shopping plaza where a medical supply store specializing in wheelchairs and walkers sits side by side with a windowless porn emporium offering a 25 percent discount for seniors. Can't beat that for convenience—a bedpan and a porno in one stop.

Quarter of a mile later, the car moves into the right lane and does a U-turn to the northbound side of the road, then turns into the parking lot of a dilapidated motor lodge advertising efficiency apartments starting at $99 a week. O'Hara turns off her lights and follows the car to the back of the building, where the old man parks in front of a ground-floor unit. After a few minutes, the woman and girl leave the car, and when the old man sees that they're safely inside, he pulls out of the dark lot and back onto the Tamiami Trail.

O'Hara, however, isn't going anywhere. She turns off the ignition and reaches into the backseat for an Amstel, stares at the door through which the mother and daughter disappeared, sips her beer. Although the old man hasn't been harmed physically, what she's observed over the last forty minutes is as disturbing as violence. Fucking with the very old seems no less heinous than messing with the very young.

O'Hara drinks a second beer, stares at the curtains in the back window, and thinks about the hard business of facing the end alone. She thinks about the old man in Publix, Levin in his condo, and Gus in his basement, and wonders if that will be her fate too. It certainly looks that way. Her grandmother, near the end of her life, told O'Hara that denial was underrated. Maybe dementia is just a stronger version of the same thing. Vicodin instead of Advil. The beers calm O'Hara slightly, till she sees a figure move past the window, and the thought of the woman inside plotting her next move on the old man.

What torments O'Hara is the realization that nothing can be done to make the old man less vulnerable. O'Hara has the old man's plates; she could get the address, and ask Wawrinka to send someone by his place to warn him, but what can they offer that will enable him to reject the overtures of a younger woman who seems to care about him when his only other option is to sit in his little box, lock the door, and wait to die? O'Hara should do the same thing. She should go back to her little box, turn on the ball game, and drink the rest of her beer. But she can't do it either.

O'Hara scans the lot for a car that might belong to the woman, but it's empty. Did the two take a bus out to Longboat Key on spec? The building doesn't seem to have an office or a front desk. As O'Hara tells herself to do the sane thing and leave, a tiny econobox, dwarfed by the dorsal fin of a pizza sign on the roof, screeches into the back lot. When a pimply teen hops out with a greasy box, O'Hara steps out too.

"I was just out for a smoke. I see you got my pie."

"Room nineteen? Mushroom and sausage?"

"Congratulations. You actually got it right this time. What do I owe you?"

"Seventeen ninety-five."

"And still nice and hot. Excellent." She gives the kid $25 and waits for him to leave, then takes the box to her car. What does she intend to do? Her legs are shaking because the box rattles on her lap. She reaches behind her and pulls the tube of aluminum foil from one of her grocery bags, removes and wraps up every slice except one, and drops them on top of her groceries. Then she rips a piece of paper from her rental agreement and writes the woman a note.

"If you ever talk to the old man again, I will hunt you down like the whore you are."

Is that it? No. Not quite. She pulls out the one slice still left in the box, takes three large bites, and drops it back inside, facedown. Then she slips the note into the box, gets out of the car, and walks toward Unit 19.

CHAPTER 31

O'HARA RAPS LOUDLY on the door, "Pizza."

After a sizable wait, the door opens a crack. The woman, no longer in her kerchief, peers through the opening.

"Pizza," says O'Hara again. Seeing the box, the woman opens it a bit wider and stares at O'Hara hard. Hard enough for O'Hara to wonder if she recognizes her from Publix.

"What happened to the kid?"

"He had to go to a funeral," says O'Hara. "His grandfather died."

"That's too bad."

"It is. Apparently he was a real sweetheart."

The woman studies O'Hara's face, and O'Hara stares right back. Say one fucking word, thinks O'Hara, and I'll pull you into the parking lot and beat the living crap out of you.

"Do I know you?" asks the woman.

"I don't know. Do you?"

"Aren't you kind of old for this kind of work?"

"I'm the manager. We're all filling in."

Harsh TV sounds come from the far corner of the room. O'Hara turns in its direction and sees the girl parked directly in front of the set, watching the show on MTV where three skanky girls sit in the back of a bus and take turns trying to win a date with a moron. Seeing the girl makes O'Hara feel bad about the pizza.

The room, which has a foreign funky odor, is a shambles. The small kitchen table is covered with fast-food trash, empty cans of soda and beer, and liquor bottles. Sweat-stained T-shirts and shorts hang over the backs of the chairs and couch. In front of the couch is a coffee table, bearing two overflowing ashtrays, a notepad, and an old-fashioned steel Rolodex, and beneath it are a boat-size pair of lime green Crocs that turn O'Hara's stomach.

The woman twists her head in the opposite direction of the girl and the TV and yells, "Pizza's here."

"I'm on the crapper," replies a deep male voice. "Just pay the kid, Gab. The money's on the dresser."

"TMI," says the girl under her breath, "gross."

After a wary glance at O'Hara, the woman disappears into a back bedroom. With the girl glued to her show and the woman gone, O'Hara takes two steps into the room. As she reaches for the Rolodex, the girl turns from the TV and stares into her eyes. "Hi. I remember you from the grocery store."

O'Hara smiles at her and puts her finger over her lips. "I remember you too. Our little secret." O'Hara is still standing beside the girl when her mother returns with the money.

"My cousin was a contestant on the show," says O'Hara. "Beautiful girl, but she didn't get the date."

"Am I supposed to give a fuck?" The woman hands O'Hara a sweaty rolled-up twenty.

"Not much of a tip," says O'Hara.

"I thought you were the manager."

"I still drove out here. I still delivered your pizza."

"I don't care. That's all you're getting."

"Suit yourself."

O'Hara retreats to her car, turns on the ignition, and glances at her watch. She doesn't have to wait long. In less than a minute, there's a flash of light and a bang as the door swings open and crashes into the brick wall. A dark shape fills the doorway and bellows an unintelligible curse.

CHAPTER 32

THE VOICE IS elderly but firm, and even in desperation, polite.

"We need an ambulance at 5265 Gulf of Mexico Drive immediately, Unit 306. The owner's name is Benjamin Levin." Now the high-pitched wail of a lawn mower straining to power through Florida crabgrass intrudes on the tape, and when the woman raises her voice to be heard, O'Hara and Wawrinka lean forward in their chairs.

"Please hurry," says the woman. "I heard . . . gunsho . . ." before the mechanical din drowns her out.

"I think she said she heard gunshots, plural," says O'Hara.

"I have no idea," says Wawrinka. "It's those damn two-cycle Briggs and Stratton engines. They should make them put mufflers on them."

While O'Hara devoted her evening to delivering justice of the greasiest variety, a detour she has chosen not to share, her new partner kept her Hawaiian eyes on the ball and her Polish nose to the grindstone. After an hour and a half at the gym, she returned to her desk to review the original paperwork filed on Levin's suicide, then tracked down the tape of the 911 call placed by Levin's neighbor, Sharon Di Nunzio. O'Hara and Wawrinka, sitting in a closet-size space in the basement of the Sarasota PD, have just replayed the tape for the third time and are still not sure what's on it, although O'Hara's faculties might be more acute if she hadn't ended her night with two six-packs in her motel room.

"Is Di Nunzio still alive?" asks O'Hara.

"Alive *and* in town. I spoke to her last night. Like a lot of people down here, she can't afford two places anymore and couldn't sell this one. So she lives here year-round."

"And how's the senility quotient? Sharon still playing with a full deck?"

"Sounded pretty sharp on the phone."

"That can be misleading," says O'Hara, glancing at the police report. "After all, she's eighty-nine."

"The tape is six months old. She's ninety now."

"In that case," says O'Hara as they get up and head to the garage, "better use the siren."

DI NUNZIO HAS the Banyan Bay unit directly above Levin's, with the identical layout, and when she guides O'Hara and Wawrinka to the dining room table, the tidy condition of both the place and owner are encouraging. Despite her frailty, Di Nunzio is still lovely and painstakingly put together, and wears the kind of chic little antique dress they feature in the windows of East Village boutiques. Di Nunzio has set out cookies and a pitcher of iced tea. Once refreshments have been graciously served and introductions made, O'Hara asks her to recount what she remembers about the morning Levin died.

"I had just come back from the Ringling Museum," says Di Nunzio, "where I'm a docent, two mornings a week. The cheap bastards don't pay, but it gives me a reason to get up and get dressed. I was putting away my groceries when I heard what sounded like a gunshot coming from Benjamin's place."

"What did you do?"

"I called his phone number, but there was no answer. So I called again, and while the phone was ringing I heard a second shot."

"You sure about that second shot?" asks O'Hara.

"Yes," says Di Nunzio with a piercing look.

"Then what?"

"I ran down to Ben's place and rapped on his door."

"You're a brave woman, Sharon," says O'Hara. "You hear gunshots and run toward them. I know cops who wouldn't do that."

"This old-age bullshit isn't for cowards."

"So I gather," says O'Hara.

"Not that I think Ben's suicide was cowardly," says Di Nunzio forcefully. "Ben was the opposite of a coward. You know I saw him punch a man at Sweet Tomatoes?"

"No way," says O'Hara. "You were there?"

"As close as you and me. It was thrilling. Some asshole tried to cut the line, and Ben leveled him. He'd never admit it, but I think he did it to impress me. In any case, it certainly had that effect. In fact, it made me wet."

O'Hara glances at Wawrinka, who barely gets the napkin to her lips in time to catch the iced tea flying from her mouth. O'Hara gives her partner a moment to compose herself, then turns her attention back to the spry Di Nunzio.

"So you knocked on his door," says O'Hara. "Then what?"

"As fast as I could, which I'm afraid wasn't fast enough, I ran up those awful stairs and called nine-one-one. Of course, I should have called immediately."

"When you first got back from the museum," asks O'Hara, "did you see anyone going in or out of Ben's place?"

Di Nunzio shakes her head. "No."

"And when you came down the stairs to Ben's place, did you see a car leaving?"

"No."

"I realize it was six months ago, but did you notice if a car was parked in front of his place?"

Di Nunzio concentrates. "Yes. There was a dark green van in visitor parking, which is right in front of his place. I remember because it was from the Sarasota Water Authority, and it scared me. It made me think there was something wrong with the water, and I shouldn't be drinking it."

"And your memory is clear on the color, even after six months?"

"Yes. Dark green with black letters."

"When the police and EMS arrived," asks Wawrinka, "was the van still there?"

Di Nunzio squints, as if spooling back the tape behind her eyes. "It couldn't have been, because the police cars and EMS parked where the van had been."

"You mentioned having dinner with Ben at Sweet Tomatoes. Were you two close?"

"I'm a cheap date. That evening must have cost him all of nine bucks, but I didn't care. I've known Ben for thirty years, and I adored him. I thought his wife was perfectly lovely too, but I can't deny that after she died I had my hopes. I was crazy about him. I'd roast him a chicken, and then I'd give him every man's favorite dessert."

"Oh, yeah, what's that?" asks O'Hara.

"Head."

A choking sound comes from Wawrinka's direction.

"Like I said, I was crazy about him. But he was a sucker for younger women. They all are. It's vanity."

Di Nunzio grimaces and puts her hand to the side of her ear.

"You okay?"

"My hearing aid. Sometimes it makes this awful piercing sound."

"Does it sound like a gunshot?" asks Wawrinka.

"Not really. But it's excruciating, which is why I don't wear it half the time."

"And how's your hearing without it, Sharon?"

"Without it," says Di Nunzio, taking her first bite of her own cookie, "I can't hear a fucking thing."

CHAPTER 33

JUST INSIDE THE door of the Longboat Key Public Library is a wooden phone booth that must be forty years old. When O'Hara pushes the hinged door shut behind her, a tiny ventilating fan goes on with the light. From the hush of the booth, she looks out at the nearly-as-quiet room, where a male volunteer pushes a cart up and down the short rows. Every few feet, he stops to lift a book from the cart to its old spot on the shelf. He looks like a farmer unpicking fruit and returning it to the tree.

When O'Hara stepped out of Di Nunzio's apartment and back into the scalding light, she was in need of a quiet place to mull things over alone, and remembered the little library next to the post office behind Publix. Di Nunzio is the most encouraging representative of her demographic O'Hara has encountered since Paulette walked into the precinct and the drumbeat of senescence and dementia began. If Di Nunzio's recollection of a second gunshot is accurate, it's the first major break in the case. From the moment O'Hara got the call from Sarasota about the ballistic report, she has been trying to connect the old man and the kid. If two shots were fired that morning in Levin's condo, it essentially puts the two victims side by side.

But how much stock can O'Hara put in the memory, eyesight, and most of all hearing of a ninety-year-old woman who by her own admission is just about deaf, rarely wears her hearing aid, and when she does is often besieged by rogue sonic blasts? O'Hara can imagine the reaction if it gets out she tried to build a case on something a deaf person heard.

Open on her lap is a sketch pad, purchased from Publix the night before. On the first pristine page she writes:

s. di nunzio: 2 gunshots, a couple minutes apart
green van, black letters
Sarasota Water Authority

O'Hara takes another look through the porthole-sized window. In the center of the room, in front of the librarian's desk, is an old-school wooden card catalogue. Beside it on a stand is a well-thumbed medical dictionary, and above it, on the wall, the Plaque of Honor, inscribed with the names of volunteers who died in the line of library duty. What does it mean, she wonders, that she now delights in silence as much as the twang of a beat-up Stratocaster and that libraries are up there next to dive bars on her list of favorite places? She knows exactly what it means. She's getting old.

A fat phone book, as much of an anachronism as the booth itself, dangles from a chain by O'Hara's knee, and she opens it to the section in front listing municipal agencies. When she can't find anything close to the Sarasota Water Authority, she uses her cell to call the city's main information number and asks what agency handles water issues for condos on Longboat Key.

"Sarasota doesn't handle Longboat," says the receptionist, "that's Manatee County. Let me give you that number."

O'Hara calls it and is connected to the Department of Engineering.

"This is Darlene O'Hara, NYPD Homicide. Can you verify for me if your department sent a vehicle to 5265 Gulf of Mexico Drive on March 3?"

"I'm going to have to put you on hold."

While O'Hara waits, she cracks the door and compares the two qui-
ets. Then she looks down at her mostly blank page, and starts a drawing that turns into a fairly decent facsimile of the wooden cooking spoon
O'Hara found on Levin's TV stand. It looks like this:

Below it, she writes,

no sign of food/no sign of cooking

Still on hold, and in possession of pen and paper, she lists another
unexplained detail:

Bullet entered boy at upward angle

The voice returns, and O'Hara pushes the door shut.

"I checked the logs. We didn't dispatch anyone to that address that
day. We haven't sent a vehicle there for months."

"Your vehicles," asks O'Hara, "what do they say on them?"

"Manatee County."

"That's it? You don't have any vehicles with writing that refers to
water?"

"No, ma'am."

"And the vehicles, are they dark green?"

"Correct. With black lettering."

"Are they vans?"

"No. We use pickups."

"Thanks for your help." It looks like the only thing Sharon got right
was the colors.

Speaking of colors, a woman with orange hair and a lavender blouse enters the library. Observed from inside the booth, her silent movements resemble a tropical fish. O'Hara feels underwater too, as if looking out from behind the glass helmet of a little Diver Dan in the corner of a fish tank. All that's missing is a trail of bubbles.

Is it possible Sharon got it all wrong? Fuck.

That Di Nunzio is such a brave and buoyant piece of work makes O'Hara even sorrier that her recollections don't check out, but her disappointment is muted by the double cocoon of quiet and the soft whir of the fan overhead. Forty minutes later a tap on the glass from the concerned librarian rouses her from sleep.

CHAPTER 34

AT 1:30 O'HARA meets Wawrinka at a Waffle House just north of downtown, where the letters of the sign look like they've been typed directly on the sky. Wawrinka orders three eggs, a short stack, sausage links, and grits, O'Hara a short stack with bacon.

"Where you been?"

"The Longboat Key library, right behind Publix."

"I know where it is, Darlene. What the hell you doing there?"

"Thinking about two gunshots and a green van."

"Don't tell me you're one of those pervs whose mind only works in public."

"Like those cretins at Starbucks?"

"Yeah, fingering the devices on their laps and loitering outside the bathroom for strange."

"That doesn't sound like me."

Their petite waitress, working name Samantha, delivers two coffees, and Wawrinka's eyes follow her butt back into the kitchen.

"I could eat that baby girl for breakfast and still have room for three eggs, a short stack, sausage links, and a cup of grits."

"Connie, you sure talk a whole lot of shit. Any of it true?"

"Nah. It's pretty much all talk."

Wawrinka really is a guy, thinks O'Hara.

"I also made a couple phone calls," says O'Hara. "I found out there is no such thing as the Sarasota Water Authority."

"I could have saved you the roaming charge," says Wawrinka. "Besides, Longboat is under Manatee County."

"And they didn't send a vehicle to Banyan Bay on March 3 either. Or anytime in March."

"And they don't use vans, they use pickups, although they are green with black letters. So maybe Di Nunzio's memory is as lousy as her hearing. Sharon's not exactly a spring chicken."

Samantha returns with their food, and O'Hara waits for her glutes to recede from view.

"Actually," says O'Hara, "Sharon is a spring chicken. In fact, the springiest fucking chicken of all time. And not only does she remember the van from the Sarasota Water Authority, but she remembers seeing it made her anxious about her drinking water. That's not just one memory, it's two, and they make sense together. That's a pretty complete and coherent little nugget to spin out of thin air."

Wawrinka responds by bursting a sausage with her fork, and O'Hara does her best to conceal her disappointment that Wawrinka's sausages look about twenty times better than her three strips of undercooked bacon.

"You think the van was a fake?"

"What I'm saying is that Sharon Di Nunzio has earned some credibility. And if she wasn't ninety and deaf with a fucked-up hearing aid, we wouldn't be so quick to dismiss what she had to say, and I wouldn't be making calls to discredit her."

"You're saying we're ageists?"

"That's exactly what I'm saying. Because every single thing Sharon says checks out with what we've already got. For starters, she heard two rifle shots."

"Claims to."

"Well, we got two bodies with bullets in them from the same ancient twenty-two, and we didn't tell her anything about the second victim. The two gunshots corroborate what we already had. She should have heard two shots. It only makes sense that there were two shots. And although we don't know anything about the whereabouts of the kid, or anything else, there is no evidence the old man had traveled to New York in the months before he died, and if he did, it's highly unlikely he would have taken his trusty rabbit gun, so Sharon's memories bolster the scenario that already makes the most sense, which was that the kid was shot in Levin's place along with Levin that morning."

"Except there was no blood. No evidence of anyone else there."

"But now there is. Two gunshots and a van that wasn't there by the time the cops and EMS arrived. If they got the kid out of there quickly, there wouldn't necessarily have been any blood. It's a twenty-two. There was barely any of Levin's blood either, and he was lying there for over an hour. I understand that had also to do with where he shot himself, but still."

O'Hara looks at Wawrinka for some sign of approval, and although she sees none, takes comfort from the fact that Wawrinka hasn't put anything in her mouth in twenty seconds.

"If the kid was shot at Levin's place that morning, and it certainly looks that way to me, he had to get there and he had to leave and he had to travel eleven hundred miles north so that he could end up buried in a hippie garden in the East Village. And since you can't get a bleeding kid on an airplane, the van makes sense too."

"You might be able to get him on a bus. There're some sketchy bus lines down here."

"Not likely," says O'Hara. She flashes on the scene in *Midnight Cowboy* when Ratso Rizzo dies on the bus just short of Miami and Jon Voight closes his eyes.

"You're saying someone went to all that trouble to create a fake van?"

"It's not that hard."

Wawrinka's lack of enthusiasm is chipping away at O'Hara's confidence.

"I don't know what happened at Levin's place that morning, or why a kid would be there, but something went very south."

"And whoever was there took off with the kid?"

"Yeah. And if you leave Levin's place in a van with a kid who's been shot, what are you going to do next?"

"Take the kid to an ER."

"That would be the right thing to do, but considering where he ended up, I don't think anyone took him to a hospital. According to the ME in New York, who traced the line of the bullet from where it hit the first rib to where it ended up in his shoulder blade, it might have barely nicked the kid's lung. With prompt medical attention, the kid could have been fine. So if a perp just left someplace where two shots had been fired, in a van with writing on it that even a ninety-year-old can remember six months after the fact, and a kid inside bleeding all over it—"

"Now he's bleeding—"

"He would have started to bleed soon. If I was the perp or perps, what I would do, first chance I got, is dump the van." O'Hara looks across the table again, but Wawrinka is concentrating on her nearly empty plates. "And I say we find it."

Wawrinka drags her last bite of sausage through the maple syrup and pops it in her mouth.

"So what you're saying is that if a ninety-year-old deaf woman is all we got, that's all we got, and we go with it until someone better comes along, like, an eighty-five-year-old who uses his hearing aid."

"Basically."

"Fair enough, but I hope you're not doing this just because Sharon is the Helen Gurley Brown of Longboat Key and still likes to give head at ninety."

"And still gets wet too."

"That is something, I'll give you that."

In the neighboring booth, a man clears his throat, and a trucker's cap clocks a half turn. "Ladies, no disrespect to Sharon or Helen, but we're eating lunch, and we'd like to keep it down."

CHAPTER 35

O'HARA FOLLOWS WAWRINKA back to the Sarasota PD, where Wawrinka fires off a dispatch to every municipal, county, and state law enforcement agency within five hundred miles. She inquires if any of them have recovered an abandoned green van with black writing, believed to have been the getaway vehicle in a homicide on Longboat Key March 3 and presumed to have been abandoned later that day or soon after that.

"Feels like writing a personal," says Wawrinka as the two eye the blank screen. "Dropping a hook into the ether and waiting for a nibble. Ever try it?"

"No," says O'Hara, and thinks of those night fishermen casting their lines off the bridge into Sarasota Harbor.

"Why not? It's like shooting fish in a barrel. Almost too easy."

O'Hara feels the conversation moving toward that awkward silence, which she'll be expected to fill with a recap of her checkered relationship history, including her breakup with Leibowitz, his not wanting another child, et cetera. To avoid that, O'Hara wanders to an empty desk and turns on the computer.

"Getting right to it?" asks Wawrinka. "Rare Irish beauty looking for stud . . ."

Instead of Nerve or Match, or whatever, O'Hara brings up Mapquest. For the starting location, she types in the address of Ben Levin's condo: "5265 Gulf of Mexico Drive, Longboat Key, Florida 34228." For the destination, she types "East Sixth Street and Avenue B."

In seconds, it generates a map of the Eastern Seaboard. It affixes a red *A* just south of Tampa on the Gulf of Mexico and a red *B* in NYC, and connects them with a blue worm. The preferred route runs northeast in a wiggly diagonal through the top half of Florida from Tampa to Jacksonville, continues on the same approximate line past Savannah, Raleigh, and Richmond, detours around Washington, then turns more sharply east toward Trenton. Before the worm slithers into the Hudson and emerges in Lower Manhattan, the bulk of nearly twelve hundred miles are on 95 North or its extensions 295 and 495. The estimated driving time is 23.9 hours.

Despite the warp speed with which the map and route were spat out, the map itself has an analogue grammar-school concreteness that takes O'Hara back to a Brooklyn classroom. O'Hara returns to the present and refocuses on the route. She sees a green van with the boy bleeding inside it as it travels north through Florida, Georgia, and the Carolinas. How far did he make it? When did the van become a hearse?

As O'Hara studies the route, she imagines the van morphing from one vehicle into another and that gives O'Hara a thought. After printing out the map and the directions, she walks back to Wawrinka's desk. "Anything?"

"No."

"I think looking for the van was the wrong approach."

"Ye of little faith," says Wawrinka. "It's been twenty minutes."

"I mean looking for it directly. If we're right and they dumped the van, they had to steal another car. Instead of just looking for the van, let's look for a car that was stolen around that time, somewhere north of Tampa. Depending on how good of a job they did getting rid of it, the van could be hard to find, but someone gets their car stolen, they're going to report it right away."

"Good idea. The kind of thing I look for in a partner."

Unlike the query for the missing van, hits on stolen cars pour in imme-diately. Like Wawrinka's would-be paramours, there are almost too many. In the first hour, they get over forty, mostly around Tampa, but few are promising. They are the kind of expensive rides that always get stolen—Mercedes, BMWs, Porsches, 'Vettes. Most have been recovered since, and in any case are an unlikely choice for someone trying to stay under the radar. As the hits come in, O'Hara plots their locations to see their proximity to the blue worm. Then she plugs the location of the theft into Mapquest to determine the driving distance from Sarasota, and checks whether that is consistent with someone heading north from Longboat Key.

At 9:00, they break for some surprisingly decent Mexican. When Wawrinka gets back to her computer, an e-mail is waiting from the state police barracks in Monroe, South Carolina. A white 1993 Volvo station wagon was reported stolen by Alfred Vanderhook, eighty-three, of 1560 Western Highway, Walterboro, South Carolina, at 11:05 p.m. on March 3, or about twelve hours after the van left Levin's parking lot.

"A nondescript vehicle like that is what we're looking for," says O'Hara. She types in the address of the home from which the car was stolen and sees that it's 450 miles, or an estimated seven hours and nineteen min-utes, north of Longboat Key. Allowing for a couple brief stops, the time required for the perp or perps to find their new target, and for the victim to notice the car was missing, location and timing both work. And when O'Hara goes back on Mapquest, she sees that Walterboro is less than four miles from I-95.

Location, timing, kind of car, are all pretty much perfect, thinks O'Hara, while still trying to maintain a realistic degree of skepticism for what she knows is a Lotto-esque long shot. The age of the car theft victim—that feels right too.

CHAPTER 36

A MATTE BLACK Crown Vic screeches into the parking lot of the Marriott Courtyard, and the tinted window spools down. Behind it, Wawrinka holds up her pinkie and forefinger, grins in a way that ought to be illegal at 5:15 a.m.

"Road trip."

A pair of iced coffees sweat in the cup holders and there's a stack of CDs between the seats, but Wawrinka, in wifebeater and jeans, is the real wakeup call. On the job, O'Hara buries her ample curves under Clintonian pantsuits and reinforces the effect with self-administered haircuts and rubber-soled shoes. Wawrinka's butch aesthetic is kept under wraps even more thoroughly.

"Look at fucking you," says O'Hara. "Nothing but baby girls and muscle cars."

"What else is there?"

"For one thing—dogs."

Neck to wrists, collar to cuffs, every bit of skin that would otherwise be concealed under Wawrinka's buttoned-up oxford shirts is tattooed with a female or an automobile or something that pertains to either. Circling her neck like a choker is the inscription "need for speed," and on her breastbone the heavy metal band "Rage Against the Machine." On her right shoulder a sailor-style tart in a negligee rides a wrench like a broomstick, and bumper-to-bumper down her left arm are scaled-down illustrations of a '68 Camaro, a '72 Malibu convertible, a '74 Chevy Monte Carlo, and finally a dull black 2001 Crown Vic. "That's what we're in now," says O'Hara, pointing at a spot above the elbow.

"Very good. I bought it when it was decommissioned by the department three years ago. Did all the work myself." When O'Hara makes the mistake of asking what that involved, she hears more than she needs to know about MagnaFlow mufflers, 2.5-inch piping, K&N cold air, and a custom tune. "She can do one-forty all day without breaking a sweat," says Wawrinka, and as she rips out of the parking lot, the pleasure she takes in her inked-up persona is so palpable it makes being a freckled Irish hetero feel like a bore and a half.

A dull black Crown Vic with big side mirrors earns a certain amount of goodwill from local law enforcement and removes whatever stress a couple cops might feel about mocking the speed limit. Slouching in her seat like Richard Petty, Wawrinka rolls the speedometer up to 110 and sticks a pin in it, and when she spots a state trooper lurking behind some bushes in the dim predawn, taps her brights instead of her brakes. A deep sonorous growl percolating beneath them, they do 260 miles in their first three hours, and that includes a stop to use the bathroom and get more coffee.

The sun comes up north of Tampa, and by Jacksonville, O'Hara's face has settled into the squint that has become her default expression. By now, she takes as a given that the old man and the kid were shot at about the same time in Levin's condo, but what connects them, beyond being in the wrong place at the wrong time? Why was the kid there at all, and why did he make the trip from New York? From there she turns to the obdurate riddle of Levin's wooden spoon and the upward flight of the bullet that struck the kid.

When Wawrinka's energy lags, she shoves early Stones into the CD player, or one of her compilations of garage punk with bands who sound like perps—Little Willie and the Adolescents, the Intruders. When Wawrinka joins in on a chorus, O'Hara discovers another advantage of being a lesbian beside the most obvious. Nine out of ten rock songs are about girls. If you're gay you don't have to transpose the gender. When Mick croons about some Siamese cat of a girl, Wawrinka can sing along without losing a thing in translation.

The tricked out Crown Vic devours the miles, and they're half an hour into Georgia, west of the Okefenokee Swamp, before O'Hara associates her queasy stomach with the growing realization that this entire trip is a fool's errand. The closer they get to Walterboro, the more tenuous her belief/hope/hunch/prayer that the Volvo was stolen by the same people who raced out of Banyan Bay in a green van. Now O'Hara has an even more disquieting thought. One detail that helped her zero in on the Volvo is the age of the victim, which seemed to fit a pattern, but short of a handicapped parking sticker, how would the perps have known the owner was old?

Eighty minutes later, they cross into South Carolina. A couple miles after that they exit the highway and pull up to the barracks of the Colleton County Police Department. Deputy Sheriff Carter Barnwell is waiting and drives them in his vehicle to 1560 Western Highway, the address where the '93 Volvo wagon was stolen from the driveway six months before. O'Hara has driven to Florida a couple times over the years but never strayed from the interstate. The country roads are her first taste of the rural South.

At 1560 Western Highway, they find a well-kept but faded ranch house, and O'Hara is relieved. As long as there was enough light, the perps would have had little trouble discerning that the home was occupied by an older person or couple. From the curtains in the windows to the porch furniture to the mailbox, everything is dated. At the top of the drive there is only a single garbage can, and in the garage window an ancient sticker commemorating the Veterans of Foreign Wars. Before 9/11, which this clearly predates, the only people who put up VFW stickers were people old enough to have fought in World War II.

For the next couple hours Barnwell patiently works his way out from the spot where the car was stolen, taking them to a dozen locations where there is a chance, however remote, that an abandoned van might have escaped attention, and as the sleepy tour enters its third hour, O'Hara's pessimism blooms anew like a dark spring. For some reason, Walterboro has five high schools, and they check them all, as well as the hospital, the playgrounds, the cineplex, and the shopping centers.

"The problem," says Barnwell as they're idling in a parking lot, "is that, except for the hospital, these lots are empty by ten or eleven, midnight at the latest. Anything in them after that is going to get noticed."

In the early afternoon they stop at a diner on Main Street, where Barnwell steers them to the meat loaf and key lime pie, and O'Hara picks up the tab, the least she can do for wasting half the man's day. "Any gay bars in town?" asks Wawrinka.

Jesus Christ, thinks O'Hara. This is all we need.

"A couple. Why?"

"For one thing, they tend be out of the way, particularly in a little town like this. And if someone did leave a vehicle behind one of them, people might be hesitant to report it."

Pretty far-fetched, thinks O'Hara, but no more than driving to Walterboro in the first place.

Without batting an eye, Barnwell shows them all gay Walterboro has to offer, which consists of a piano bar attached to a motel at the edge of town and a lesbian joint called Christy's in the basement of a bed-and-breakfast in the boonies.

"Ever been here?" O'Hara asks Wawrinka.

"No, have you?"

In the midafternoon, both are closed, but at Christy's two old cars are parked in the dirt lot, and to O'Hara's annoyance, both are VW Jettas. I drive a dyke car, she thinks. Great. Depressed by the folly of their excursion, she summons the little self-discipline she has not to ask Barnwell to stop at a grocery so she can pick up a couple six-packs.

"Sheriff," says Wawrinka, "you said that everything in Walterboro shuts down by midnight. Any big twenty-four-hour shopping centers in the vicinity?"

"There's a Walmart superstore. That big enough for you?"

"How far?"

"Four miles north on 95. Couldn't miss it if you wanted to."

Barnwell drives them back to Wawrinka's car, then has them follow him to the highway. "Sorry about this," says O'Hara.

"What are you talking about, Darlene? The meat loaf alone was worth the trip."

"By the way," says O'Hara, "guess what kind of car I have?"

"A Jetta," says Wawrinka.

"How'd you guess?" says O'Hara, laughing.

"Pretty obvious to me what you'd be driving."

CHAPTER 37

THE WALMART PARKING lot is the size of Luxembourg. Toward the rear is a modest structure of cinder block and corrugated steel, and standing immodestly in front of it, his posture and accessories exaggerating his authority, is a man who looks like a mediocre high school football player gone to seed. He holds a two-way radio, a clipboard, and Styrofoam coffee cup, and wears pointy western boots that look to be ostrich, although his own view of his pricey footwear is challenged by his ample gut. As O'Hara and Wawrinka approach, he welcomes them by lifting the coffee cup and catching the thin brown sluice of saliva and tobacco he squirts through his lower teeth.

"Good afternoon. I'm Connie Wawrinka, with the Sarasota Police Department. This is Darlene O'Hara, a homicide detective from NYPD. Are you in charge of parking lot security?"

"Clint Eakins," says the man, rearranging his items so that he can steady them with his left hand and extend the right. "And yes, I am. What the hell have I done now?"

"I have no idea, Clint," says Wawrinka. "And I'm not sure I want to know."

Because the language and customs of South Carolina are closer to Florida than New York, the two determined that Wawrinka would do the honors. "What I am concerned about is a vehicle involved in a homicide," she says. "Specifically a dark green van, which may or may not have 'Sarasota Water Authority' written on the side. We have reason to believe it was left in this lot several months ago."

"Doesn't jump to mind. What makes you think it was left here?"

"We'd rather not get into it right now, Clint. Let's just say that we do."

"I can appreciate that, but like I said, nothing like that comes to mind, and I've run this lot for the better part of two years."

"All that responsibility, Clint. How do you sleep at night? In that time, how many cars have you recovered?"

"About thirty-five."

"I would have thought there would have been more. When someone leaves a car here, how long before it comes to your attention?"

"Two, three weeks. This lot holds twenty-five thousand cars. In the run-up to Christmas we'll get forty thousand vehicles passing through in twenty-four hours. My men do a complete cruise-through twice a week. They notice a car been here long, we chalk it up, go back in a couple days for another look. Once we determine it's been abandoned, we call the state police in Columbia. It can take them a week or two to get around to it, but eventually they come down and haul it away."

"You got a list of every vehicle abandoned here in the last year?"

"Of course I do, or should I say, I did. Until two weeks ago, when my silly computer crashed. Everything on my hard drive was wiped out."

"You got to back that shit up, son."

"I learned that the hard way, didn't I?"

Something over Wawrinka's shoulder distracts Eakins.

O'Hara turns to see an enormous bearded man lumbering in their direction. From his bandana to his work boots, everything is smeared with grease.

"Who do you deal with in Columbia?"

"Where?"

"With the state police. Who's your contact person?"

"It's not any one person," says Eakins.

"Give me a couple names, then?"

"It's no big deal. Whoever I can get on the phone."

"Well, they would have a list of every car they picked up, wouldn't they? Or have they had computer issues too?"

"Not as far as I know."

Eakins raises his palm to stop the progress of the approaching man, but it's like trying to stop an ocean liner. It takes a couple steps for his boots to grab and bring him to a stop. "Buddy, as you can see, I'm kind of tied up here right now. I'll call you in a few."

"Suit yourself," says the man and turns around.

"Who's that?"

"That enormous son of a bitch is Terrence Porter, old fishing buddy."

"Oh yeah. What kind of fishing you boys do?"

"Depends on the season, of course, but this time of the year we're still doing some grabbing. What you do is take a hook and dangle it from an overhanging limb. When the fish, suckers mostly, come schooling by, you yank them right out of the water. I live for grabbing suckers. Of course, you need to know the right spot, and I'd tell you."

"But then you'd have to kill me," says Wawrinka.

"'Fraid so."

"Clint," says Wawrinka, "you got a card, in case we need to get in touch with you again?"

FIVE MINUTES LATER, back in the Crown Vic, Wawrinka is still holding Eakins's card by one corner.

"Something not kosher about that boy," she says.

"I don't think there's anything kosher about him. That thing still damp?"

"Yes."

A diesel gurgle cuts through their air-conditioning, and an eight-wheel tow truck with custom paint job slowly passes in front of them, dragging a five-year-old Saab. According to the fancy gold script, the tow has a name, *Mabel*, like a yacht.

"I'll be amazed if the state police have even heard of this mother-fucker," says O'Hara, pulling out her cell and making the call. O'Hara is connected to the State Police barracks, where she is promptly put on hold. While she hangs on the line, the big diesel comes back into earshot and stops three lanes in front of them. The promised thirty-second wait turns into minutes, and she is still on hold when Eakins steps out of the security hut and walks up to the side of the truck.

"You have binoculars in here?"

"Right in front of you. Glove compartment." O'Hara pulls them out and focuses on the driver's-side window.

"Whoever's in the cab just slipped the Archduke of Parking a rather fat envelope," says O'Hara.

"Nothing sadder in this world than a rent-a-cop turned bad."

As the truck pulls away, O'Hara pans down the side of the cab to the name of the company: "TP Salvage, Ruffin, South Carolina."

"Connie, what was the name of that biker dude who Eakins waved off—Terrence something?"

"Terrence Porter."

"Well, a Saab just got pulled out of here by a tow named Mabel working out of a place called TP Salvage."

"For once in his life, that slimy son of a bitch Eakins was telling the truth. He and Porter are fishing buddies."

"Porter pays Eakins to fish in his pond."

CHAPTER 38

THE RESOUNDING COLLISION cuts through the drone as cleanly as a howitzer. It's the sound of a car hitting a wall head-on at sixty miles an hour, and although in this case it's the wall that's moving, not the car, the effect on the car locked inside the compactor is the same. The first blow compresses the hood like an accordion. The second flattens it flush against the engine wall. At the same time the rear and sides are also being battered, and after four mighty blows, what was once a Buick Skylark is a two-ton piece of carry-on. At first, O'Hara found the violence disturbing. It reminded her of the highway horror shows they made her sit through in drivers' ed. But after a while the violent rhythm is soothing.

"It kind of takes the edge off," she says, "like watching the breakers hit the beach in Montauk after a storm."

When O'Hara and Wawrinka rolled into TP Salvage forty minutes earlier, it was already 6:00. *Mabel*, with the Saab still hanging off the back, was parked just inside the wire fence. Behind her was a long, low shed with a marquee-style sign listing in press-on letters the newest additions to the inventory of parts on sale inside. The back of the shed, which is open but unattended, looks out on a clearing filled with hundreds of cars, arrayed in tall rusty stacks. In the midst of the wreckage squats the hulking three-story compactor, whose violent mastications are the only movement in the seventy-acre vista. Despite the scale of the operation, there's only one visible employee, the eponymous Terrence Porter. He sits fifty feet off the ground in the throbbing cab, bunkered so deep inside his Spector-esque wall of sound, the horn of the Crown Vic can't pierce it. All O'Hara and Wawrinka can do is repair to the shade of the back porch and wait for Porter to shut down for the day. Since then, they've sat witness to the final moments of a Camry, a Hyundai, and this light blue Skylark, which, having been stubbed out like a cigarette, is nudged down a rusty chute into a railroad car.

"It's also pretty damn depressing," says Wawrinka. Sitting at their feet, her mottled tongue hanging from her mouth, is the mongrel bitch who crawled out from under *Mabel* soon after they settled in the shade, and Wawrinka reaches down and rubs her neck. "Knowing that sooner or later, the same thing is going to happen to my Crown Vic."

"And my lesbian Jetta."

"Not to mention the three of us. You were right about dogs. They definitely make the short list."

To take her mind off the grim eventualities, Wawrinka gets up and walks back to the car, and returns with the binoculars. Back on the bench, she aims them at the compactor. Although still rattling, the cab is empty, and she sees that Porter has moved to the even higher cab of an adjacent crane.

"How late is this guy going to work?" says Wawrinka, handing the binoculars to O'Hara. "Now he's in the goddamned crane."

Porter is using the second machine to reload the first. As she watches, he clamps the teeth of his shovel down on the roof of a Pontiac Fiero and pries it off the stack like a bouncer separating combatants in a brawl. He carries the Pontiac to the compactor, drops it into the chute, and rolls back to the stack for seconds.

"He's like a kid playing with his Tonka toys," says O'Hara.

Now the vehicle at the top of the stack is a Cimarron, without question the lamest model to wear the Cadillac badge, not really a Caddy at all, and below it a Cherokee and a nondescript box of a van. As Porter lines up to grab the Cimarron, O'Hara sees that the van is dark green, and when she screws up the magnification, sees that the side panel is flecked with black. Panning the full width of the side panel, she can make out the outline of a *W* in the center.

"Jesus fucking Christ," says O'Hara, jumping to her feet, "it's our van. We got to get this toddler's attention."

"I got it covered," says Wawrinka, getting to her feet.

"What are you going to do?"

Wawrinka reaches for the Sauer automatic holstered in the small of her back, undoes the safety, aims it straight over her head, and fires three times.

CHAPTER 39

IN THE FADING light, the green van is little more than a dark rectangle. It's not until the Caddy and the Cherokee have been shunted aside, and the van brought closer to the ground, that O'Hara can see that the tires and wheels have been stripped along with all the glass—front windshield, passenger windows, and side-view mirrors. There are no windows in the back of the van.

Using a forklift, Porter lowers the van to within four feet of the ground, then turns toward the edge of the clearing. As he navigates the rutted track between the outer stacks and the first line of surrounding woods, O'Hara, Wawrinka, and the dog walk behind the front-loaded vehicle like mourners following a loved one to the grave. The evening smells of damp clay and pine, and the air buzzes with moths, gnats, and mosquitoes. After half a mile, a clean boxlike structure materializes in the woods. "Could you pull up the door in the middle," asks Porter over the idling engine, "then pull it shut as soon as we're in. Maybe we can keep most of the bloodsuckers out."

O'Hara grabs the handle and braces her back, but the door flies up the well-oiled track so easily she nearly loses her balance. Inside, the darkness is complete. The echo of Porter's clomping steps are followed by an electrical *thwunk*, and a bank of fluorescent lights come on in succession across the high ceiling. Rather than a backwoods shed, O'Hara finds herself in an immaculate three-bay garage with whitewashed cement floors.

Porter parks the forklift in the center bay and gently lowers the rusted axles to the floor. To the left an automotive shape is covered by a tarp, and to the right on a jack is number 57—a black dirt-track racer, its front end almost as banged up as the Skylark after the first blow inside the compactor. Surrounding the number in scripts of various size and color are the car's sponsors—MABEL'S TOWING, EZ EXCAVATING, TP SALVAGE, and BO'S BAR & GRILL—and on the wall behind it a large poster: CHEROKEE MOTOR SPEEDWAY, THE PLACE YOUR MAMA WARNED YOU ABOUT.

Slowly, O'Hara circles the van. She is so stunned and relieved to have found it and so riveted by the dazzling sight of it in front of her in the operating room light, she is half afraid it's a mirage, and for several minutes forgets she isn't the only person in the garage. Outside, there was just enough light for O'Hara to make out the little bits of black and the *W* in the middle. Under the powerful fluorescent lights of the garage it's clear that those flecks of black are what remain after someone hurriedly scraped off letters painted on the side panel with a stencil. Standing to the side, the outlines of even the most thoroughly scraped-off letters are plain: SARASOTA WATER AUTHORITY, word for word, letter for letter, exactly what Sharon Di Nunzio remembered seeing briefly in Banyan Bay visitor parking more than six months ago.

"God bless her heart," says O'Hara, talking out loud for the first time. "That ninety-year-old slut got it exactly right."

"Excuse me?" Porter's drawl brings O'Hara out of her thoughts and back into the room. Porter, who goes about six-four, two-fifty, with the kind of NFL lineman infrastructure that could handle fifty more, stands in front of her, both hands shoved into the pockets of his greasy jeans. Size notwithstanding, Porter doesn't evince a shred of menace. His fleshy jug head, and furrowed brow, suggest a benevolent mastiff. On the other hand, Porter has every incentive to put his best foot forward, and since O'Hara and Wawrinka abruptly got his attention, he has been projecting goodwill in buckets.

"I need some answers," says O'Hara. "They are sufficiently important that for the moment, I'm going to move off to one side your dealings with that Clint Eakins and how you happened to come into possession of this vehicle. First of all, what is it exactly?"

"A 2004 GMC Astrovan."

"How long have you had it?"

"I picked it up about five months ago. Except for my sister's boy, who comes in a couple afternoons and Saturdays, it's just me here. So the vehicle would have sat in the yard for another two months easy before I got around to doing anything to it."

"As in stripping it for parts?"

"That's right."

"So how long has it been exposed to the elements?"

"About three months, and unfortunately, this time of year, you can count on a thunderstorm every week."

"One last question for now. What's the name of your dog?"

"Mabel."

CHAPTER 40

CAREFUL NOT TO touch the side of the car, the five-foot-four O'Hara takes her first look inside. The height of the opening makes it difficult to see much, and even in the bright light the interior is in shadows. Without prompting, Porter rolls a metal chest of Snap-on tools to the driver's-side, locks the wheels, and helps O'Hara onto it, giving her platform from which to peer down into the front of the van. Then he drives the forklift to the opposite side of the car, attaches two hanging lights to the lift, and raises it just short of the roofline. The lights, aiming downward from the top of the missing passenger window, illuminate the entire front interior.

Three months without a windshield have subjected the dash to a furious aerial assault, and it's caked with a thick omelet of bird shit. They say that a roomful of monkeys equipped with typewriters will eventually tap out the plays of William Shakespeare. That may or may not be true, but with a couple months and a sky full of birds you get a Jackson Pollock.

"I've never seen pigeon shit like this," says O'Hara.

"Neither have I," says Porter. "This is crow and blackbird, a little osprey and hawk, and maybe a couple seagulls who took a wrong turn."

"Kind of like you, Porter. For a car thief, you certainly know your bird shit."

Porter's only response is to continue to offer the same high level of personal service, which combines the anticipation of a valet and the resourcefulness of a gaffer. He rummages through a drawer and grabs a spackling knife. "How about I try to dig out the vehicle identification number?"

"That would be lovely." As she surveys the garbage-strewn interior, Porter chips and scrapes the left side of the dash until he unshits a metal tag. He wipes it with a soaked rag, then reads the numbers to Wawrinka, who calls them in to Sarasota PD. Watching them interact, it occurs to O'Hara that Wawrinka has finally encountered someone butcher than her.

O'Hara returns her attention to the interior. The foot wells on the driver and passenger side hold a foot of gray water, and the seats, as well as the raised area between them, are littered with a sodden mess of greasy food wrappers and cardboard containers representing the major enablers of American obesity.

Although the light is good, leaning into the car's window without being able to touch any part of it for support requires the strength and flexibility of the contortionists whose portraits hang in the Ringling Museum. O'Hara can't do it for more than thirty seconds at a time before her back starts to give, but that's enough to see that there is more trash than would have accumulated in a twelve-hour sprint from Florida to South Carolina. That suggests the perps have been using this van for several days or weeks before Levin was killed.

This is confirmed when Wawrinka gets a return call from Sarasota PD. "The VIN bounced back," says Wawrinka. "The van was rented from Alamo at the Sarasota Airport on February 18, thirteen days before Levin got shot. It was put on MasterCard by a Nicholas Adams of 187 Parade Hill Road, Dearborn, Michigan, and when the bill wasn't paid and the address found to be fake, was reported stolen three months later. According to his Michigan driver's license, which has the same phony address, Adams is twenty-three, five-seven, a hundred and thirty-five pounds. No priors under that name."

"They have a picture?"

"No. Michigan is one of only two states where they don't have license pictures in the system. All we got is the description."

Like a snorkeler, O'Hara takes a breath and leans back into the car. In addition to the bird-shit-speckled garbage, there's a flotilla of trash on the water. O'Hara can make out a half dozen Pepsi and Coke cans, several water bottles, and a plastic Advil tub. Beside it, floating on its back in a clear pouch is a Happy Meal toy. The green figure is the first thing she has seen that makes her think of the kid rather than the perps, and the thought of his agonizing death hits her in the chest. As she unfolds from the window, Wawrinka returns from the small kitchen in the back of the garage.

"Darlene, I just got off the phone with my sergeant," says Wawrinka, and for the first time since O'Hara met her, she sounds uneasy. "For starters, he sends his congratulations."

Okay, thinks O'Hara, what's the lousy part?

"He's sending a crime scene here first thing in the morning with a flatbed to haul the van back to Sarasota."

"And?"

"He wants us to shut it down for the night. He doesn't want us to risk anything that could compromise the scene. He knows when we left this morning and how tired we are at this point, thinks we've done enough for the night."

"Sounds like a helluva guy," says O'Hara "Compromise the crime scene? Why would he think we would do that?"

It's bad enough, thinks O'Hara, I have to deal with my own sergeant. Now I'm getting another layer of supervision from Sarasota?

"I don't know," says Wawrinka. "He doesn't want us to take any chances. Like I said, he thinks we've done enough for the night."

Rather than responding, O'Hara acts like she hasn't heard a word and turns to Porter, as if Wawrinka isn't in the room. "Terry, could you raise the lift an inch or two so more light hits the water." Once Porter has done that, O'Hara twists her upper body back through the window. With the improved light, she notices two additional objects floating on the water. They are boxes of some kind, but more substantial than the containers for Whoppers and McNuggets, and they are both dark red.

"Terry, do me another favor. Stick your head in here and take a look at the two red boxes floating on the water. Tell me what you see." O'Hara comes down off the tool chest so Porter can slide it aside. Then he carefully sticks his massive head into the car. It takes him a second to find the boxes she is referring to.

"I see them. One box has gold trim, and so does the other. There's writing on the top of it, on top of the box, starts with a *C*, 'Carter,'" he says. "You know what, I think it's a ring box. It is. An empty ring box. Both of them. They're a set. Same color. Same gold trim."

"Carter, you sure about that? How about Cartier?"

"That's it. There's an *i*."

"Darlene," says Wawrinka, "we got to shut down."

"I just want to see if there's any way to see into the back."

"That's a bad idea. Listen, there's something I didn't tell you. Apparently your sarge and my sarge have gotten all chummy. In the process, your sergeant warned mine about you. Said you're a great detective, but a loose cannon, that you sabotage yourself. Here's the thing, I don't give a shit about my sergeant or your sergeant. I'm sure they deserve each other. But I don't want to let you do something stupid for my own reasons, because you're my friend. You found this van, and I don't know one other detective that could have done that. Now let's get drunk."

CHAPTER 41

BO'S BAR & GRILL is a hillbilly version of an East Village dive. The light and clientele are just as murky, the jukebox (Haggard, Atkins, Jones, Jagger/Richards, Plant/Page) as good, and the ladies' bathroom, where O'Hara slaps up a Flat Screens sticker, a half step better than a latrine. The only difference is that no one is sporting a fedora or arrived on a bicycle, and no one's parents are paying the rent.

While Wawrinka and Porter detour to the pool table, O'Hara grabs a bottle of Maker's Mark, and a glass of ice and settles into a tattered booth with her new best friend, who happens to be a dog. O'Hara's strength as an investigator is that she's a world-class muller, willing to roll over the same pebble as long as it takes to yield a fresh drop of blood. The flip side is the tendency to aim the same obsessive attention at herself, which can feel like falling asleep under a sunlamp. The great perquisite of finding the van is knowing that for the next several hours, she'll be gnawing on the case instead of herself.

As she imbibes her first hard alcohol in a week, she makes a mental list of everything she now knows or is close to knowing about the perps, some of which she shares aloud with Mabel. Based on the discarded empty ring boxes and the bogus but official-sounding "Sarasota Water Authority" painted on the side of the van, they're burglars. They knock on people's doors. They bullshit their way in, and they rob them. Based on their MO, and efficiency at carrying it off, they've done this many times before. They're pros. They've got skills. With a stencil and a can of spray paint, they turn a generic rental into an official vehicle and themselves into municipal employees. O'Hara rattles the ice, and tells Mabel, "Despite being from New York, they rent the van with a credit card and license from Michigan, which just happens to be one of two states that doesn't store photographs in their computer files."

O'Hara refreshes her glass with ice and bourbon, glances at the pool tournament in progress, then returns her attention to Mabel. "One thing that's a little odd," she tells the dog, "is that they're a burglary outfit from New York, but work a thousand miles away in Sarasota. That's a long way to go for a couple old rings, don't you think, even if they are from Cartier." Thinking about it more, she sees the advantages of working in a random destination far from where you live—the cops don't know who you are, and if the cops don't know you, there's no way for them to lean on you or your friends and no one to rat you out, and you don't have to worry about bumping into one of your victims at the corner bodega. It's just another example of their professionalism. But why bring along the kid? Why involve a kid at all? If they walk up to some apartment and claim to be with the water company, doesn't having a kid contradict the story and make the whole thing less persuasive? And despite the empty jewelry boxes and the bogus writing on the van, there was no evidence Levin's place had been ransacked or anything stolen.

When O'Hara looks away from Mabel, Wawrinka and Porter have joined them in the booth. "There's something you got to see," says Wawrinka. Her eyes sparkle, and her face is flushed with a tequila glow. "Show her, Porter."

Porter, in the outside corner of the booth, pulls his jeans over a massive calf and unveils a tattoo portrait of the junkyard proprietor as a very young man. The young Porter who already has his distinctive jug head, sits astride his plastic Big Wheel. The seat is red, the fork and handlebars yellow, and the wheels black with yellow inserts. Beneath the pedals is the slogan—"Fast, Furious & Fun."

"That's his first vehicle, Darlene. His first set of wheels. That's where it all starts."

"In the beginning," says O'Hara, "was the Big Wheel."

"Exactly," says Wawrinka, and as O'Hara chinks glasses with her partner, she shares an eye roll with Mabel.

"And you know something else, Dar," says Wawrinka, slurring slightly. "That fifty-seven car on the lift. Porter built that himself from scratch. Fabricated the body, everything."

"Too bad I can't keep it on the track," he says.

O'Hara has been so immersed in her thoughts, she hadn't noticed that all the other customers have left, and now the barkeep approaches their booth.

"Go home," says Porter. "I'll lock up."

"Sure?"

"No problem."

"You own this bar, don't you," says O'Hara. "You brought us to your own goddamn bar. No wonder the name of the place is on your car. I guess that means you also own EZ Excavating, and God knows what else."

"A little real estate is all," says Porter, embarrassed.

"I always figured 'entrepreneur' is just another word for 'criminal'," says O'Hara, chinking his glass. The departure of the bartender reminds her how exhausted she is. "I need to pack it in too," she says.

"I got a little apartment upstairs," says Porter, "in case my friends or I get too drunk to drive home. A guy like me doesn't need a DWI, right? Two beds in each room, and I just washed the sheets. Swear to God."

"I'm going to take you up on that," says O'Hara, "as long as I can borrow your dog."

"Mabel's a grown woman," says Porter; "she can do as she pleases."

"I'll be up in a bit," says Wawrinka, heading back to the table. "I don't want to end the night on a losing streak."

O'Hara and Mabel climb the stairs to a bedroom as clean as Porter's garage where they barely stir until 10:00 the next morning, when Wawrinka makes a clumsy attempt to discreetly slip into the other bed.

CHAPTER 42

WHEN CRIME SCENE unlocks the back of the van revealing the blood-smeared gray metal walls, O'Hara's mind reels, and retreats to the Chelsea gallery where she first glimpsed the kid, and fell hard. Despite what her eyes see now, she smiles at the remembered image of that shirtless gink, all skin and bones and attitude, his arm cavalierly draped over the shoulder of a topless girl, as if it's the kind of thing that happens to him all the time. The photographer must have seen that the kid was a natural, and no doubt the kid nailed it, gave him exactly what he wanted, but he also threw in a little mockery for himself.

O'Hara loves that sparkle in the kid's eyes, is unlikely to ever forget it, but as a mother, O'Hara is even more defenseless against the sight of the kid's belly, his smooth skin stretched tight over his ribs and skinny arms. It reminds her of a picture she took of Axl when he was three or four. A friend of O'Hara's came over and was playing with Axl in her mother's backyard, holding a baseball bat sideways as Axl clung to it like the bar of a jungle gym. In the picture, the friend lifts the bat in the air, and as Axl hangs on for dear life, his shirt rides up over his navel, and whenever she looks at the picture she recalls exactly how the cool skin of her son's stomach felt on her hands and lips. She knows it's all evolution, like the sweet smell of a baby's head, a way to make parents adore their offspring, take care of them, and even die for them. But did they really have to make the smell and touch that sublime? Obviously they did, because for some parents it's still not enough.

O'Hara's mind jumped from the back of the van to the last known image of the kid alive, because she knows that here, alone in this window-less cell, is where he died. While the perps stuffed their faces in front, the kid slowly bled to death behind them on a thin foam mattress stained maroon black. Surrounding the mattress are mangled packages of gauze, cotton balls, and antiseptic wipes, and empty bags of M&Ms and Cheetos and two *Superman* comics, and everything is dabbed with bloody finger-prints, even the paint bucket the kid used as a toilet.

Of all the stains, the most disturbing are the handprints on the flat gray metal walls. They are the same size as the ones stamped out of the gate at the community garden, but these are the prints of someone trying desperately to get out.

When O'Hara stands up and turns away, she searches the garage for her new friend. "Hey, Porter, what happened to Mabel?"

"As soon as they opened the van, she scratched on the back door and asked to be let out. She didn't want any part of it."

CHAPTER 43

FRAN LEBRIE SITS at the kitchen table and rubs the spot on her finger where her ring had been. She wears a large floppy hat tied by a string beneath her chin, and her delicate cheekbones are slathered with a silverish cream. "They said there might be a problem with the water," says Lebrie, "and they were going to have to do a few tests. Had I drunk the water this morning? Had I used it to make tea or coffee? Had I washed my hands with it, and if I had, was I wearing my ring when I did?

"I wasn't sure if I had washed my hands, I told them. I'm not one of these people who wash or use a hand sanitizer every five minutes, but I knew that if I had, I certainly wouldn't have taken off the ring, and I told them that.

"'Better safe than sorry,' he said, 'do you have any milk in your refrigerator?' I was about to make a cake, so I actually had two kinds of milk—regular and nonfat. I asked, what would be better? 'The regular,' he said, 'and I'll need a bowl.' He got a bowl down from the cabinet and poured in about a cup. I remember my cat was going crazy for the milk, or maybe she was alarmed by my stupidity. Then he had me take my ring off and put it in the milk. 'If there are any impurities in the water,' he said, 'the milk will counteract them.'"

"How many men were there?" asks O'Hara.

"Two."

"Two men?" asks Wawrinka.

"And a boy."

"Can you describe them?" asks O'Hara.

"They were such an odd group. One man was very big and heavy and dark, in his forties. The other man was slight and short and in his mid-twenties, if that. The boy was about nine, very thin with long blond hair, and had a limp. I still remember his smile.

"I think that's why I let them in," continues Lebrie. "Because of the boy. I'm sure it was. The older man said his son had the day off from school, and had brought him along so his son could get a clearer idea of what his father did for a living. When he was growing up, he said, he didn't have a clue what his father did all day at his job, and he vowed that when he had children they would get a chance to see him at his job. That's why I let them in. Because of the boy and that story."

The afternoon they headed back from South Carolina, Wawrinka was still such a mess, she surrendered the keys to her precious Crown Vic and let O'Hara drive. For O'Hara it was refreshing to wake up less hung-over than the person she was with, although in this case Wawrinka was dealing with too many tequilas as well as sex with someone of the wrong gender. In any case, it gave O'Hara time to think.

Among the things she focused on were those Cartier boxes floating in the rancid water. If the jewelry hadn't come from Levin's place, and based on the condition of Levin's place, it didn't seem like they had, it meant that the perps had gotten into at least one other home, and more likely many. When they got back to Sarasota, O'Hara checked the logs between February 18, the day the van was rented, and March 3. She found that on March 2, Fran Lebrie, seventy-nine, had reported a burglary at her bayside home half a mile south of Levin's, and that the responding officer found her so distraught, he concluded she would be of no value as a witness and gave her name to Elderly Outreach.

"Can you give any more details about the men?" asks O'Hara. "You said the bigger of two men was huge. Do you mean tall or heavy?"

"Both. He was well over six feet, and obese. I would say, more than three hundred pounds. And dark. Swarthy. He didn't look at all like his son, but I didn't think about that till later. Or maybe I did, and was just scared." The woman rubs her hands together, and winces, reliving the incident.

"The smaller man was less memorable," continues Lebrie, "although I think he had earrings in both ears. He didn't say much. The bigger one was in charge and did the talking."

"The boy," says O'Hara. "Did he say anything?"

"No. I remember him looking at the art. He liked it. I could tell. All the work is mine." For the first time, O'Hara glances at the art hanging on the walls. Mostly it consists of assemblages of plastic action figures arranged in provocative ways—wrestlers from the WWF, athletes or superheroes. Perhaps, thinks O'Hara, they reminded the boy of the inflated characters in his comics.

"What happened then?"

"He asked me where my water heater was, and when I told him it was in the basement, he walked me down and had me show it to him. On the way he grabbed a spatula out of the drawer in my kitchen cabinet, and when we got to the basement and were standing in front of the water heater, he handed the spatula to me. 'When I get back to the kitchen,' he said, 'I need you to knock on the water heater with the spatula and not stop until I tell you. That's very important, and it's important that you not stop or we won't be able to figure out what the problem is. ' He went back up the stairs, and I did as I was instructed and knocked the heater with my spatula. I did it for quite a while. I must have kept it up for five minutes or maybe even longer. Then I started to feel stupid, and then I started to feel scared. I was scared the whole time."

For the perps who prey on them, these old vics must seem like manna from heaven, well worth traveling a thousand miles for. They're physically weak and easily intimidated. Even the plucky Di Nunzio recalled that the sight of the van made her fearful. And once they've been fleeced, they're all but useless as witnesses. Their hearing, eyesight, and memory are rarely intact, and even when they are, the police dismiss them anyway, as the Sarasota cop did with Lebrie—and as she herself nearly did with Di Nunzio.

"I called out to them and there was no response, and when I got upstairs they were gone. I took the bowl to the sink and poured out the milk, but by then I already knew that the ring would be gone. In my bedroom, drawers were open and other precious things were missing too, including a pair of matching watches my husband bought to celebrate our fiftieth anniversary."

The old people, thinks O'Hara, come for the sun and the beaches and the golf courses and each other, and the perps come for them. Like fishermen, or that woman and her daughter trawling the aisles at Publix.

"You know," says Lebrie, "I got married when I was twenty, which of course was much too young. On the day of my wedding, I looked at my new husband and realized I barely knew him. But I was lucky. He turned out to be a perfectly lovely man. As you get older, everything gets taken from you. My husband died three years ago, but he had already lost his memory. Every month you lose something else or someone or some part of yourself. That jewelry is the least of it, but I had worn that ring for sixty years, and my hand feels funny without it. And I feel like such a fool."

"Well, I love your pin," says O'Hara, referring to the bold geometric shape on Lebrie's sweater.

"Bakelite," says Lebrie with a gentle smile. "And please don't be alarmed by my appearance. It's just sunblock. I came to Florida and discovered I was allergic to the sun."

CHAPTER 44

"YOU ALL QUIET because you're sorry to see me leave, or you still suffering from your little indiscretion?"

"It doesn't seem little to me," says Wawrinka. "I feel like a sellout."

"Imagine how I feel after spending the night with Mabel. I still haven't decided if I'm going to tell Bruno."

"Some free advice, Darlene."

"What's that?"

"Don't."

O'Hara's flight is in less than three hours. Wawrinka intended to take O'Hara to her favorite seafood shack, a spot under the drawbridge called Ernestine's, but O'Hara insists they use the time for one last look at Levin's apartment. Now that they know the perps' MO, she wants to see if something had been stolen that they hadn't noticed. Once there, she figures they might as well polish off Levin's last two Amstels, which they are doing on the small porch off the living room, which looks out over some spiky crabgrass and then the beach and Gulf.

"From the gut-shot way Porter was staring as the car drove off, you must be a real natural. First time out of the gate like that."

"A natural slut more like it. Like our old pal Di Nunzio."

"To Sharon," says O'Hara, extending her Amstel.

"To Sharon," echoes Wawrinka, meeting it halfway. "And I guess Lebrie's spatula clears up the mystery of Levin's wooden spoon."

"Yeah," says O'Hara, "sometimes a cigar is just a cigar, and sometimes a spoon or spatula is just something to bang on the water heater so the perps know it's safe to ransack the rest of the place."

"Those are some canny motherfuckers. They talk their way in, so it's not breaking and entering. Then they pepper her with questions and knock her off her balance."

"Fuck them," says O'Hara. "They think they are so smart, but really they're goons, scaring old people as much as fooling them. And the kid is just a prop. A way of taking the stink off them, reducing suspicion, getting folks to let down their guard. A throwaway prop they let bleed out on a sponge in back while they're eating burgers and fries." She thinks of the mother and daughter at Publix, and all those Madonna and Child paintings at the Ringling Museum. Every scam goes down a little easier, she thinks, if you throw in a kid.

When they've finished their beer, they do a final walk-through, O'Hara smiling wistfully at the useless angel asleep at her post, her cheeks and thighs as chubby as those old-time circus performers'. Nothing seems to have been taken, and there's no sign that anyone swept through the place with bad intent.

What they do find—in a bowl on the dining room table—is a small key for a safe or lockbox. If the box is gone, maybe the perps took it on their way out, removed the contents, and dumped it somewhere before they unloaded the van. But five minutes later O'Hara spots it, apparently undisturbed on a shoulder-height shelf of the bedroom closet. It's less a safe than a container, shaped like a small suitcase, made of heavy-gauge plastic designed to protect the contents from fire or flooding. However, it's nearly as heavy as a safe, and it takes the two of them to get it down off the shelf and carry it to the dining room table.

The key works, but there's not much of value inside, at least not to thieves. What it contains is the memorabilia of an illustrious boxing career, starting with a stack of old newspaper stories chronicling the teenage exploits of Bunny "Schoolboy" Levin. One yellowed clipping from November 15, 1937, is illustrated with a photo of Levin in shirt and tie and sweater vest being mobbed by his adoring classmates. "After his stunning knockout, Levin returns to South Newark H.S. a conquering hero," reads the caption. Beneath the brittle pages, with their antiquated typefaces and layout, is a small cardboard box containing the pin Levin earned for winning the lightweight division of the 1937 Golden Gloves, and beneath the box, in the well of the compartment, a plastic bag. When O'Hara peers inside, she sees Levin's old silk boxing trunks with the Star of David on the leg and his shockingly delicate lace-up shoes.

"Like going to war in boxers and ballet slippers," says O'Hara.

"I say we give the pin to Sharon," says Wawrinka. "God knows she deserves it. Besides, she saw Ben's last bout. February 5, 2007, Sweet Tomatoes, stopped after three seconds of the first round by knockout."

"If you count Sweet Tomatoes and the golf course, Levin may have had the longest career in boxing history. How about you give the pin to Sharon, and I'll call Sol about the rest."

While Wawrinka climbs the stairs to Di Nunzio's place, O'Hara heads back to the tiny porch and gets Klinger on her cell. "Sol. It's Darlene O'Hara. I'm at Ben's place right now. I found some things you need to see."

"Can't it wait till the morning?"

"No, you gotta come right now. I'm heading to the airport in less than an hour."

"But Pettit's working on a one-hitter. He's pitching a gem."

"Sol, don't be a schmuck. Get your ass over here pronto. And come round the back to the porch."

Twenty minutes later, O'Hara hears the big Lexus turn into the driveway. Then she hears the *thunk* of the heavy door and Klinger's footsteps, first clicking on the cement, then crunching the crabgrass. When he turns the corner, O'Hara can see his white leather loafers.

"Sol, up here."

"I see you, Darlene. This is nuts."

"I got a question about those nights when Ben had a fight and would come by your building and stand under your window. You remember how he would whistle?"

"Like it was yesterday," says Klinger. "Two at a time, one long, one short, like this."

Klinger tries to whistle but starts crying before he gets out more than a little stream of air. Nevertheless, O'Hara leans over the railing and lowers the bag to within a couple feet of his outstretched hands.

"Hey, Sollie, catch."

PART III

CHAPTER 45

O'HARA BROUGHT TWO things back from Sarasota—the seeds of a cold, courtesy of JetBlue, and the twenty-four-sheet Strathmore sketchbook she tossed into her shopping cart at Publix—and on her first morning back in the city, she drops the pad on the bar of Milano's, beside her grapefruit juice and vodka. As she reacquaints herself with the ghostly chiaroscuro of the downtown dive and stews over the lack of progress in her homicide, she flips the pages until she stops at the sketch of Levin's wooden spoon she made in the phone booth of the Longboat Key Public Library. The crude rendering reminds O'Hara of her and Wawrinka's visit to the home of Fran Lebrie, and in the space below the spoon, she scratches out a companion drawing of Lebrie's plastic spatula.

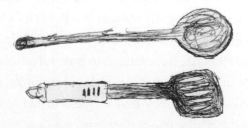

The drawings aren't half bad, thinks O'Hara. With the right frame, maybe she could sell them to the Chelsea gallery that shows the late great Freek Staps. Call it *Cop Art*. Then O'Hara starts to hear them, not the drawings but the utensils, or at least the sounds they'd make smacking the steel casings of the water heaters. Soon a nice little geriatric rhythm section is percolating inside her head, the slap of Lebrie's plastic spatula punctuated by the pop of Levin's spoon. The spatula sounds delicate and feminine and more like jazz. The spoon is more rock 'n' roll, like that drumstick on a cowbell at the start of Mountain's "Mississippi Queen."

The distinct sounds draw O'Hara's attention to a difference between the two drummers. At some point early on, Levin stopped banging and returned to his bedroom to confront the perps, while Lebrie did as she was instructed and kept the beat going in her basement. Why did Levin figure out that the two guys from the water authority were impostors before Lebrie? Lebrie is a sharp lady, yet she kept slapping till the perps and her jewelry were long gone, while Levin grabbed his gun and headed back down the hall. Did he notice something she didn't, or was it simply a disparity of nerve? Or was he more foolhardy? Certainly, her fear of what might happen if she walked in on the perps as they rifled through her drawers was sensible.

O'Hara takes a sip and picks up her pen again. In the space below the drawings, she writes "Gus Henderson" and shifts her attention from the Gulf of Mexico to East Third Street. Ever since O'Hara buckled herself into her seat for the return flight, she's been sorting through the perplexing disparities and consistencies between what Henderson claims to have done and what she now knows. Combining and recombining the various pieces is like trying to line up the squares in a Rubik's Cube, and the fruitless twisting and turning is starting to mess with O'Hara's equilibrium.

According to Paulette, Gus claimed to have killed a large black man, then buried him under a shady tree in the community garden. Instead of the victim he described, they find a nine-year-old blond boy, but the location is spot-on, and now one of the perps, who was with the boy, turns

out to be not large and African American but large and swarthy. Is that
a coincidence? If so, it contradicts a fundamental axiom of investigative
work, which is that there are no coincidences.

Obviously Henderson didn't kill the perp. As far as O'Hara knows, he
is still alive. But maybe the old man so desperately wishes he did that he
almost came to believe it, and time and dementia did the rest. Maybe Gus
sees himself like one of the caped crusaders in the kid's comics, aveng-
ing wrongs and protecting the innocent. What's frustrating is the suspicion that somewhere in the corroded synapses of Henderson's brain is an
image of exactly what happened in that garden, as clear as that Polaroid
of the willow, but digging it out would take a pickax.

O'Hara savors the cocktail and quiet. Milano's feels as sealed off from
the world as the inside of that old phone booth, and the studious way her
two fellow regulars apply themselves to their beverages, they could be in a
library. Witnessing the slavish routines of addiction might even be sober-
ing if she let herself dwell on it. Instead, O'Hara concentrates on the drink
and case at hand and, to goad herself into sharper thinking, recalls the
galling spiel the larger perp gave Lebrie about wanting his son to know
what his old man did for a living. The depth of cynicism required to come
up with that upside-down version of Bring Your Kid to Work Day makes
O'Hara's head hurt. Is that perp really his father? If so, no one understood
more clearly what his old man did for a living than Herc, and no one has
displayed less parental concern than someone who let his nine-year-old
son bleed to death for however long it took.

Images of the blood-soaked mattress and bloodstained comics reap-
pear of their own volition. O'Hara returns to her drawing of the spoon and
thinks about the eighty-seven-year-old, 118-pound bantamweight who
stood up to those assholes. To O'Hara, courage is the most miraculous
human trait. It defies all logic and self-interest, and as she pictures the
drama that played out when the old man returned to his bedroom with
his antique .22, it generates a second question. Why did Levin bring the
spoon back to the bedroom? Why didn't he leave it by the water heater?

Wouldn't he have dropped it among his shoes and sneakers when he reached into the closet for the gun?

O'Hara has an answer for this one. Bunny "Schoolboy" Levin brought the spoon back from the water heater because at eighty-seven, he was still representing his buddies at Newark High, letting them know he hadn't gone soft. Levin brought back the spoon along with the gun because he intended to shove it up that big perp's ass. Schoolboy was going to take that splintery utensil and insert it where the sun don't shine, not even in goddamn Florida in fucking August.

CHAPTER 46

JANDOREK WELCOMES O'HARA back to homicide with an arched eyebrow and a breath mint.

"I thought Florida was going to do you some good."

"Florida in the summer doesn't do anyone any good. But thanks."

When O'Hara turns on her computer, she has a new e-mail from Wawrinka, the gist of which is that there's nothing new. Despite the assault of wind, rain, and bird shit at TP Salvage, Sarasota Crime Scene was able to scrape some DNA from the inside of the van, along with two sets of prints, but they don't match anyone in the system, and there's still no trace of the white wagon the perps stole from the old man's driveway.

With nothing of value coming out of the van, the charges on Adams's MasterCard are the only trail for the perps north of the Walmart, and O'Hara opens up the account file on her screen. A total of seven charges were made on the card, and by calling the credit card company and the merchants, Wawrinka has been able to put together an itemized list of purchases:

2/17/07, 5:28 p.m., Sarasota Airport: van rental from Alamo ($399 per week)

*3/3/07, 11:45 a.m, Longboat Key, FL, Circle K: six packages of gauze,
2 containers of Advil, two different kinds of antiseptic cream, adhesive
tape, and four six-packs of water ($83.78)*

*3/3/07, 12:05 p.m., Bradenton, FL, CVS: 5 bottles of hydrochloric
solution, 2 thermometers, six packages of gauze, sterile pads, cotton
balls, 3 gallon jugs of distilled water, 1 six-pack of Coke, 4 Hostess
Twinkies, 1 Superman comic ($147.38)*

*3/3/07, 1:12 p.m., Tampa, FL, CVS: 5 bottles of hydrochloric solution,
8 packages of gauze, sterile pads, 3 tubes of CVS antiseptic cream, 3
containers of Aleve, 3 six-packs of water, 1 six-pack of Coke, 1 package
of Oreos, 1 Superman comic ($118.07)*

*3/3/07, 11:53 p.m., Vance, SC, Sunoco Service Center: 14.8 gallons of
regular gas, two bottles of water, one six-pack of Coke ($56.10)*

*3/4/07, 10:16 a.m., Baltimore, MD, Exxon Service Center: 17.7 gallons
of regular gas, two bottles of water, one large Coke ($67.49)*

*3/4/07, 3:09 p.m., Kings Ferry, NY, Citgo Service Center: 7.53 gallons
of regular gas, 1 six-pack of Corona ($40.93)*

The first time Adams used the card was to rent the van on February 17. The next was on March 3, seven minutes after Di Nunzio called
911. That was a minimart half a mile west of Levin's condo in Banyan
Bay, where more than $80 was spent on first aid supplies and water, pre-
sumably to clean the boy's wound as much as drinking. Twelve miles and
twenty minutes later, they stopped again for more supplies at a CVS in
Bradenton, and a little more than an hour later, they stopped at a CVS in
Tampa.

The short intervals between those first three stops, as they race to plug the boy's wound, are heartrending. So is the attempt to bolster the boy's spirits with the comic books, which this time someone actually got right. But after Tampa, the medical efforts stop, and O'Hara sees that the conflict between regard and disregard evident at the grave site was also being played out in the front of the car. The kid needed a lot more than gauze and Advil and a comic book, but one of the perps seemed to care about the kid, while the other didn't give a rat's ass. O'Hara assumes that somewhere between Walterboro, South Carolina, where the Volvo was stolen, and Vance, where they stopped for gas but no more first aid or comic books, the boy died.

The last three charges are all at service centers—in Vance, Baltimore, and finally thirteen miles north of Manhattan on the Palisades Parkway, and since they are all O'Hara has, she pores over them. She determines the distances between the stops and the amount of gas purchased, in case a change in mileage might suggest they switched vehicles a second time. But there isn't one. In Baltimore, which is 512 miles north of Vance, they put in almost 18 gallons, and in Kings Ferry, New York, on the Palisades Parkway, which is 209 miles north of Baltimore, they put in a little over 7.5 gallons, and in both cases that works out to about 28 miles per gallon. And because she can't think of anything else to do, she looks up the specs for a 1993 Volvo wagon, and sees it has an eighteen-gallon tank.

Since the last charge is at the Kings Ferry service center on the Palisades Parkway, the focus has been on New York and New Jersey, but in fact the car could be anywhere, and despite her efforts, O'Hara can't get the data to yield anything that might pinpoint the search. All she gets is a white wagon that looks like an ambulance, but is in fact a hearse.

CHAPTER 47

THE FLAT SCREENS are up third, scheduled for 10:30, and O'Hara meets Krekorian at Lakeside at 10:00. Arriving at 10:00 for a 10:30 show is a mistake only a mother could make. At midnight the second band hasn't started, and forty minutes later, when they're down to the ice chips in their third Maker's Mark, K taps out.

"I'm too old for midweek shows," he says. "Before I go, you got to promise me you're not going to embarrass Axl, yourself, or the NYPD."

"I'm already embarrassing the NYPD. A month since we dug up the boy, and I don't know his name."

"I'm more concerned about your immediate family."

"You afraid I'm going to wander onstage, blubber into the mike, and fall on my ass?"

"Yeah."

Despite her nascent cold and a long day, O'Hara is all keyed up for Axl's show. Based on the knots in her stomach, you'd think she's about to watch him step into the ring at one of those smoke-filled joints where Sollie cheered Schoolboy from the front row. Then again, the stakes aren't much different. One seat over is a twentysomething who looks as much of a wreck as she, and he's wearing a Germs T-shirt. All hands, forearms, and spiky black hair, he taps out a beat on the rim of his glass with a red swizzle stick.

"The Germs were a hell of a band," says O'Hara, shamelessly passing on information recently acquired from her new pal Holly. "Too bad Darby Crash killed himself."

"The Germs? Never heard of 'em. I swiped the shirt from some chick's drawer."

That's what you get for being full of shit, thinks O'Hara. Although it wouldn't take much to convince herself she needs another drink, she remembers K and pushes from the bar. Rather than stand around awkwardly waiting for the show to start, she steps outside and walks past the smokers clustered by the door toward the corner. Across the street, Tompkins Square Park looks like a zoo closed down for the night, the animals asleep in the shadows. Like any woman killing time on a street corner at one in the morning, she pulls out her phone. One voice mail. One text. O'Hara starts with the text from Ashworth in evidence:

> Darlene, you know the marble and the fake pearl? Along with
> the victim's DNA, we found traces of beeswax on both of them.
> Based on that, I'd say they weren't there as currency but placed
> in the boy's nostrils. The only people I know who do that to their
> dead are the ancient Egyptians, king tut, etc. There aren't a lot
> of folks keeping it Egyptian so I thought it could be helpful.

O'Hara reads the text again and shakes her head. "I don't see it," she mumbles.

"You're talking to yourself?"

O'Hara turns over her shoulder and it's the kid from the bar.

"Was I disturbing you?"

"Not at all. Mental illness runs in my family."

"I hope it skipped a generation."

"No such luck." He tosses his thumb toward Lakeside, "I'm up next. With the Flat Screens."

At this point, O'Hara should identify herself, if not as NYPD, as the mother of the front man, but when she hesitates and the kid continues, it seems too late.

"Their original drummer quit—a job, business school, something pathetic—and I've been rehearsing with them for a couple weeks. Basically, this is an audition. It goes well, I'm in like Flynn. I suck, it's sayonara cupcake. You should stick around, they're awesome."

"I just might. Good luck, then."

"I'm Silas."

"Darlene."

"To be honest, I'm nervous as hell. How about a kiss for luck?"

"Can't I just say, 'Break a leg?' "

"I suppose."

"Fine," says O'Hara. As she plants a kiss on the drummer's cheek, he helps himself to a generous handful of her Irish butt, squeezes it emphatically, and darts around the corner.

"Nervous, my ass!"

"Exactly."

Like any self-respecting woman who has just been groped on a street corner by her son's new drummer, O'Hara takes out her phone again. This time, she plays back the voice message.

"Hey, Darlene, it's Sollie. I remembered something. Fricking miracle, right? Thought I better share it before I forget it again. At dinner, I told you Bun got conned into paying tuition for some gold digger's son. That was the first woman. And the smaller amount. The second woman took him to the cleaners. She said her kid was born with one leg shorter than the other and needed an operation to lengthen it. I'm pretty sure he paid the whole tab—or at least thought he did—which was some serious cabbage, almost a hundred large."

In terms of shamelessness, thinks O'Hara, that's up there with Perps'

Bring Your Kid to Work Day. You got a kid walking around with a limp, because no one bothered to fix his broken leg, and use that as the pretext to scam an old guy out of $100,000.

In the last week, the Flat Screens have been touted in several blogs and an item in the *Village Voice*: "Are the Flat Screens the next Television?" Every seat in the back room is taken, and she's lucky to find a spot to stand between the jukebox and the photo booth. After a week among the frail olds of Longboat Key, it's a pleasure to be squeezed tight on all sides by electric youth, and when her own twenty-year-old steps up to the mike with his big beard shaved off, the beauty and vulnerability of his pale, freckled skin almost make her weep.

"Welcome," says Axl, "to the all-important second show. Someday we may be good enough for Williamsburg or Bushwick or even Red Hook. But for now, we're just humble apprentices of rock, grateful to play wherever, even in Manfuckinghattan. So thanks for coming. I know what a pain in the ass it is to get here, and how depressing once you arrive." Like a restless ballpark crowd cheering over the national anthem, the tattooed boys and girls clap and stomp their feet, and one nearly middle-aged female detective sticks two fingers in her mouth and emits an ear-piercing whistle.

At last the band begins to play. The tempo is funereal and the sound muddy, until the outline of "When You Were Mine" bubbles to the surface. Of all the songs in Prince's catalogue, it still strikes O'Hara as the best, and she recalls the night she first played it for Axl. In the Flat Screens' version, the synth pop of the original has been replaced by three miles of bad road. It underlines the heartbreaking simplicity of the chorus—"I love you more than I did . . . when you were mine"—and drives home how hard it is to appreciate anyone enough at the time.

The Prince cover is followed by five originals, only two of which she recognizes from the Ukrainian Center. Despite the noise and excitement and jostling, O'Hara can't stop her mind from returning to Sollie's voice mail. In the midst of the sweaty din, it occurs to her that Sollie might have answered the first question she asked herself at Milano's, which is why Levin stopped banging the water heater before Lebrie.

Maybe Ben saw the kid's limp, remembered the money he had sent to fix it, put it together, and reached for his gun. Then O'Hara realizes Sollie's rekindled memory does more than explain why Levin might have seen through the scam before Lebrie. It means that around the same time Levin was targeted by distraction burglars, he was also being scammed by two different women, and in all three cases the kid seemed to have been involved and used as a kind of prop to soften the mark. The burglars said the kid was along to see what his father did for a living, the second woman sought the money for an operation to fix his leg, and the first woman, the one who nicked Levin for the smaller amount, featured him too. *My kid's having problems at school. Other kids pick on him. I want to send him someplace new so he can get a fresh start, but I can't afford it.* Instead of a random knock on the door, Levin was being worked over by a tag team of scammers operating in concert to milk him dry. Meanwhile her own kid is singing his ass off on the small stage twenty feet away, but in her effort to process, the band's last couple songs pass in a blur.

CHAPTER 48

NINE HOURS LATER O'Hara is back in Tompkins Square. In the midday heat, the juicers on the benches sit as still as the leaves in the trees, and the jungle gym, handball and basketball courts are all on hiatus. From the skateboard park, however, comes listless grinding, and O'Hara is relieved to spot Ben, Jamie, and minions bogarting the shade of a large elm. Based on the strong smell of reefer, she's arrived thirty seconds too late.

"I need you slackers to concentrate for five minutes," she says. "We got a description of two perps with Herc when he was shot. I want to run them by you, see if they spark anything. One was in his early forties, Caucasian but really dark, at least six feet and over three hundred pounds. The other was half his size, about twenty three, five seven, and a hundred and thirty-five pounds. Wore diamond studs in both ears. They target old people, talk their way into their homes, and rob them. Remember either of these scumbags coming by the park?"

"I don't see how we could have forgotten a pair like that," says Ben.

"How about separately?"

"The smaller one," says Jamie, "sounds like the one I told you about, the one Herc got along with."

"I've seen him a couple times," says a kid she doesn't know by name. "Herc called him Bones or Sticks, something like that."

"You said two women came by, and one was unattractive. Can you try again to remember what made you think that? Was she overweight?"

"It was her face," says Ben.

"What about it? Her features? Her nose, her teeth?"

"She had bad skin."

"Sure about that?" Asking a teenager, stoned by noon, if he was certain about something, seems absurd, but his description matches what she got from Sollie. Not only that, their memory of Herc's affection for the smaller perp corroborates her own observations about the contradictory behavior in the van, with one perp trying to help the kid far more than the other.

"How about an old guy name Gus? Short, bowlegged, black hair, thick black glasses? Moves slow, thinks slow? Ever see him with Herc?"

These last questions fail to get a rise from any of them, and a scan of their faces indicates that their window of attention has closed. "If you remember anything, give me a call," says O'Hara. "But try not to call me when you're stoned. I'm a cop. Remember? . . . You know what? Nix that. You think of something, call me any time."

"Darlene, you okay?" asks Ben.

"Just tired. Had a long night."

"You sure?"

"Yeah. But thanks."

O'Hara traverses the park, passing a tree where she once spotted an owl the size of Bruno. South of the dog runs, she enters an elegant paved plaza where a tribe of bike messengers meet in the early evenings, their beloved single-gear bikes stacked at their feet. Today the Caribbean and African health-care workers from the old-age home on Fifth Street have wheeled out a dozen old-timers and aligned their chairs in a half crescent facing the sun. Side by side, they soak up vitamin D, their drooling, farting, and nodding off a modest last stab at camaraderie.

On her way downtown, O'Hara called Paulette and asked her and Gus to meet her at the garden. O'Hara spots them inside, beneath an arbor, Gus sitting at the end of a bench, and Paulette standing beside him, and as O'Hara watches through the gate, Gus reaches up and grabs Paulette's ass. It reminds O'Hara of the previous evening. Still, she can't help but smile, surprised to see that Gus has a little more game left than she thought. The audacity of hope, she thinks. Or is it the audacity of grope? Paulette takes her time before she loosens the old man's grip, and even then she does it with a warm smile, which strikes O'Hara as well beyond the call of duty and the reasonable expectations of minimum wage.

"Hey, Johnny Depp," says O'Hara when she reaches them, "I see you're feeling your oats."

"Why not? I ain't dead yet."

"Nowhere near, apparently."

As O'Hara takes a seat beside Gus, she can see Christina Malm-strömer tending to her salad greens and peppers.

"Gus, remember the big guy you told Paulette you killed?"

"The big white guy?"

"Now he's white? You said he was black."

"Did I? All I know, he went down like a sequoia."

"Gus, no bullshit. Was he black or white?"

"What does it matter? The point is, he was a bastard, big as a house, and I killed him."

"Oh, yeah. Why?"

"Because the bastard deserved it a hundred times over."

O'Hara had hoped meeting in the garden might jar loose some memories, but this exceeds her hopes.

"What I hear, the big guy had a partner. A younger guy, much smaller fellow, about your size. Wore diamond studs in both ears. You kill him too?"

"No," says Gus. "No, I didn't."

And then he starts to cry.

"Come on, Gus, don't waste your tears over these guys. Save them for people who deserve it."

"Maybe I got enough to go around?"

For the same reason that O'Hara arranged to meet in the garden, she has brought the catalogue from the show in Chelsea. When Gus recovers, she pulls it out of a plastic bag and opens it to the picture of Herc and the girl.

"Gus. You ever seen this boy? His friends called him Hercules."

Gus runs a fingertip along the profile of the boy's face and stares through the branches at Malmströmer weeding her plot. "Nice paper," he says, "thick." Then he turns the catalogue over and glances at the cover. "You shelled out two-fifty for this?"

"No way. I impounded it."

O'Hara tries again to get Gus to focus on the photo, but it's no use. Between the demented and the addled, O'Hara hasn't gotten a straight answer all morning, and when her cell phone rings, she is relieved.

"Steve Baginski with the New York State Police. We found the stolen vehicle. It was right there at the service center, a hundred feet from the pumps."

CHAPTER 49

THIRTEEN MILES NORTH of the George Washington Bridge, O'Hara turns off the Palisades Parkway into the Citgo service center that sits in the grass divide between the north- and southbound lanes. It's 8:10 p.m., the end of the evening rush, and as O'Hara rolls past the pumps and minimart, the northbound traffic lays down a carpet of sound and orange taillights thread through the trees.

At the north end is a parking area for commuters. Crime scene has put up a tent, and O'Hara parks nearby between a New York State cruiser and the NYPD communications van. O'Hara is relieved by the lack of TV turnout. Without a body, the recovery of the stolen vehicle didn't rate a segment on the evening news, and without the cameras there won't be any brass to pontificate in front of them. That means O'Hara will be on her own and not obliged to kiss anyone's ass. Considering the way she feels and the length of the night ahead, that doesn't seem like a minor detail.

O'Hara climbs out of her Jetta and steps into the tent. Somewhere between the Bronx and New Jersey, O'Hara's cold burst forth into full majestic bloom, and she feels like utter crap. Nevertheless, the sight of the car under the crime scene lights is an enormous relief.

Moby fucking Volvo, thinks O'Hara, the great white wagon. It's about friggin' time. At the same time, she can see why it went unnoticed so long, particularly in this liminal strip of a nonplace, with traffic sweeping by at sixty miles an hour. The boxy lines are so straightforward, they look like they could have been drawn with crayons by a kindergartner, and the original fourteen-year-old paint has faded into something between white and invisible.

All five doors are open so crime scene tech Jack Marin can photograph the interior. O'Hara has worked with Marin before and trusts him. Rather than stand over his shoulder, O'Hara steps outside. The highway is wooded on both sides and, despite the proximity to the city, feels rural. Before the mosquitoes get a bead on her, she gazes at the stars and wishes Axl rock 'n' roll success.

O'Hara makes her way to the twenty-four-hour minimart, where the shelves are stocked for passing motorists and indigenous late-night stoners. On one side of the register is a medieval-looking apparatus that makes doughnuts, on the other a gleaming new machine that spits out Lotto tickets. ALL IT TAKES IS A DOLLAR AND A DREAM, reads the placard, and O'Hara finds it even more offensive than usual. She takes her chances instead on the iced coffee and a packet of Advil, washed down with her first sip.

Rather than returning to the tent, she walks to the idling communications van. The vehicle, outfitted with an arsenal of real time telecommunications, is alleged to have cost taxpayers a couple hundred thousand dollars, but the way O'Hara feels, the AC alone is worth that. For the first time in her experience, the computer actually works, and there's Wi-Fi.

O'Hara updates Wawrinka and Jandorek on the recovered vehicle and congratulates Axl on the show. She replays her voice mail from Sollie and thinks about the confederacy of perps preying on one old retiree. How, she wonders, did he fall into their clutches? Then she rereads the text from Ashworth and his arcane theory that the marble and pearl found near the remains had originally been placed in the boy's nostrils.

O'Hara turns back to the computer and Googles "pearls in nostrils."

She braces for porn—on the Internet all roads lead to smut—but the first result is an ad for a fourteen-karat gold, two-millimeter akoya pearl right nostril nose ring, for sale on Amazon. The second ad is for a similar nose ring for the left nostril. The third result is for a "faux pearl dangle navel ring," "pearl bezel nostril piece," and "nostril-piercing retainers with dome."

O'Hara modifies her search to "beeswax and pearls in the nostrils of the dead." The first item is "pediatric pearls for parents," which offers tidbits of parenting information; the second for a "100% organic bee propolis beeswax lip balm from the Philippines." The third result reads: "Death in Ancient Rome—Wikideath": "A common practice was to place pearls or beeswax in the nostrils to prevent evil spirits from taking control of the dead body." Ashworth didn't get the civilization right. It's the Romans, but still. The text continues: "The libitinarii would then ensure . . ." The fourth item is an excerpt from something called "The Patrin Web Journal—Romani (Gypsy) Death Rituals and Customs," with the text "Some tribes may plug the nostrils of the deceased with beeswax or pearls to . . ."

When O'Hara clicks on it, she lands on a site bearing a large title—"Patrin"—and the subhead, "Romani Customs and Traditions: Death Rituals and Customs." It is illustrated by an old black-and-white photograph of a Romani or Gypsy funeral procession, the mourners following a coffin through the woods. Another click opens an academic entry several pages long, which she scans through.

> *All Roma tribes have customs and rituals regarding death. . . .*
> *For Roma, death is a senseless unnatural occurrence that should*
> *anger those who die. . . . According to traditional Romani beliefs,*
> *life for the dead continues on another level. However, there is a*
> *great fear among the survivors that the dead might return in some*
> *supernatural form to haunt the living. . . . Some tribes may plug*
> *the nostrils of the deceased with beeswax or pearls to prevent evil*
> *spirits from entering the body . . . another important step is the*

*gathering together of those things that will be useful to the deceased
during the journey from life, to be placed in the coffin. These can
include almost anything, such as clothing, tools, eating utensils,
jewelry, money.*

O'Hara thinks of the artifacts excavated from the community
garden—the cash, the subway token, the lighter, the Swiss Army knife,
the CD. Now she adds the random bits of Gypsy hearsay she's absorbed
over the years—that they yank their kids out of school after third or
fourth grade, constantly pull up stakes and move, often on a day's notice
and usually because the police are closing in, and their suspicion about
modern medicine. It all fits. The perps are Gypsies. Rom, Roma, Romani,
whatever the PC term may be. Dark scamming outsiders operating in the
margins and governed by their own obscure, inverted code.

Why had none of this occurred to her earlier? It was the kid's hair.
Who has ever heard of a towheaded Gypsy? But now that she runs everything she has learned through this new Gypsy filter, the pieces fall into
place: the physical description of the two perps—swarthy but not African
American—the kid's untreated broken leg, the lack of school records.

O'Hara flashes back to that night in Sarasota when the woman and
girl sank their hooks into the elderly shopper at Publix and she followed
them home. She recalls the smells emanating from their motel room
and the curse howled from the doorway, which must have been a choice
bit of Rom. Somehow Benjamin Levin fell into the clutches of a tribe of
Gypsies, and unlike the times he stepped into the ring to face an opponent who in most ways was his double, he didn't stand a chance. Hauling
aboard the ramifications requires so much of her depleted brain, it takes
three knocks to distract her from the screen. In the window is the wide-
brimmed hat of a New York State trooper.

"Steve Baginski," he says when O'Hara opens the door. "We talked on
the phone this afternoon. Jack Marin asked me to come get you."

CHAPTER 50

THE REAR PASSENGER door of the Volvo is open, and Jack Marin crouches behind it like a man praying to his backseat. His broad back blocks whatever he's looking at from view, but glancing over him into the front of the car, O'Hara can see that the perps didn't improve their diet between South Carolina and Jersey. The passenger well is strewn with the same collection of soda cans and fast-food wrappers that littered the van. The backseat of the car, however, is nothing like the back of the van, showing only slight traces of blood. In a way, that's as disturbing as the blood-soaked mattress. It means that by the time the boy had been transferred to the Volvo, he didn't have much blood left. It also confirms what O'Hara had deduced from the receipts, which is that by now even the most meager efforts to help him had stopped.

Marin twists to face O'Hara and points at the upright tube of Pringles open on the floor of the car. "I found it under the front seat," says Marin. "It's too heavy for chips, and there's something shiny inside. Since these aren't Cracker Jacks and you said the perps were burglars, I thought you'd want to see it."

With his gloved hand, Marin carries the orange tube, about the size of a can of tennis balls, to a foldout table at the back of the tent and tilts it over a plastic tray. After a couple greasy napkins fall out, there's a sound of metallic objects bumping into each other as they slide along the cardboard. Then a gold ring and two gold watches, their delicate bands intertwined, fall into the tray. The diamond has been plucked from the ring, but the watches, which have blacked-out circular faces unmarked except for a small gold disk at the top to signify noon, are intact and lovely, not at all crass.

The smaller is inscribed "hers," the bigger "his," and both engraved "6/1/51," presumably the date Lebrie and her husband got married. The ring must be the one Lebrie slipped off her finger and dropped into the bowl of milk. O'Hara remembers her gentle knowing eyes, her broad sun hat, and her paper-thin skin slathered in zinc. Lebrie told her that in old age one thing after another gets taken away. Now, three of them are about to be returned.

"These were stolen from a woman on March 2," O'Hara tells Marin. "The next day they tried to rob the old man."

"What's the name of the woman?" asks Marin.

"Fran Lebrie."

"And the man is Benjamin Levin?"

"Yeah. Why?"

"I found both their names on a piece of paper in the driver's-side door. It's in the container on the other table. Don't touch it—I'm hoping to get some prints off it—but you can read it."

On the far side of the car, O'Hara bends toward a ripped sheet lying faceup in the container. It's a printout, generated by an organization called Ambex Marketing, working out of a P.O. box in Tampa, and contains some twenty-five names in alphabetical order. "Lebrie" and "Levin" are next to each other in the middle of the list, and like all the names, are followed by their addresses, ages, and a date. For Lebrie, the date is 4/1/05, for Levin 6/14/06.

"Is that it?" asks O'Hara.

"So far," says Marin.

When O'Hara steps out of the tent, it's after midnight, too late to share this small piece of good news with Lebrie. With no traffic, the odd isthmus sandwiched between four lanes of blacktop feels even more remote. O'Hara walks beneath the chilly stars to the highway bodega, where she replenishes her supply of iced coffee and ibuprofen and returns to the van. Before being summoned by Marin, O'Hara forwarded her findings about the Gypsy connection to Wawrinka. Now she finds Wawrinka's reply, titled "Fudgesicle & Popsicle."

"Darlene," reads O'Hara, "meet Johnny George and Nick Adams." She stops reading and opens the attached mug shots. George is the larger, darker one. He is listed at five-eleven, shorter than Lebrie thought, but at over three hundred pounds he must have loomed far larger than his actual height.

Rather than overtly vicious, he looks like someone who has never been able to afford the luxury of giving a shit about another human being. His face is scarred by acne, his chin a crease in his jowels, and in his eyes is the weariness of pushing his massive bulk through the world. Adams, five-seven and 135 pounds, is a no-account little grifter. His ears are too big for his face, and he's got diamond studs in both. His eyes are large too. According to Wawrinka, Johnny George goes by: George Johns, Skigo, and Fudgesicle; and Adams's aliases include Nick Miller, Tom Marks, and Popsicle.

The rest of Wawrinka's message reads: "When you told me our perps are Gypsies, I went online and found a retired detective in San Diego who maintains a national database of Gypsies and other con artists. These guys rarely do real time and often don't have rap sheets. Old people make terrible witnesses, and no one believes them anyway. That means they almost never get convicted. When they do, they pay restitution, write it off as the price of doing business. That's why they didn't show up in the big computer. But based on the name on the credit card and the description, he found Nick Adams, aka Popsicle, and through him, his most frequent accomplice. Quite the duo, these two. The Laurel and Hardy of distraction burglary."

O'Hara returns to the brooding face and sleepy eyes of Fudgesicle and imagines him in Lebrie's doorway. These assholes think they're outsmarting every one, but all they're doing is bullying people at the end of their lives, when their strength and resolve are depleted. Lebrie was smart to keep slapping the spatula until she knew they were long gone.

She Googles Lebrie and finds a small site devoted to "Fran Lebrie—Assemblage Artist." "Fran Lebrie," reads the introduction, "is an assemblage artist whose imaginative constructions reflect both her background in philosophy and her skills in product design." The site includes photos of Lebrie's work, including several O'Hara and Wawrinka saw on their visit. Among the other results is an obituary for Alfred Lebrie in the *Longboat Key News*, dated 4/8/05. Looking at her notepad, she sees that the date is a week after the date on the list. An obituary in a weekly paper would probably run the week after a death, and the obituary confirms it. "Alfred Lebrie, who wintered for 36 years on Longboat Key, died last Monday, April 1st, at the age of 86. A veteran of World War II, who served as a lieutenant in the 93rd infantry division . . ."

Now O'Hara Googles Levin and scrawls down the list of items until she finds the obit on his wife, Evelyn. The date of her death also matches the date on the sheet. Apparently targeting the elderly isn't enough of an edge for these motherfuckers. To find victims even more vulnerable, they search out those who have just lost their spouse.

CHAPTER 51

THE STEEL STAIRS are treacherous, particularly in three inch heels. At the bottom, a round-shouldered crone in a Bart Simpson T-shirt points at a plastic chair. O'Hara takes it, the damp seat sticking to her thighs. With wobbly shoes, clinging dress, and deranged orange lipstick, O'Hara is cultivating early forties reality-show tragic, a guise she realizes is hardly a stretch, and as she dangles a shoe on her toe, her keeper assesses her from a cement ledge. Soft light leaks from behind the curtains of a basement window, and trickling down from the curb the Friday-night bustle of the Lower East Side.

After ten minutes, a metal door scrapes open. A surprisingly presentable young woman clambers to the street, and the crone slips inside. She reemerges with a toothless smile. "Miss Marla can see you now." O'Hara steps from the stairwell into a small, dark, airless space, and as her eyes strain to take in the scene, the heavy door swings shut behind her. At her feet is a low table with a candle, and behind it, all but her face in shadow, squats Miss Marla. O'Hara sits across from her on a shabby ottoman.

"You seem troubled, my dear. What brings you to me this evening?"

"A decision," says O'Hara. "An important one."

Outside, O'Hara was handed a menu of offerings and prices, and when O'Hara slides over a stack of twenties and ponies up for the full $220 reading, Miss Marla springs for a stick of incense, which she lights with a plastic Bic. A brown plume corkscrews toward the ceiling, its spicy scent mingling with the smell of burned meat that seeps from behind a blanket partition.

In the dim light, O'Hara takes the measure of the woman across from her. Miss Marla has sad, shrewd eyes, a broad nose, and a defiant mouth that cuts through her fleshy face like a line drawn in the sand. It's a face born and bred for a mug shot, and O'Hara puts her in her late fifties. Marla's lower body is wrapped in a dark skirt, her enormous bosom covered by a cotton pullover, and like Sollie, her reading glasses hang from a string around her neck. She slips them on and reaches for O'Hara's hand, turning it palm up beside the guttering flame.

Minutes pass in silence as the psychic pores over O'Hara's palm and from the frowns that play across Miss Marla's face and the anguish in her eyes, it's clear that little of what she sees is anything to write home about. When the strain becomes too much, she looks away or glances sympathetically at O'Hara, gathers her strength, and dives back in.

Jesus, thinks O'Hara. I know I'm a mess, but what the hell? She tunes her ears for sounds of life beyond the blanket. The purr of a cat? The whisper of an old woman? O'Hara can't be sure. "I see that you are a serious person," says Marla at last. "That's obvious. And ambitious. You are determined to accomplish a great deal in this life and have the ability to do it. Unfortunately, you are your own worst enemy. You behave rashly and impulsively, and these misguided actions undermine the effect of the many good things you do. It's a problem in your work, but worse in your personal life. Again and again, you jeopardize relationships that are most important to you."

When Miss Marla glances at O'Hara, she can't conceal her satisfaction at having hit the mark. "You mentioned an important decision. What kind?"

"I'm about to sign a lease on a new apartment," says O'Hara. "In fact, I withdrew the money this afternoon, so I can give it to the landlord tomorrow. Now I'm getting cold feet. Like you said, I tend to be rash, and I want to be sure I'm making the right decision."

"Interesting," says Miss Marla, and returns her attention to O'Hara's hand. "Rash in matters of the heart, cautious and diligent when it comes to finances."

"I worked hard for that money."

"I know you did. Where is it . . . the apartment, I mean?"

"A few blocks north," says O'Hara, and studies the eyes studying her. Like many things about Miss Marla, they seem both defeated and unyielding. "East Sixth Street, overlooking the garden."

Marla's eyes hold O'Hara's for a second, then dip to her palm. "Your new apartment will be a wonderful home," she says, "exactly the fresh start you've been looking for—" Miss Marla is about to continue, but catches herself, stopped by something troubling, like a malignancy, she has spotted near the base of O'Hara's ring finger. "The place is a good choice, I have no doubt about that, but I'm seeing a dark spot . . . it's just a matter of figuring out where . . . it's on your money. Yes. I'm sure of it now. Somehow, a curse has attached itself to your money. Do you have any idea how that might have happened?"

"Not at all. Is there anything you can do?"

"Child, there's always something Miss Marla can do. But I'm going to need your help. It's going to take all your strength as well as mine. I can tell you're not a person for whom money is the most important thing in life. The people you love are far more precious. But ignore the curse, and it will spread until it poisons everything. Did you say that you have the money with you tonight?"

"I do. Just over three thou—"

"The amount is unimportant," says Marla, cutting her off. "I don't want anything to distract me." From the same dark space below the table from which she pulled the mangy stick of incense, Marla removes a red kerchief and a flacon of perfume. She flattens the kerchief on the table and sprinkles on a few drops. "Now," says Marla, "it's okay to take out the money. Just place it on top, but do it carefully. Place it directly in the middle."

No sooner has O'Hara produced a fat envelope marked "Rent/Security" than Marla pushes to her feet and disappears behind the blanket. In less than two minutes, Marla returns to her seat and drizzles a few more scented drops on the envelope. Then she enfolds it in the kerchief, and secures it with a knot.

"Because our foe is dark and underhanded, we will fight it with what it fears most. We'll fight darkness with darkness," she says, and as she swoops across the table and grabs O'Hara's hands, she blows out the flame. The darkness is so sudden and complete, it feels as if the floor has been pulled out from under them and they're falling together through black space.

Miss Marla speaks softly at first, but soon is stomping her feet and rocking in her chair as she spews a torrent of what must be the vilest oaths and imprecations. At one point, Miss Marla becomes so enraged she pulls one paw from the sweaty pile and shakes her fist at the ceiling. Marla maintains this violent intensity as long as humanly possible, and when she pulls out her Bic and relights the candle, her ravaged face is flushed.

"Should I take out the money?" asks O'Hara.

"Not yet," says Marla, fighting for breath. "The curse is too strong. Even after what we've done, it will take three days for it to die. Take the kerchief home, place it in the back of a dark drawer, but don't go anywhere near it until Monday morning. This is very important. If you don't wait, little bits of the curse will remain, and eventually return as powerful as ever."

Mindful of her instructions, O'Hara carefully deposits the fragrant bundle in her bag, then peers at Marla. Marla stressing the importance of not touching the kerchief till Monday reminds O'Hara of the warning Fudgesicle gave Lebrie. "Whatever you do," he told her, "don't stop hitting the water heater." As O'Hara considers how the scams and scripts are refined and honed over the years, she feels as if she is looking through Marla at the dark face in Fudgesicle's mug shot. Marla is nothing if not observant, reads the shift in O'Hara's eyes.

"Is something the matter?"

"Depends how you look at it."

"What is it, my child?"

"You're under arrest."

CHAPTER 52

FIVE BLOCKS AWAY on Pitt Street, O'Hara and Miss Marla face off again across a second crappy table in an even less pleasant space. Round two is in the interrogation box in the second-floor detective room of her old precinct, the 7, and Marla's right wrist is cuffed to her chair. "Sorry about the harsh light," says O'Hara, nodding at the bare overhead bulb. "Someone keeps swiping the candles."

Between them, giving off a heady bouquet, are two rectangular bundles in matching red kerchiefs. As Marla looks on glumly, O'Hara unknots one, unveiling a stack of filthy newsprint. "Why, Miss Marla, there's nothing here but worthless paper! No wonder you preferred I wait to open it till Monday."

Now O'Hara undoes the second parcel, the one she found under Marla's ass after she yanked it out of the chair to read her her rights. "By the way Marla, what's this fragrance—Shalimar?"

"Tommy Hilfiger."

"Oh, yeah? It's ghastly."

This kerchief contains the rent money, and O'Hara counts every last one of 106 twenties. "It's all here—five thousand, three hundred. Since it's over three thousand, we got you for grand larceny, third degree. You're going away for a while."

"What do you want from me?" Earlier in the evening, O'Hara got consults at three other neighborhood parlors, and cooling their heels in the holding cell are Dame Olga, Madame Irma, and Lady Nadia. As O'Hara got Marla printed, she made a point of parading her past their crowded cell.

"Information," says O'Hara, "about these two." She removes the kerchiefs and replaces them with the mug shots she received from Wawrinka. "This one goes by Johnny George, George Johns, Skigo, and Fudgsicle, this one by Nick Adams, Nick Miller, Tom Marks, and Popsicle. Fudgesicle and Popsicle are a burglary team and work out of town. Sometimes they work with this boy." O'Hara adds a closely cropped picture of Hercules. Just seeing the pictures of Herc and the two perps side by side pisses O'Hara off.

Marla leans over and studies the pictures with the same ostentation she brought to O'Hara's palm. But this time, she comes up empty. "I've never seen any of them. I'm certain."

"Really? A striking pair like this doesn't jog your memory?"

"No."

"Same thing with a blond Rom kid? I suppose there are so many they all blend together? Marla, I'm beginning to think you're a lot like me, your own worst enemy."

"I've never seen or heard of any of them. I swear it."

"How about two female Gypsies who work with them? One with bad skin, the other kind of a hottie? Both bilked the same old man, and both used the boy."

Marla makes a sign, then mimes spitting over her shoulder. "I don't associate with burglars."

"You're better than them?"

"I don't break into homes."

"No, that would be bad *kasa*," says O'Hara, throwing out a word she picked up online.

"You speak Rom?" For a second the apprehension in her eyes seems almost genuine.

"Marla, I agree with you about one thing. I don't think you're as bad as those two. They're scumbags. You're a scoundrel. But it's eleven twenty on a Friday night, and the only one you've given up is Tommy Hilfiger. That means you're going to spend the weekend in central booking. You been to central booking on a weekend? It's a warehouse of lost souls. People screaming and fighting, going to the bathroom in front of you. On Monday, if you make it that long, you're going to Rikers, another bad place, full of people with nothing to lose."

"For telling a fortune?"

"For grand larceny. Third degree. But most of all for lying to me."

"I don't know them. Any of them."

O'Hara reaches across the table for Marla's uncuffed hand and turns it palm up. "I see awful things, Marla. Things you don't deserve, Blood and death . . . actually, it's not all bad. I see good things too . . . like love."

"Yeah?"

"A very big love. African American. She's going to introduce herself in the shower along with five of her friends, and she's going to hold something sharp to your neck. . . . After that it gets fuzzy. Probably just as well."

"Pizza," says Marla.

"You hungry?"

"That's her name. Pizza Denikov. I heard she scammed an old man in Florida pretty good. She lives in Union City. Got a pencil, I'll give you her address."

CHAPTER 53

WITH ITS PROXIMITY to the city, low rents, and low profile, Union City Is a perp haven, like the woods around a medieval fortress. Its harsh clogged streets are a parking nightmare, particularly on a Saturday, and because you never know when a Jersey cop with a hard-on for the NYPD will tow you for sport, O'Hara circles for twenty minutes rather than pull over in front of a hydrant.

The address she got out of Marla, written on newsprint in the block letters of a five-year-old, is on a block of dreary two- and three-family homes. A raspy voice barks through the intercom, and a door opens on the third floor. "Pizza," calls O'Hara.

"Who is it?"

"Darlene O'Hara, NYPD. I need to talk to you."

At the top of the stairs, O'Hara displays her shield. As she catches her breath, she tries to determine if the woman in the doorway is the woman with bad skin referred to by Sollie and the skaters. The woman, who is petite and wears a dark skirt, is not unattractive, and although her skin bears a few residual acne scars, they're not striking this morning. "Come in," says Denikov, "My house is your house. Make yourself at home."

The apartment contains no rugs, pictures, or curtains. What little furniture there is could be packed up in an hour. Nevertheless, the hospital-
ity appears genuine. Soon after O'Hara sits at a stark white table, Denikov
places a steaming paper bowl in front of her. The reddish broth contains a
stub of corn, a carrot, and a chunk of meat.

"A simple *boyash*," says Denikov, "a stew, but we like to dress it up a
little." She slides over a tray crowded with mysterious condiments.

Throwing caution to the wind, O'Hara takes a spoonful. It tastes as
advertised—a simple stew—and feels good on her scratchy throat. From
the corner of the room comes a burst of gunfire. A boy about thirteen lies
on his stomach in front of a large TV. He wears a headset and wields a joy-
stick. On the screen are images of urban warfare, soldiers fighting house
to house. Beside him is an acoustic guitar.

"Giuseppe is playing with his friends on the phone," says Denikov.

"A handsome young man," says O'Hara. "Your son?"

"Grandson."

"I take it he's already dropped out of school."

"Make up your mind," says Denikov as she lights a Menthol 100. "You
NYPD? Or you children's services?" Behind her, a young man in his early
thirties enters the kitchen from a back room, ladles some stew into a bowl,
and retreats to wherever he came from.

"And him?"

"Juice, my son. Giuseppe's dad. He sits in his room all day and takes
Vicodin. It makes my heart sad."

"I got your name from a fortune-teller named Miss Marla."

"Oh, really. And how is Marla?"

"About the same, I guess."

"Still running scams out of her little *offisa* on Clinton? Still got the
hunchback working for her?"

"Yeah. In fact, Marla read my fortune last night. Discovered I had a
curse on my money that had to be removed pronto."

"I bet she did," says Denikov. A smile ignites her brooding face.

"Then I read hers in my little *offisa* at the back of the Seventh Precinct. It didn't look so hot either."

"At least, until she offered up my name. Out of curiosity, what did that fat, lying whore have to say about me?"

"Good things, mostly. She thought you might be able to help me. I'm working on a case involving an old man who ended up dead in his condo outside Sarasota and a boy who ended up dead in the East Village. Marla said you took some cash from the old man in Florida."

"There are lots of old men in Florida, Detective. The state is full of them."

"Makes it convenient, doesn't it? Having so many in one place. This one was named Ben Levin."

"Sounds like a nice old guy. But the name doesn't ring a bell."

"Give yourself a second." O'Hara deals out pictures of Fudgesicle, Popsicle, and Hercules. Again, seeing the three together disturbs her. "In the meantime, maybe this will help. These two are a burglary team. They were in Levin's condo the day he died. This boy, who had blond hair and a limp, was with them."

O'Hara leans forward and nudges the picture of the boy closer to Pizza. "They let the boy bleed to death in the back of a van. How would you like it if someone treated your grandson like that? Like a piece of trash?"

Pizza pushes the picture back and crosses her arms.

"I don't recognize any of them," she says. The playful tone is gone.

"Do you mind if I ask why you call yourself Pizza?"

"That's what they used to call me when I was young. I had bad skin."

Why would a person with bad skin give herself a name so loaded with adolescent cruelty? Particularly a woman? It makes no sense. At the same time, however, the story of Pizza's name and how she got it convinces O'Hara that the woman in front of her is the one Sollie was talking about; a person who would name herself Pizza, who would take what they called her and appropriate it for her own purposes, is the same kind of person who would use her bad skin to convince an old man she could care about him. It's how her mind works.

"Never heard of a blond-haired gypsy boy with a limp? Sure? Or this three-hundred-pound bag of shit? They let the boy bleed to death for a couple days in the back of a van. Like an animal. Now that Giuseppe's out of school, how's he going to earn a living? He's going to end up in one of those burglary teams too, right? You want the same thing to happen to him?"

"No one treats a child like that."

"They did. Believe me. You should have seen the mattress. It was soaked with his blood. And I think you know who all these people are. If I find out that's true, I'm going to make it my business to track you down, I don't care how many times you jump in your caravan."

"I know Ben Levin," says Denikov, her arms still crossed. "But I never met him, I swear. I just talked to him on the phone."

"How did you meet him?"

"The lava line."

"The lava line?"

"Yeah. For lahvers."

"You mean the love line?"

"Yeah. A chat line. I talked to him, got to know him a little, became friends, and he lent me a little money. And I mean a little. I have too much conscience, it's my fatal flaw. But I know someone who doesn't have that problem, who took him for a lot. A whore named Crisco."

What's with these names, thinks O'Hara. Pizza, Juice, Crisco. "So what, you passed the old man's number on to Crisco?"

"Look around. Look out the window. Now look at me. Do I look like someone who can afford to be generous?" Denikov turns her attention from O'Hara to the back of the living room. "Giuseppe," she says, "sing a song for Darlene. Giuseppe, please."

"What do you want me to play?"

"Something pretty."

He strums his guitar and without self-consciousness hums along to what sounds like an old Gypsy ballad but turns out to be the theme for *The Godfather*. Giuseppe's voice and playing are lovely, but the effect is undermined by O'Hara's knowledge that Denikov is using her grandson the same way the perps used the kid, the same way the woman in the Publix used her girl. Giuseppe, with his sweet voice and grandmother's soulful eyes, has probably been burglarizing homes for years.

"Giuseppe, knock that shit off," comes the pissed-off voice of his father from the other end of the apartment. "I'm trying to get some sleep."

CHAPTER 54

AN HOUR AFTER crawling out of the armpit of southeastern Jersey, O'Hara is rolling down a country lane in a bucolic Westchester village called Waccabuc. Instead of three-family houses, it's three-acre zoning. Instead of warehouses, short-stay motels, and toxic waste, it's gentlemen farmers, bed-and-breakfasts, and horse manure.

Crisco resides in a sprawling '70s modern hewn from stone, cedar, and glass. In the gravel drive are a little white Mercedes and a mud-splattered GMC pickup with "T & C Contractors" on the cab. The his-and-hers vehicles play off each other nicely, the automotive yin and yang of upscale suburbia, but O'Hara knows how fond these perps are of trucks and vans. Working vehicles evoke honest skilled labor, and provide a legitimate reason for them to be parked in an elderly stranger's driveway.

From the scammers' database, she's learned that phony home repairs are a cornerstone of elder abuse. A guy knocks on an old man's door and offers to fix a couple loose shingles on the roof, then tricks/ intimidates him out of $3,000 for ten minutes of work. Or a guy sprays some old lady's driveway with gasoline and charges her as if he repaved it. Thanks to the database, O'Hara is current on seal-coat suspects and paving and roof-repair suspects. "When the suspect was pulled over," read a typical police account, "his truck bed contained a spray rig with five gallons of Dewitt blacktop sealer. Recovered from the vehicle, along with multiple receipts from pawnshops and a prescription for Xanax, were two-way radios and a police scanner tuned to San Antonio area police agencies. . . ."

The lady of the house is in her late forties, early fifties, tall, attractive, stacked, and although her tits could have been acquired anywhere, her eyes and attitude could only come from the streets. She seems as out of place in leafy Waccabuc as O'Hara. "I'm Darlene O'Hara with NYPD Homicide," says O'Hara, displaying her gold shield. "Pizza says hello."

After a contemptuous once-over, her host waves O'Hara inside. A flagstone entry opens dramatically on a two-tiered living room that looks out on a lake and nothing else. No neighbors in sight, just hundreds of acres of preserve. If Pizza's strained circumstances are a poor inducement to a life of crime, this place is more persuasive. Based on the view, they could be a thousand miles from New York, not fifty.

"Pizza's a hater," says Crisco.

"I can see why. How many old people you have to scam to pay for this?"

"My husband has a successful landscaping business."

"T & C Contractors," says O'Hara. "Of course. I jotted down the name in case I ever need some quality work done or want to pass it on to the IRS. Right now, though, I need to talk to you about Benjamin Levin." O'Hara takes out the picture of Levin sprawled on his bathroom floor and places it on the glass coffee table. "I understand both you and Pizza were crazy about him."

"I never met this man in my life. I haven't been to Florida for years. It's too depressing. I need sun, I go to St. Bart's."

"Maybe you never met him, but you took him for over a hundred thousand, and that's not just from Pizza. I also know you used this boy in your scams, and he's dead now too."

'O'Hara takes out the cropped gallery shot of Hercules and places it beside the photo of the old man.

"Negative again," says Crisco.

"You don't know him either?"

"Of course not."

"A kid like him must have seemed like a gift from God. With his white-blond hair, no one thinks Gypsy for a second. But I would have thought you'd have treated such a valuable asset a little better."

O'Hara takes in Crisco's sneer along with her lake and trees. The disparity between Pizza's Union City apartment and this is so wide, it seems unfair, even to O'Hara, and Crisco and Pizza were playing with the same pieces. With the same mark (Levin) and the same prop (the kid), Pizza extracted rent money, and Crisco, enough to live large for months. The only difference was their level of shamelessness, and that might be the only distinction that matters.

NOW O'HARA LAYS out the two mug shots. "This one is Fudgesicle, and this is Popsicle. They're a team, and like your husband, they do distraction burglaries. They use a van that reads Sarasota Water Authority instead of a truck that says T & C Contractors. I suppose you don't know them, either."

"Of course not."

"Well, they know you, because they robbed the same guy you and Pizza were milking, and they also used the boy. In the process, they got him killed. I'm getting pretty close to these two, and I'd be concerned about that if I were you. Because once I get them in the box for murder, they'll give up their sister if they thought it would help. For all I know, you are their sister, or cousin." And then, to piss her off, "Or mother."

Crisco's expression doesn't waver, but it does piss her off.

"I'm going to have to ask you to leave now," she says.

"Could I use the bathroom? It was a long ride from Union City."

Crisco points past a large open kitchen, and O'Hara walks down another stone corridor. From behind a door comes the hollow sound of a daytime studio audience. O'Hara makes sure Crisco hasn't followed her, then cracks the door of a guest bedroom. On a recliner facing the TV is a sparrow of an old lady in a black dress and shawl.

"I adore Dr. Phil," whispers O'Hara.

Without taking her eyes from the set, the old woman nods in agreement. "He's very reasonable."

"Maybe he's part Gypsy," says O'Hara.

"Could be," says the woman, smiling at the screen. "You never know."

"The golden child, the blond-haired boy," says O'Hara. "Do you miss him?" The old lady doesn't respond or turn from the TV, where Dr. Phil interviews a teenage girl with an eating disorder.

"Can I ask you another question?" asks O'Hara softly. "Why did they risk him? Why did they put the boy in danger?"

The old lady glances at O'Hara for the first time, then turns back to the screen. "If the bear don't hunt," she says, "the bear don't eat."

O'Hara hears Crisco's angry heels in the hallway, but by then it's too late. When Crisco flings open the door, O'Hara stays where she is, right behind the old lady's shoulder.

"I said you could use the bathroom," says Crisco, "not disturb my family." She says something cold and clipped in Rom to the old woman, who shrugs.

"We're just a couple ladies watching Dr. Phil," says O'Hara.

"Actually, I'm glad you've had a chance to meet my mother. Now you know why people preying on the elderly is not a problem for Gypsies. Unlike you, we don't entrust them to strangers, or leave them to fend for themselves. We take care of them. Let me show you out."

O'HARA EATS SOME suburban "Chinois" in a shopping center and gets on the Saw Mill River Parkway back to the city. Southbound traffic on a Saturday evening is slow, and O'Hara is worn to the nub by her cold and the strain of navigating the upside-down Gypsy universe. Despite the twisted logic, that last sanctimonious salvo from Crisco didn't entirely miss the mark. If O'Hara's mother had a medical crisis and couldn't take care of herself, would O'Hara set up a hospital bed in the living room and have her move in with her and Bruno?

A call from Wawrinka saves her from having to answer. "Dar, how you doing?"

"Been talking to Gypsies all day. My head is spinning."

"Got something. We located Popsicle."

"Where?"

"South Carolina. A couple hours' drive north of that Walmart, a town called Quinby."

"He liked the area so much he decided to settle down?"

"Yeah . . . to the bottom of a pond right next to Ninety-Five. The pond is on a golf course in front of the seventeenth green. Every summer they hire a diver to dredge up all the golf balls the hackers hit into it. Then they wipe them off and sell them back to the same hackers."

"Last night, this guy wades in in his wet suit and hauls out eight huge bags like he's picking cotton underwater. As he's going in for another, he steps on something soft. Fortunately they don't have gators, or there wouldn't have been anything to step on."

"How do you know it's Popsicle?"

"Everything checks—height, the studs in what was left of his ears. Plus the timing. The coroner puts him in the soup six months, which is when he and Fudgesicle and the kid were passing through. But here's the clincher. They do an autopsy, and guess what they find in his lower intestines?"

"I'd rather not."

"The one-point-five-carat stone missing from the ring you found in the Volvo. Before Popsicle stashes the ring, with the rest of his private swag, he pops the stone and swallows it."

O'Hara isn't surprised Adams turned up dead, but is sorry to hear it. With another witness dead, the chance of learning what happened that morning in the old man's condo is that much less, and after soaking at the bottom of a pond for six months, she doubts the corpse will offer any clues.

"So Popsicle got caught with his hand in the cookie jar?"

"Looks that way. The little guy was beaten to a pulp. All the bones in his face were shattered."

For the remainder of the drive, O'Hara considers the scenarios that might have led to the final encounter. Had Fudgesicle been aware of his partner's poaching for a while and waited to kill him until it was convenient? He couldn't do it until they'd stolen the Volvo, because he needed a second driver to drop off the van or maybe he waited till he had a spot to dump the body. The severity of the beating, however, suggests something more spontaneous.

Due to the traffic, it takes another hour to get back to the city and another thirty minutes before O'Hara is clomping down the steel stairs to Miss Marla's *offisa*. "Someone's in there," says the toothless homunculus.

"Then give her a rain check." A woman in emotional disarray gets the bum's rush, and O'Hara takes her still-warm seat. "I hope it didn't interrupt anything too lucrative."

"Darlene. The only fortunes I give now are happy ones." Marla pulls a tissue from her sleeve and honks her nose. "By the way, thanks for the cold. You talk to Pizza?"

"And Crisco."

"That one's a sharpie," says Marla.

"With a view to prove it. But some of what I'm hearing doesn't make sense. Pizza told me that she snagged the old Jew on a chat line. She charms him, gets him to send her a few thousand dollars."

"Working a Willie," says Marla. "That's what they call it."

"So Pizza is working her Willie, and Crisco snatches him out from under her nose and proceeds to work him for a hundred times more."

"So what's your question?"

"How did Crisco even find out about him? Would Pizza pass a mark on to someone she hates?"

"Would you turn over a big case to another detective because you thought he would do a better job? Well, Pizza wouldn't either."

"Does she get a finder's fee?"

"Why would Pizza give up the whole for a piece? And how could Pizza trust Crisco not to stiff her?"

"So if Pizza doesn't run her mouth, how would Crisco know she has someone on the hook?"

"I don't know for sure. But I can tell you it wouldn't be hard. Let's say that Pizza is on T-Mobile, then all Crisco has to do is make a friend at T-Mobile. The friend makes a copy of Pizza's phone bill and sends it to Waccabuc, where Crisco spreads it out on her kitchen table. She sees that on Wednesday night, Pizza spent twenty minutes talking to someone in Saint Augustine, Florida, which I know from *Jeopardy* is the oldest city in America. The next night she calls the number again and talks for half an hour. That month's bill, half is spent gabbing to one number in Florida. Since Crisco knows for a fact that Pizza doesn't have a family in that part of Florida, and doesn't know any Gypsies who live there either, that means Pizza is talking to a *gadje*, an American, and the only reason Pizza would be calling an American is if she is working him. So one afternoon Crisco dials the number herself. She comes up with some story—it wouldn't take much for a lonely old man—starts flirting and telling him how hard it is to find a good man even at her age. The next thing you know, the American belongs to her."

"How do you know he's an American?"

"American, *gadje*, whatever." For Marla, anyone who isn't a Gypsy is an American. That means American is just another name for a mark. P. T. Barnum couldn't break it down more succinctly.

"Doesn't Pizza have any recourse?" asks O'Hara. "I read that when a Gypsy feels himself wronged by another Gypsy, he can call for a trial, or a *kris*."

"No one is going to stop what they're doing and travel hundreds of miles to settle a dispute over day-to-day hustling. Most *krisa* have something to do with a dowry—a marriage is arranged and falls apart so quickly the family of the groom demands the return of the dowry."

"So marriage doesn't work any better for you than Americans?" In the candlelight, O'Hara catches a Gypsy eye roll. "Please," says Marla, "and if it's not about a dowry, it's about something important. A serious accident or a death. One Gypsy kills another, and the family of the victim demands a payment. The last one I heard about involved the murder of someone's grandson."

"You remember what happened?"

"Nothing. They blew him off. In the end, it all comes down to money. Money makes the monkey dance."

"And if the *kris* doesn't go your way?"

"You're stuck. Submit to a *kris*, you have to accept the decision, good or bad. Refuse to comply, you risk *marime*, which means you are expelled from the world of Gypsies. After that, no Gypsy will have anything to do with you. For a Gypsy, that's the same as death."

"So what could Pizza do?"

"Strike back or get over it."

"Make her own friend at the phone company?"

"Why not? It's a free country."

"And a new American is born every day."

"That's a good one, Darlene. I like that."

CHAPTER 55

AFTER PUTTING UP with her cold for a week, O'Hara decides to throw everything she has at it, sweat it out or die. As soon as she gets back to her apartment, she strips off the clammy clothes she's been in all day and replaces them with two T-shirts, sweatpants, and thick cotton socks. Then she puts a teapot to boil and does an inventory of her cabinets. When she's done, three bottles and a puckered tea bag are lined up on her kitchen table. The green one is NyQuil, the orange Theraflu, and the brown Maker's Mark. None is more than a third full, and according to the stamp, the NyQuil expired in February '03.

When the kettle whistles, she pours three fingers of bourbon over the tea bag, adds boiling water and the viscous remains of the NyQuil, and stirs it with a chopstick. With Bruno looking on anxiously, she transports the steaming concoction to the living room, where two towels and a blanket have been spread over her couch. Before it can cool, she downs it in its entirety, crawls between the towels, and pulls the blanket to her chin.

Although O'Hara feels the weight of her beverage, it doesn't quiet the chatter in her head, and despite the help from Marla, one question keeps tripping her up. Why would they rob Levin when he was already volunteering the contents of his bank account? What could they hope to find that would justify the risk? Were they lured by that safe in his closet? Had they somehow found out about it, but didn't know all it contained was an ancient pair of trunks and shoes? Or maybe they were convinced they'd already extricated all the cash they could by other means. But still. A good Willie is like an oil well. It can keep pumping for decades. Why chance closing the spigot?

Beads of sweat line the creases of her forehead like planes on a runway, but she's still wide awake. She pulls one arm from under her blanket, opens her laptop, and returns to the entry about Romani death rituals. "For Roma, death is a senseless, unnatural occurrence that should anger those who die," she reads. "At the approach of death, Roma are concerned not only with the pain and heartbreak of the final separation from a loved one. They are also worried about the revenge that the dead, or *mulo*, might seek against those who are living."

Later in the entry, the writer repeats the theme. "The dying Rom must never be left alone. This is not only out of compassion for his condition, but also out of fear of possible anger. . . . According to traditional Romani beliefs, life for the dead continues on another level. However, there is great fear among the survivors that the dead might return in some supernatural form to haunt the living. It is for this reason that the name of the dead should not be mentioned, that the body should not be touched, and that all objects that belonged to the dead must be destroyed. The survivors must be protected in every way from the evil spirits the dead can emit. To avoid this, stones or thornbushes are sometimes placed around the grave."

When O'Hara stumbled on these passages at the service center, she'd never met a Gypsy in the flesh. Now that she has spent quality time with Marla, Pizza, and Crisco, they resonate more vividly. To a Gypsy, death is nothing more than the worst version of bad luck, like scratching off the numbers of a black Lotto ticket or pulling down the arm of a slot machine and watching five skull-and-crossbones fall into place. Naturally the person doing the dying is pissed off and jealous of those lucky enough to still be alive. When tools, money, and gifts are tossed into the grave, it's less out of generosity than fear of reprisal.

When O'Hara learned that the crew preying on Levin were Gypsies, she imagined a confederacy of perps, who shared information and resources. In fact, they are more like rival hyenas fighting over the same infirm caribou, and the infighting and distrust extend into the afterlife. If Barnum was right, the supply of Americans is bottomless. Every day another batch of pink little suckers open their eyes for the first time. So you would think there would be more than enough to go around, and they wouldn't have to poach each other's Americans. But when you spend all your time and energy fucking with people, even if you designate them as subhuman, it spills over and fucks with your head and turns everything toxic, even your relation with other Gypsies. That's the fly in the ointment of all criminal societies. The members turn on each other.

Still unable to sleep, O'Hara peels herself off the couch and heads back to the kitchen. The water takes forever to boil, and O'Hara and Bruno stare at it together. When it finally does, she fixes herself another, this time with Theraflu, and returns to the couch. It tastes even worse than the first, but she drinks every drop and is crawling back between the damp towels when Wawrinka calls again.

"Hey, Con."

"Darlene, you sound underwater."

"Do I?"

"I just sent you a piece of video. It's from the ER at the Mother of Mercy Hospital in Florence, South Carolina, seven miles from where we found Popsicle. The light isn't great, but you can make out all three of them."

O'Hara struggles to understand what Wawrinka means. "They took the kid to an ER?"

"Almost. Just watch it."

"Almost? How did you find this?"

"You know how we figured Fudgesicle killed Popsicle for stealing his swag? When I thought about it some more, that didn't make sense, because Fudgesicle didn't know about it."

"I don't follow you," says O'Hara groggily.

"If Fudgesicle knew about the swag," says Wawrinka, "he wouldn't have left it in the car. And based on the beating he gave Popsicle, if he knew about the diamond, he would have cut it out of his stomach. So if he didn't kill Popsicle for stealing from him, there had to be another reason. I thought maybe it had to do with the boy, particularly since one perp seemed to be trying to help him a lot more than the other.

"On a flier, I called all the hospitals anywhere near where we found Popsicle, and had them go through their logs for the night of March 3, when we know the three passed through. A couple hours later, Mother of Mercy got back to me. According to their records, someone called the ER that night at 1:07 a.m. on March 4 and told them that they were about to bring in a sick child, but there was no record of a child being admitted. I asked them to look at their security footage, and they found this. It's only thirty-eight seconds. I'll stay on the line."

The hospital camera is mounted above the entrance to the ER, aimed at a piece of driveway beneath a concrete overhang. At the center of the overhang moths swirl around the bulb. A white station wagon pulls into the frame. Although the car stops just short of the light, O'Hara can see through the windshield that Popsicle is behind the wheel and Fudgesicle in the passenger seat. Fudgesicle's chin rests on his massive chest, and he slumps in his seat as if asleep.

The door on the driver's side opens. A small man steps out and hurriedly opens a back door. He bends out of view and comes up with the boy in his arms. From the limp way Herc's head and limbs hang, he appears to be unconscious. As Popsicle gathers the boy in his arms, there's a sudden movement in the front seat and a flash of light as the passenger door flies open. A large blur passes in front of the car, and when Popsicle turns from the backseat with the boy and steps toward the glowing entrance, he and the boy run straight into the oncoming blur.

As Popsicle stands defenseless, the boy in his arms, Fudgesicle strikes him in the face with vicious force. The first blow sends the smaller man reeling against the side of the car, the next knocks him onto his back, but neither gets him to release the boy. As Popsicle lies in the driveway, with the boy sprawled across him, his partner stomps him in the head, glances over his shoulder, then brings his full weight down on him again. Even when Fudgesicle tosses them into the backseat, Popsicle clings to the boy. After Fudgesicle shuts the back door, he drops to one knee and reaches behind the rear tire. Whatever he finds, he slips into his pants pocket, then clambers into the front seat. When the car pulls out of the frame, Popsicle and the boy are as good as dead.

CHAPTER 56

O'HARA SITS UP between the soaked towels, and with the back of one hand wipes the gunk out of her eye. In her other hand is a phone. "Dar," says Krekorian, "I just backed out of my driveway. What are you doing?"

O'Hara looks at the light streaming through the window, then turns over the Casio on her coffee table: 10:43. She slept thirteen hours. "Not sure."

"I was thinking I'd swing by and give you a ride downtown. There's something I want to talk to you about."

"Okay." It's been four days since O'Hara saw her old partner at Lakeside, but it feels like forever. "It's good to hear your voice, K," says O'Hara before she can catch herself.

New City is forty minutes from her side of the bridge. That's enough time to walk the pooch and shower, not a makeover.

"What the hell, Dar, they giving away Maker's Mark in Riverdale?"

"Not that I'm aware of. The only thing I've been abusing is NyQuil and Theraflu."

"Together?"

"You think I'm crazy? Consecutively."

Krekorian pushes his way into the traffic crossing the Spuyten Duyvil into Manhattan.

"Like I said, I want to talk to you about something."

"Okay. But I need some coffee."

K reaches into the backseat and hands her a Red Bull.

"It's about your homicide," says Krekorian. "Yesterday, I'm going through the robbery reports from the night before. I see that at 4:15 a.m., a call came in for a robbery in progress at a fortune-teller on Eleventh Street between A and B. First thing I think, is Who the fuck robs a fortune-teller? The second thing I think of is you."

"I didn't arrest anyone at that location," says O'Hara, who realizes that her cold is gone.

"I know, but seeing as you've been dealing with Gypsies, it caught my eye. I speak to the responding officer. He tells me it turned out to be nothing, or at least that's what he was told by the old lady who came to the door. 'The cat set off the alarm,' she says. The cop tells her the caller heard more than an alarm. He heard screaming and yelling and a car taking off, but the lady swears the caller heard wrong. Just a crazy old cat who doesn't see so good."

Krekorian exits the West Side Highway at Eighteenth and crosses under the rusted-out trestles of the old high line. "It was a slow night—in robbery, they're all slow—so I look to see if there's anything else involving fortune-tellers. There wasn't, but there were three other 911s around the same time—a robbery, a report of suspicious behavior, and the report of another house alarm going off. The first, at 2:45 a.m., is from Thirty-Eighth Street and Ninth Avenue, the next, at 3:05 a.m., is at Eighteenth and Eighth Avenue, and the third, at 3:50 a.m., at Sixteenth Street and Seventh. And then there's the first one I saw on Eleventh Street, another twenty minutes later. Based on the sequence and timing, it looks like one perp, working his way downtown, like he plotted his spree on Mapquest."

K drives east through the brick towers of the last public housing in Chelsea, turns south on Ninth and east on Fourteenth. "I play the calls back. In every instance the drama is on the ground floor, or basement. So I take a drive—like I said, it's a slow night—and sure enough every one of these buildings has a sign in the window—'Psychic' or 'Tarot Cards' or 'Fortunes Read'—and if I can get anyone to come to the door at all, they tell me the same thing the lady told the patrolmen. It was nothing, a lover's quarrel, a fight over a poker game."

"I didn't lock up anyone at those addresses either," says O'Hara.

"I know, but think about it. I've been in robbery over a year, I haven't heard of one fortune-teller getting knocked over. You start hocking Gypsies, dragging them in, busting their crystal balls, and a couple days later someone is out there robbing four of them in one night. You think that's a coincidence?"

"Probably not." O'Hara is as taken by his generosity as by his thinking. If the shoe was on the other foot, with her in robbery and him in homicide, would she be driving around on a slow night for him? "It's got to be another Gypsy," she says.

"Of course. It's like a drug dealer robbing drug dealers. Whoever it is knows exactly who he's dealing with and where the money is. In ten minutes, he is in and out and on to the next one. The only other possibility is a cop who specializes in Gypsies, and I don't see you turning vigilante quite yet."

"So where we headed?"

"A diner on Second Avenue. Of all the calls that came in that night, the most coherent came from a place called the B & H Dairy, a kosher place between St. Mark's and Seventh. The guy who made it is a cook, an Egyptian dude named Ahmed."

"An Egyptian cook at a kosher dairy?"

"If he wasn't Egyptian, Dar, he'd be a Mexican or a Puerto Rican. The old lady in the back, baking the challah, she is going to be a Pole or a Latvian, but behind the counter you need someone with fast-twitch muscles."

Kosher food and fast-twitch muscles make O'Hara think of Levin. "You know the other victim in this case," says O'Hara, "the old guy in

Florida—he was a boxer, a real one." For the next couple minutes, O'Hara brags on Levin so vehemently, you'd think Sollie was standing behind her whispering in her ear, which he is, in a way. "Turned pro at fifteen, beat a leading lightweight contender when he was still in high school, fought at the old Garden and the old Coney Island Velodrome."

K parks in front of a hydrant, makes O'Hara toss her Red Bull, and the two step into a diner as tight as Milano's. They sit at the counter across from the grill. Inches away, his back to them, is a tall man wearing a Nike tennis shirt who must be Ahmed. He breaks four sheets of matzo into a steel bowl, adds boiling water from the coffee urn, and drowns the shards with his fork, getting them nice and soggy. Then he cracks two eggs and empties them into the bowl, whips it all up with the fork, and empties the bowl into a hot skillet. After a couple minutes he flips it, and a couple minutes after that, slides the browned yellow disk in front of the tattooed kid at the end of the counter, along with a side serving of applesauce. Ahmed turns to face O'Hara and K. "You must be the detectives."

"Serge Krekorian," says K, "and my old partner Darlene O'Hara. We'd appreciate it if you could tell us everything you saw that morning."

"It's what I heard," says Ahmed. "My shift starts at five. I drive in from Long Island and try to get here by three thirty. At that hour, no one is on the road, and I have plenty of time to find a space. Then I go to the jungle gym in Tompkins Square, work out for about an hour before work." As O'Hara listens, she smells the omelet at the end of the counter.

"That morning it was hard to find a space, I didn't have time to exercise. I read the paper in the car, then walked over. On Eleventh, I hear an alarm go off on the ground floor of a building with a sign for a fortune-teller in the window. As I got closer, I heard a couple women screaming hysterically in a language I didn't recognize. It was like an opera, but not Italian."

"All you heard were women?" asks O'Hara.

"No. I heard one man with a deep voice and then the females, two, maybe three, shrieking for about ten seconds. Then they all shut up quick—like someone threw a switch."

"You see the guy?"

"No. I didn't want to. And I didn't want him to see me. I put my head down and kept walking. When I got here, I called the police."

"You notice anything else as you walked by?" asks O'Hara.

Ahmed wipes his hands on his apron. "There was a cab out front, double-parked on the other side of the street."

"Anyone in it?"

"There must have been. The engine was running. It was a brand-new Toyota Camry. I have a Camry too, with 180,000 miles on it. This was brand-new, the first time I've seen one used as a cab."

"Ahmed," says O'Hara, "let me ask you something. That omelet you just made for the kid. What was it?"

"Matzo *brei*."

"We'll take two. With applesauce. Please."

CHAPTER 57

AT AWESOME TAXI MANAGEMENT, days are divided into two twelve-hour shifts, one ending and one starting at 5:00 p.m. At 4:30, as the shifts cross over and the cars change hands, every bit of Forty-Fourth Street between Tenth and Eleventh, including the curbs, is running yellow. Behind the wheels sit dark, bearded men, whose stony countenances contradict the platinum strippers on their roofs. Fleet managers jockey vehicles into and out of impossible spots, hand off keys, and call out medallion numbers, while behind them in the brightly lit garages, mechanics furiously perform triage. Working on three or four cars at a time, they patch them up, and push them back out into the fray.

Among the Indians, Pakistanis, Afghans, and Ghanains are a smattering of locals, forced into cabs by hard times, and O'Hara fears that soon Axl will arrive for one of these shifts. Despite the vagaries in dress and grooming, the only substantive difference between drivers is *before* and *after*. Those who have just completed twelve hours of city driving are bleary-eyed and broken, their heels scraping the cement as they trudge to the subway. The new arrivals, whether sipping iced coffee, tea, or a muddy blend of herbs and roots, can still walk upright.

Across from Awesome Taxi Management is the back of PS 51, and Krekorian's car is tight against the fence that surrounds the playground. Working through the Taxi and Limousine Commission, O'Hara and Krekorian found that twelve '07 Camry's were on the street last night. Based on meter readings and drivers' logs, the most promising was driven out of ATM by fifty-seven-year-old Rachel Hadass, and as the two watch from K's Impala, a delicate bookish woman wearing madras shorts and a button-down shirt threads her way through the yellow gridlock.

An Indian with ferocious facial hair reroutes Hadass toward K's car, and O'Hara hops out to wave her over. Along with her iced coffee and sandwich, Hadass carries a copy of the *Quarterly Journal of Military History*. "Rachel, I'm Detective Darlene O'Hara, and this is Detective Serge Krekorian. Could you join us in our car? We need to ask you about one of your fares last night."

"Two hundred seventy-eight dollars and fifty cents," says Hadass, taking a seat behind them. "I thought I might hear from you."

"Rachel, how long you been hacking for ATM?"

"Eighteen years. That's why they gave me a new Toyota."

"They treat you pretty well?"

"They treat me 'Awesome,'" says Hadass, pointing at the sign.

"Can you describe the person you drove around for three hours?"

"He weighed four hundred pounds. Is that enough?"

"It's a start. What else?"

"About forty, very dark complexion, but not African American. Deep voice, and considering the ruckus, very calm."

"What did he tell you he was doing?"

"Collecting rent."

"And you believed him?"

"I did . . . almost. My grandfather owned a building in the Bronx. If you were feeling ungenerous, I guess you'd call him a slumlord. I learned from him that if people are dodging you, your only chance is to show up when you're not expected."

"So this guy reminded you of your grandfather?"

Hadass shrugs.

"You said he was calm?"

"Every stop was World War II, but he walked back to the cab like he was coming from the newsstand with his *Post*."

"Where'd you pick him up?"

"Ninth Street and Second, in front of Starbucks. He hands me three hundred dollars, says it's an advance on the meter, and has me take him to Hell's Kitchen. A basement apartment, not far from here. A couple minutes later I hear screaming in a strange language. Could have been Romanian, or maybe Armenian."

"Did it sound like this?" asks Krekorian. *"Tvek' indz gumar, duk' khent' bitches!"*

"Not really."

"Then it wasn't Armenian."

"Probably not. Anyway. There was a lot of carrying on and hysteria, then stone silence. Same pattern every stop. There were six all together."

"He have a gun?"

"Possible, but I never saw it. He walked in and out, carrying a plastic shopping bag."

"Where did you drop him off?"

"Seventh Street and Third, right around the corner from where I picked him up. He gave me the meter plus the three hundred dollars."

"You see which way he went when he got out?"

"Toward St. Mark's. A guy his size couldn't have gone far. There's something you should know. He asked me to pick him up again tonight. Same place I dropped him off, at one thirty a.m. When I hesitated, he offered me a thousand dollars. At that point, I figured he probably wasn't collecting rent, so I took a pass. God knows I could use the cash, but it's not worth risking all this," she says, holding up her coffee and a cucumber sandwich. Then she turns to Krekorian. "By the way, that smattering of Armenian, what was it?"

"'Give me the money, you crazy bitches.' It's my motto."

CHAPTER 58

O'HARA OPENS HER computer on the front seat between her and Krekorian, finds the video from Wawrinka, and hits play. Once again the white Volvo drives up to the ER of Mother of Mercy Hospital. "The little guy behind the wheel is Popsicle," says O'Hara. "The huge motherfucker asleep in the passenger seat is Fudgesicle." They watch the smaller man hop from the front and hurry to the rear. Because she's waiting for it and not under the influence of cold remedies, she can see the instant when the giant wakes and registers where he is, and the violence with which he turns on his partner, defenseless with the boy in his arms, is more disturbing the second time around. At the same time, she is more affected by the smaller man's resolve, the way Popsicle clings to the boy no matter what, and it occurs to O'Hara that both of the men who stood up to Fudgesicle were barely over a hundred pounds.

"What do you think Fudgesicle is picking up?" asks O'Hara. "Popsicle's wallet?"

"No," says K, "his phone." The two watch the video a second time, and O'Hara closes her computer. She and Krekorian are parked just north of St. Mark's on Third Avenue. To afford a direct view of the spot

where Hadass dropped off Fudgesicle the night before, they are facing south. Although Hadass declined the perp's offer to drive a second
night, O'Hara and K have been staked out there since midnight, in the
hope that another cabby will take him on his rounds, then deliver him
to the same spot.

"I remember when this was a freak parade," says Krekorian about the
pedestrian traffic on St. Mark's. "Now it's college kids in flip-flops."

"And have you seen the fucking Pinkberry next to Grassroots?" asks
O'Hara. "Classic dive bars should get landmark status preventing anyone
from selling frozen yogurt within fifty feet of them on either side."

Despite the knee-jerk kvetching, O'Hara still appreciates the late-
night hubbub of the downtown streets, still gets a kick out of the club kid
working out his identity crisis in hot pants and platform sneakers. "I've
been thinking," she says, "about the cabby's description of the perp. His
nonchalance, the way he didn't seem to give a fuck about anything. I'm
pretty sure he's what Gypsies call *marime*. Like cops only hang with cops,
Gypsies only hang with Gypsies, only it's much stricter. If you do something seriously wrong, you run the risk of *marime*. That means you're
shunned, and banned from all contact. For a Gypsy, that's even worse
than it would be for a cop, and that's how our perp is behaving, like a man
with nothing to lose."

"You were getting close," says K, "so they cut him loose."

"I think so. And now he's pushing back."

A young musician walks by, carrying a guitar case.

"You never told me about Axl's show at Lakeside," says Krekorian.

"It was great."

"The kid has talent."

"That's what I'm afraid of."

The conversation turns O'Hara somber. She wonders if Axl will end
up on *Behind the Music* or behind the counter of a Burger King. For a
rocker, there doesn't seem to be a whole lot in between.

"Check it out," says Krekorian. He points at the cab that's pulled to a stop on the east side of Third. The light on the roof switches from yellow to white, and after a long pause the back door opens on the traffic side. It takes another minute for a black porkpie hat to pop above the door and an immense rectangle of a man to emerge. As he walks around the back of the cab, he moves less like a person than a wave.

CHAPTER 59

FUDGESICLE LEANS OVER a curbside counter, grabs a slice, and continues north, a paper plate folded in one hand, a Duane Reade shopping bag dangling from the other. He wears a white V-neck tee and light blue surgical scrubs, and O'Hara is amazed by how little attention an obese sociopath in a porkpie hat and translucent pants receives at 3:45 a.m. in the East Village on a summer night. For O'Hara the sight of the long-sought perp releases so much adrenaline, it's a struggle to think clearly, but to pedestrians, who surrender the curb to let him pass, he is a jet-lagged tourist who stepped out for a slice and a toothbrush, or a hospital orderly just off work. He doesn't rate a second look. O'Hara suspects the incongruous hipster lid is part of it. Somehow, it helps him blend in.

Moving directly toward them up Third, Fudgesicle appears smaller and larger than his description, more like five-nine than five-eleven but also significantly heavier, as if he's packed on another hundred pounds since the last entry into the database. His face is more bloated than in the picture, his eyes little more than slits, and, with those thirty-eight seconds of video fresh in her mind, there's something obscene about the laxness in his face and the way he's barely contained by his clothes.

"We got to call backup," says Krekorian as he reaches into the glove compartment for the Taser, and attaches it to his belt. "He makes Goodman look like Buscemi. I don't think I'll be able to cuff him."

"If the two of us can't arrest this load of shit, we should pack it in. He can barely walk."

"He moved well enough to stomp his partner to death."

"Let's see where he's headed. It's too crowded to grab him on the street anyway. Particularly if he's got a piece."

When Fudgesicle gets within thirty feet, O'Hara and K scramble out of the car, and when he turns east on St. Mark's, they dodge the two-way traffic on Third and trail him from the north side of the street. From behind, Fudgesicle only appears to be rocking from side to side, his weight shifting from the outside of one green shoe to the other, yet somehow that propels him past a sunglass stall and a sports bar, where the jersey of the pitcher on TV is reflected in the window. A couple steps before Trash & Vaudeville, he turns his back on them again, and when he hitches up his pants and steps into the narrow entrance of the St. Marks Hotel, O'Hara sees that he's wearing lime green Crocs.

"So now we call backup," says K.

For a second, O'Hara doesn't respond. She's back in Sarasota in the foul-smelling efficiency with the grifter mom, the man on the toilet, and the scruffy girl staring at the TV. It's doubtful that under any circumstances, O'Hara would have the wherewithal to twiddle her thumbs on the curb as the perp disappeared into the hotel, but after realizing that she had been within fifteen feet of him before, it's impossible.

"We do that," says O'Hara, "brass will close off the whole street and turn a simple arrest into Iraq. I've been this close to this motherfucker for weeks. I'm not going wait around all night while they play soldier."

"The perp's not going anywhere, Dar. We have time to do this right."

"Let's give him five minutes to get to his room. We don't need a shootout in the lobby. Give him a chance to get separated from his gun, if he has one, maybe fall asleep. Then we go in and suss it out. If it's more than we can handle, we call in the cavalry."

Although O'Hara's voice sounds reasonable, the words coming out of her mouth aren't, and even she knows it. For a couple minutes, the two stare across the street at the fleabag SRO turned cut-rate tourist motel, the more astute hustlers in the crowd noting the twin bulges beneath Krekorian's blazer.

Since logic didn't work, Krekorian appeals to her self-interest.

"We need someone to cover the exit. What if he makes us, goes out a back door, and hails a cab. I know you've been on this guy for a long time. All the more reason you don't want to be the one responsible for letting him slip away."

"You're right," says O'Hara, stepping off the curb and nearly into the path of an eastbound cab. "We got to go in now."

CHAPTER 60

DESPITE O'HARA'S HEAD start, Krekorian reaches the entrance ahead of her. His gun, already out of the holster, is against his hip. There's no space in the old flophouse for a lobby, just another corridor that runs past a tiny office to the ground-floor rooms. The night clerk, a short-haired woman, sits in front of a computer screen. A lip ring centers her earnest midwestern face and a vinelike tat crawls out from under her shirt at the elbow and neck.

As O'Hara displays her shield, she reads the girl's name on the tag pinned to her shirt. "Anna," says O'Hara in a soft voice. "I'm Detective Darlene O'Hara, and this is my partner, Serge Krekorian. The large man who just entered the hotel fits the description of an important suspect. Did you see him go into his room?"

"There's nowhere else he could have gone."

"How about a fire exit?"

"That would have set off an alarm."

"Does his room have a window?"

"Not one that opens."

"What room is he in?"

"One eleven," she says, glancing at her screen. "Registered as Bob Geis."

"Anyone with him?"

"No."

"Has he had any visitors?"

"Not since I arrived at midnight."

"How about the rooms next door and above him?" asks Krekorian. "Are they occupied?"

Anna looks at her screen and shakes her head. "We have fourteen guests tonight. Except for an elderly man at the other end of the hall, they are on the top two floors. Most guests request that, but we don't have an elevator."

Krekorian, who now holds his gun in his jacket pocket, gestures at the computer. "Is there any way you can tell us what's going on in his room?"

"Only if he's on the phone or ordering a movie," says Anna. "He's not."

"We're going to take a look," says O'Hara, and slips down the hallway so quickly Krekorian has to hustle to catch up.

"You're scaring me, Darlene. You're moving too fast. You don't have a plan."

"My plan is to arrest this motherfucker and put him in the box. I have some questions to ask him."

"You're not thinking straight."

"Just want to take a look."

The two follow the ratty red runner down the hallway. The city is sprinkled with fleabags transformed into cash cows with little more than paint and wallpaper, but here its humble history is particularly transparent. The only flourish is a couple Mediterranean window scenes in recessed spots on the wall. Room 111, the second to last on the right, has a red door and gold numbers. A DO NOT DISTURB sign hangs from the knob.

Krekorian pulls out his gun, and O'Hara puts her ear against the door. She can't hear a thing, but considering the number of rock shows she's attended and her notion that earplugs are for pussies, that doesn't mean much. She crouches at the foot of the door and presses her fingers against the synthetic fiber, trying to clear enough space below the door to see if the lights are on inside, but the rug is too thick. It's also damp, and when she glances up and mouths the word "wet" for Krekorian, she sees that the placard dangling off the knob is wet too.

While K guards the door, O'Hara goes back to the office and returns with a coded card she uses to unlock 113, the room next door. O'Hara sees why they only get $119 a night. It's barely big enough for a queen-size bed. Instead of a closet, there's a coffin-shaped frame against one wall with a couple hangers. Above the bed is a photo of an Italian village, and beside it, on a tiny table, a stack of tinfoil ashtrays. The bathroom has a shower in the corner and black-and-white tiles. When O'Hara leans against the tiles, she can hear the shower running next door. "The guy's in the shower," she whispers when she steps back into the hallway.

"Maybe," says K, his eyes dark and angry. "Or maybe he isn't. Maybe he's on the other side, waiting for us."

CHAPTER 61

O'HARA SLIPS THE card into the lock and leads Krekorian inside. Between the closet, bed, and the wall, there is barely room for her and K to stand. In front of them, inches from the barrels of their guns, is the bathroom door. From behind it comes the sound of running water and nothing else.

O'Hara scans the cluttered space for the weapon. Clothes and trash, tossed everywhere, fouls the air. On top of the closet are the orange-stained wax paper and plate from his last meal, and hanging off the corner of the bed, a pair of mighty whities the size of a pillowcase. Maybe the gun is in the shopping bag, but O'Hara can't find the bag until she looks down and sees she's standing next to it. Inside, thousands in loose bills are piled like leaves, but there's no gun.

That could mean he didn't have one, or it's somewhere else in the room, or he's holding it in his hand on the other side of the door. In an instant, all the urgency and crap thinking of the last twenty minutes come back as its B side—panic. For the first time since she rushed them into the hotel, O'Hara appreciates the danger she has put them both in, and as she looks over at her partner, her vision tunnels.

Because O'Hara led them into the room, Krekorian stands directly in front of the bathroom door, with O'Hara just beyond him. Is K seconds away from getting shot? Is she about to get her partner killed? In her hand is a weapon O'Hara has never drawn in the field till now. The last time she fired it was ten months ago at the range for her annual certification.

O'Hara stares at the bathroom door and listens to the running shower. She wills the spout to be turned off and the water to stop, and to hear the scrape of grommets as the shower curtain is swept aside, but none of those things happen. All she hears is rushing water. When O'Hara glances at K's bullet-shaped head, his eyes are focused on the door.

If the perp has a gun in his hand, every second they delay increases their chances of getting shot. She tries to think clearly, but how can she when the reason they're in this position is that she hasn't been thinking at all? Instead, she reaches for the rage that has never been far since she saw the handprints in blood on the metal wall of the van, and turns the handle of the bathroom door.

Like the rug, it's wet, and slips in her hand. When she tries again and pushes it open, steam billows into her face, blinding her, and for the second time in a minute, she stands frozen, waiting to be run over or shot. Krekorian reaches behind her and opens the door to the hallway. Enough steam escapes for her to make out a shape in the shower. "Police officers," says Krekorian. "Turn off the water."

The perp doesn't respond, and Krekorian says it louder. "Police officers. Turn off the water." As more steam clears, O'Hara has a better view of the pale figure wedged into the corner behind the clear plastic. His dark hair is bent under the shower head, and the water cascades off his massive back. O'Hara is struck by the paleness of his shoulders, the tops pink from the rush of scalding water. For a second she wonders if they got the wrong guy.

"Police," says O'Hara. "Get the fuck out of the shower."

When O'Hara turns toward Krekorian again, he has transferred his revolver to his holster and is holding the Taser. He raises the weapon to the level of the perp's elbow, slips his finger over the trigger, and inches forward until the front of the device almost touches the shower curtain.

"Hold on a second," says O'Hara. She takes in the forward tilt of the perp's head, then sweeps the shower curtain aside. Fudgesicle's jowls are on his chest, and his arms at his side, but except for the angle of his neck and slack arms, nothing stands out, until she moves to the side and sees the part of his chest the water didn't reach. Running from neck to navel is a deep maroon stain that fans out like a '70s tie, and lying across the drain between enormous lime green Crocs is a straight-edged razor.

"I'll say one thing," says K.

"What?"

"Great water pressure."

CHAPTER 62

KREKORIAN CRACKS HIS knuckles and squints into the sun. At 7:45 in the morning, St Mark's is far quieter than at 3:00 a.m. Except for a couple employed outliers hustling to the subway, the sidewalks are empty.

"Breakfast?"

"I was leaning toward a drink," says O'Hara.

When they arrive, Milano's has only been open for minutes, but O'Hara's two fellow regulars are already perched on their self-assigned stools. Neither looks up as O'Hara and Krekorian sit between them.

"Good morning, Darlene," says Holly.

"Good morning. Holly, this is Serge."

"What can I get you?"

"A Guinness."

"And you, Darlene, the usual?"

"Please."

Krekorian waits for Holly to deliver their drinks and walk away. "'Good morning, Darlene,'" he mimics. "'Good morning, Holly.' 'The usual, Darlene?' What the hell is wrong with you? You got exactly what you wanted. You made homicide at thirty-five. And you start your day here? You haven't changed a bit."

"Isn't that a good thing, in a way?"

"Actually it's not. The idea of life is to change. That's the point."

"Really? No one told me."

"I'm telling you now."

Krekorian is too weary to press the matter. He drains half his pint in one long sip, sits back in his stool, and closes his eyes. O'Hara is exhausted too, and in the last few minutes her spirits have dipped. Seeing Fudgesicle wedged under the shower head, so drained of blood he looked like an albino, was not unsatisfying, particularly since it's what he did to the boy, but it keeps him out of the box and keeps her from ever finding out how he could toss away the boy's life so cavalierly. She wanted to put him face-to-face with what he had done, and now she can't.

"There were four people in that unit that morning," says O'Hara, "the old fighter, two perps, and the kid. Now that they're all dead. There's no one left to say what happened."

"At least you put him out of business," says Krekorian, "backed him into such a corner, he had no choice but to pull the plug."

"Although for a second there I thought you were going bring him back à la Frankenstein. If you had zapped him with that Taser, he might have turned off the water and reached for the towel."

"I guess I owe you for that one, Darlene." He clinks O'Hara's cocktail with his pint. "Tasering a dead Gypsy is probably not good luck."

"It was the least I could do," says O'Hara. "I miss you, K."

"Miss you too, Dar. God knows why."

"By the way, Holly used to be Richard."

"No shit."

"Which I guess proves your point about people needing to change. Some more than others."

Krekorian quaffs the last of his Guinness. "That's it. We had our drink. I need some sleep."

"One last shot?"

"No. And you're coming with me. I'm not leaving you here."

"Let me just go to the bathroom."

O'Hara has avoided Milano's bathroom till now, but this morning she has no choice. As she steps through the door, she sees she's gotten a text from Axl, and her spirits spike.

Hi, Darlene. Glad you liked the show. Gotten a lot of positive feedback. Unfortunately things aren't looking good for the band. The new drummer turned out to be a dick. We got into a fistfight at our last rehearsal, and the bass player is talking about following his girlfriend to Vermont. I'm afraid the Flat Screens are fading to black.

CHAPTER 63

THE GRAY-HAIRED WOMAN shuffles from the counter, clutching a Coke and a paper bag. She wears a thin cotton dress that reaches the top of her flip-flops, and her neck and wrists are a welter of beads. Despite her choice of a rendezvous, she is bone thin, the kind of woman lucky enough to have shed her weight over the decades and streamlined for old age.

O'Hara has been waiting for an hour. She sits at a table in front that looks out at the pedestrians wilting in the heat on Third. The old woman takes the seat across from her and reaches into her bag for the cardboard jewel box and two plastic containers. The box, which bears the claim AN EXCELLENT SOURCE OF HAPPINESS, contains four McNuggets. The plastic tubs hold her sauces—barbecue and sweet 'n' sour.

"You expected a man?" Through Miss Marla, O'Hara requested a meeting with the Big Rom, or whoever has jurisdiction over that part of the East Village that includes the community garden.

"Yes."

"Most people do." With cultivated precision, she lifts a tawny globule, dunks it in both sauces, and drops it into her mouth.

"I want to know what happened in Florida," says O'Hara.

"Detective," says the Big Roma, "I wasn't there. Fortunately, the person most responsible has done us all a big favor. Now the book is closed."

"I still need to know."

"Since when do you care about Gypsies?" The woman repeats her drill and licks the greasy crumbs from her fingers. Through parts not covered with grime or plastered with promotions, light slants through the window and bounces off the orange and maroon puddles.

"If the kid was a Gypsy, then I care about Gypsies."

"Because he was blond?"

"Because he was nine years old and locked in the back of a van for over a day as he bled to death. Because he had no family and no choice but to help a bunch of lowlifes prey on old people. You're right, I don't give a fuck about anyone but the boy. For the way he was treated, I hope bad *kasa* haunts all of you for the rest of your days."

The part of the room where O'Hara and the old woman sit looks more like a shelter than America's favorite restaurant. Nearby, a woman stares into space, and a bearded man nods out in his panhandling prop of a wheelchair. Those who are more alert are preoccupied with their own fresh catastrophes, but the threat of bad *kasa* gets the old lady's attention.

"What makes you think he didn't have a family?"

"If he did, he would have been better off without them. They didn't take care of him. They didn't protect him. They didn't educate him. They didn't even set his broken leg. The only thing anyone ever did for him was bury him. Tell me what happened, or I'll lock up every Gypsy below Fourteenth Street until someone does."

"Like I said, I wasn't there. I couldn't tell you if I wanted to."

"Then find out. Ask around."

"I'm too old for that. Besides, nothing would be gained."

"A few months ago, the boy's body was moved from wherever it had been to the community garden. That was a very difficult, unpleasant job. Did you order someone to do that?"

"No," says the old lady. "But I can tell you that whoever did, thought it was the right thing to do. They thought it was important for the boy to have a decent burial."

"What was decent about it? And why take the risk to move him there?"

"I don't know."

"You had a theory about why he'd been moved, take a wild guess."

"I've guessed enough for one day."

The old lady returns to her McNuggets, and O'Hara thinks about all the people who used the boy. To Fudgesicle and Popsicle, he was the master key who could unlock any door. For Pizza and Crisco, he was the little piece of business that took the stink off their scams, and to the photographer he was essentially the same thing. No doubt this bony old bitch found a way to profit from him too. Thank God, thinks O'Hara, for his skater pals. All they wanted was his company.

"By the way, whoever handled the funeral got most of it wrong."

"What do you mean?"

"The kid didn't like *Batman*. He liked *Superman*. He didn't give a fuck about the Yankees, and he thought Coldplay sucks."

CHAPTER 64

FROM HER DESK O'Hara can see the board. Whenever she makes the mistake of glancing in its direction, she sees "John Doe, 9, remains, 6th Street, Avenue B" and the blue line running through it. With his fetish for closure, Kelso wasn't going to waste any time crossing the homicide off the board. By the time O'Hara got back to the squad that morning, he had pulled a chair over to the wall and done it himself. But more disturbing than the false finality of the blue line is that the victim still doesn't have a name, and never will.

"You stop at the wheel?" asks Jandorek.

"No. I miss something?"

"A bunch of punks pushed a skell down the stairs to the R train at Union Square, fractured his skull in two places. He's not expected to make it. The vic has the same name as the old fart who thought the Terminator was our commander-in-chief."

"Got to be another Gus Henderson. My Gus wasn't homeless."

"Sixty-seven," says Jandorek, reading from the sheet. "Lifelong junkie . . . record as long as the tracks on his arm."

"What hospital?"

"St. Vincent's. My favorite."

"I'll take a look," says O'Hara, already out of her chair. "I'll call if there's anything."

"Thanks. I'll check with the MTA. See if they caught it on film."

Unfortunately the head nurse on duty is the imperious Evelyn Priestly. Before O'Hara can open her mouth, Priestly cuts her off. "No. You can't. Disturbing him now could kill him. That's why he's in intensive care."

"I don't want to disturb him," says O'Hara. "I came to see how he's doing."

"You should have called, then. Saved yourself a trip."

"Believe it or not, Gus is a friend. I met him working a case."

"Well, your friend is in pretty bad shape. He's got a compound fracture in his skull, and he wasn't exactly a model of health to begin with."

There's nothing worse than the ICU at night. What's intensive is certainly not the care. As O'Hara walks by the open doors, she sees wispy old people alone on their backs, their eyes enlarged and scared. In the endless corridors, there's no help in sight, only the somnambulant shuffle of the occasional nurse's aide or a janitor walking behind his polisher. What is intense is the quiet and sense of incipient death and the smell of the disinfectant used to scrub it out.

O'Hara sits on a bench across from the nurses' station, finds Paulette's number, and sends her a text. "Paulette, I just heard Gus got mugged in the subway. How did that happen?" Out of the corner of her eye, O'Hara watches Priestly at her desk. When the nurse leaves her station and steps into the elevator, O'Hara finds Henderson's room and slips inside. From a chair in the corner, she stares at Gus's bandaged head, his fragile hold on life reflected in the rising and falling numbers on the monitor above his bed.

O'Hara looks at her phone again. Still no response from Paulette. She should be here, thinks O'Hara, and is surprised that she isn't, particularly when she recalls how gingerly she removed Gus's hand from her ass that afternoon in the garden. How the hell could she have let Gus slip out of sight? The guy can barely move. How was that even possible?

Gus's personal effects are in a plastic bag on the table. O'Hara doesn't recognize any of them, and there's no sign of his glasses. She gets out of her chair and walks to the head of the bed. Without glasses, Gus barely looks like himself. In fact he isn't Gus, not the Gus Henderson she knows.

O'Hara bends closer to the battered face and realizes she got the math of junkiedom wrong. A sixty-seven-year-old who has been an addict for forty-six years doesn't necessarily look eighty-five. He just looks like crap. But that's not the real issue. If this guy is the real Gus Henderson, who is the demented old fart she's been dealing with?

Her Gus Henderson wanted to get something off his chest. He knows about a body buried in the garden that he has no good reason to know about. He has a picture of a willow in his cigar box. He said he killed a big black guy, and one of the perps is dark and very big. And then he changed his mind and decided that maybe he was white. One fucked-up detail and coincidence after another. But if Gus Henderson isn't really Gus Henderson and is someone else with an actual connection to the perps, all these details become a lot less fucked up and a lot less coincidental.

The implications put O'Hara's brain on tilt. As she sorts them out, the pale stranger on the bed opens his eyes as if from a nap. "How you feeling, pal?"

"Perfect."

"Seriously?"

"How do you think I feel? I feel like shit."

"Gus, there's a guy going around saying he's you."

"Why would anyone do that? I don't even want to be me."

"I'm wondering the same thing. He's about ten years older than you at least. Thick black glasses. Jet-black hair."

"He have a pretty black girlfriend?"

"Girlfriend?"

"Tall woman, from the islands, way too young and cute for that bow-legged old fart?"

"Now that you mention it."

"His name is Emmanuel Robin. Everyone calls him Manny."

"How do you know him?"

"I don't even remember anymore. It's been so long. He's got a repair shop in Alphabet City. Does a little bit of everything—luggage and jewelry repair, haircuts and shaves. You got a high pain threshold, you could probably get a root canal. You're a cop, right? A detective?"

"Yeah."

"Mind if I ask you something?"

"Sure."

"You give even the slightest shit about the motherfuckers who tried to kill me, or you just come here to ask me about an old Gypsy?"

"I do care about you, Gus. Really."

The basement apartment, thinks O'Hara. The stew burning on the stove twenty-four hours a day. The simple fucking *boyash*.

"Did you say Manny's a Gypsy?"

"So you don't give a fuck about the people who rolled me down the stairs? You couldn't care less."

"That's not true, Gus. Tell me what you remember about last night." O'Hara reaches into her bag and takes out a notebook. "Did you get a good look at any of them?"

"I get it—now you're going to act like you care. Very convincing. Nurse!"

"Gus, you got to calm down. You need to rest."

"Fuck you! Nurse! Nurse!" Gus pushes himself up so violently, he disconnects several tubes from his arm. That sets off an alarm in the nurses' station. When Priestly rushes into the room, she finds O'Hara beside the bed, notebook in hand.

"How do you live with yourself?" asks Priestly, euphoric with disdain. "Gus, I'm very sorry that you were disturbed. Detective O'Hara assured me you two are old friends. Is that true?"

"I've never seen this cunt in my life."

CHAPTER 65

MANNY'S FIX-IT IS in a First Street basement that smells hospitably of leather, stain, and heated glue. When O'Hara steps through the door, the stooped repairman is conferring with a would-be It Girl in culottes and heels, and if he notices the arrival of a homicide detective, he keeps it to himself. He focuses instead on the vintage bag the girl has dropped onto his counter, and shakes his head in dismay at the many areas in need of repair. Now that he's playing himself, instead of a doddering old codger, Manny seems a decade younger.

Having assessed the damage inside and out, Manny looks up apprehensively and breaks the bad news. "One hundred and twenty-five dollars."

"Manny, that's more than I paid for it."

"I would hope so." With a look of resignation, he reaches for the bag again, and O'Hara notices the black-and-white pin: OBAMA. CHANGE WE CAN BELIEVE IN. Apparently, he is now up-to-date on presidential politics.

While Manny reappraises, O'Hara takes in the cluttered space. Completed repairs are stuffed between shelves. Repairs-in-progress crowd his workbench, along with umbrella ribs, trunk locks, and other replacement parts. In the back corner is an old barber's chair, and above it a hand-drawn sign advertises haircuts for $14, hot shaves for $7. Between Manny and his customer is a display case featuring items for sale—vintage jewelry, flatware, several watches, and a couple cameras, including a Polaroid Swinger. They could be flea-market finds, but more likely they're the purloined harvest of junkie thieves like the real Gus in ICU.

O'Hara leans toward the photographs on the side wall. In one, Manny stands beside Paulette, his too-young, too-pretty girlfriend. In another, his arm is draped around a slight young man O'Hara recognizes as Popsicle. Side by side, their resemblance is striking.

"It's a big job," Manny tells the girl. "The whole back has to be cut out . . . a new lining sewn in . . . the lock replaced. . . ."

"Can't you just patch the back and fix the lock?"

"I could try."

"Manny. You're such a doll!" Before she leaves, O'Hara has to watch her dip across the counter and kiss him on the cheek.

"HI, MANNY."

"Hi, Darlene."

"That picture on the wall, that your grandson?"

"Yeah."

"That's interesting, because not long ago I saw a fortune-teller named Miss Marla. Perhaps you know her. I've been seeing a lot of fortune-tellers lately. She mentioned an old Gypsy who sought reparations for the murder of his grandson. According to Miss Marla, a *kris* was convened, but in the end they told the old man to take a hike."

"Darlene, you believe what you hear from fortune-tellers, I got a good deal for you on a bridge that connects Manhattan to Brooklyn."

"Manny, you already sold me that fucking bridge three times over, and a river full of bullshit to go under it. I were you, I wouldn't push my luck."

"How can I help you, Darlene?"

"Let's start in Florida, the old man's condo, right after Fudgesicle and your grandson go in posing as employees of the Sarasota Water Authority."

"Sounds like you already got it figured out."

"Tell me anyway."

"According to my grandson, it was the usual drill. They tell the old man they're checking for contamination and have him bang on his water heater. Two minutes later the guy comes back into the bedroom, banging whatever it is they gave him on the barrel of a rifle."

O'Hara had grown attached to her version, the one in which Bunny brings back the spoon so he can shove it up Fudgesicle's ass, but this makes more sense. By knocking the spoon on the gun, Bunny could make it sound like he was still hitting the water heater and take them by surprise.

"Then what?"

"The old man points the gun at Fudgesicle, tells him to get on his knees, or he's going to kill him. I wish he had. Instead, Fudgesicle bends down and grabs the boy."

"What do you mean?"

"Fudgesicle picks up the boy."

"To run?"

"The kid doesn't need help to run. Limp or not, he can run faster than Fudgesicle. Even I can."

"What are you saying?"

"He picks up the kid to hold him up in front of him—as a shield . . . so the old guy won't shoot."

O'Hara had played out the scene a hundred different ways, but not like this. She feels like she's been kicked in the stomach.

"Holding the boy, Fudgesicle rushes past the old man toward the door. He hits the gun, the gun goes off."

"I don't understand," says O'Hara, although it's more anger than an inability to comprehend. "What made Fudgesicle think he could treat the boy like that?"

"I can't answer that one, Darlene. Maybe he'd say 'cause he was the one who adopted him, or maybe because the boy wasn't a real Gypsy. But he treated my grandson no different or worse, so who cares what that piece of shit thought?"

"How do you know about all this?"

"My grandson called me right before he took the boy to the ER. He thought it might get him killed. I guess he was right, because I never heard from him again."

O'Hara leans against the counter. The smells that were pleasing when she walked in have turned noxious.

"If the boy was a *gadje*, why'd he rate a Gypsy funeral?"

"He was born *gadje*, raised Gypsy. His mother was Christina, the woman from the garden. That day you came with your book, I thought you'd see it. She has the same face. When she was fifteen, she got pregnant. The only one who noticed was the Big Roma who lived on her block. She arranged the whole thing. She had the girl tell her father she was sleeping over at a friend's house, delivered the baby that night, and sold him to Fudgesicle and his wife, a Gypsy named Gabriella. "

"I ran into that bitch in Florida," mutters O'Hara, more to herself than Manny. She winces at the memory of Herc's stepsister, staring at the TV.

"At the *kris*," says Manny, "the old lady came up with the idea of burying the boy in the garden. As if having him back near his real mother made everything right again. She didn't care about my grandson, just her own bad *kasa*. So she had Fudgesicle get his body from wherever he'd dumped it and move him to the garden."

"And who the hell are Pizza and Crisco?"

"His Gypsy grandmothers. Pizza is Fudgesicle's mother. Crisco is the mother of Gabriella. At one point they were partners, but they had a falling out and have hated each other ever since."

"Why didn't you go straight to the cops?"

"I didn't want to be expelled. Demand a *kris*, you have to abide. Something called *marime*. You wouldn't understand."

The basement air is suffocating. O'Hara does one last scan of the premises and lands on the sign above the barber's chair: HAIRCUTS $14, SHAVES $7. She remembers the straight razor across the drain, the wet carpet just outside the door, and the damp corner of the DO NOT DISTURB sign. "Manny, when was the last time you gave someone a shave?"

"Been a while. Kids all growing beards like the sixties all over."

"You didn't, by any chance, give one the other night to a shit bag at the St. Marks Hotel?"

"I don't think so. But you know how it is, Darlene. My age, you forget half the things you do soon as you do them."

CHAPTER 66

BE CAREFUL WHAT you wish for, O'Hara's mother likes to say. You might get it. For the next couple weeks, the weight of her long-sought answers feels like a backpack full of stones, and she's almost nostalgic for the ignorance with which she arrived that morning at Manny's Fix-It.

The onset of fall always knocks O'Hara off balance—something about the crisp air and the school-bell chill--but this year the malaise seems deeper. She knows K is right. It's time for a change. Long past it. She should call her old boyfriend Leibowitz and ask for another chance, or at least have him give her the name of a good Jewish shrink. But of course, she does neither. Instead, she calls in sick, takes a subway downtown, and wanders the East Village.

It's mid-October, midweek, midafternoon. Few people are out, and those who are seem underemployed and at loose ends, marooned by the day. At the bodega on Sixth and B, O'Hara buys a coffee and carries it across the street to the garden, where the entrance, with its garland of tiny stamped-out hands, is locked. O'Hara sips her coffee and peers through the bars at the overgrown quarter acre. That the Big Roma made Fudgesicle rebury the boy in here almost makes sense. Having brought the kid into the world and brokered his adoption, it was on her to send him out of it, and if possible, square things with the boy's mother.

This afternoon the garden feels as slack as the streets, adrift on the same autumnal lull. From the entrance, O'Hara has a good view of Christina Malmströmer's garden. Even dormant, its tidiness stands out. While other plots have been abandoned in haste, Christina's has been thoughtfully shut down for the season and a layer of loam spread over it to rejuvenate the soil. As Christina told O'Hara, she's the one in the family who is good at growing things.

O'Hara was so much luckier. Eight months into her pregnancy, she was in such denial about her predicament that she almost forgot about it. Had the bulge been detected by a sharp-eyed baby broker instead of the school nurse, and had that person promised to make it all go away without anyone being the wiser, she couldn't have resisted the offer any more than Christina had. And after Christina saw how the old man treated her sister for infractions that were so minor by comparison, she would have feared the worst. Then again, old man Malmströmer didn't get off any easier, spending his nights making furniture while his flesh and blood hopped around the neighborhood on a broken leg.

O'Hara tosses her cup into the trash and pushes from the gates. She walks past Malmströmer's basement workshop and a fortune-teller's window and keeps going, all the way to Lafayette. At St. Mark's, she dodges the skaters around the Cube and enters the subway at Broadway and Eighth. As she waits on a bench, whose inhospitable angles have been designed to deter the homeless, a schizophrenic at the end of the platform goes off in a sputtering rage. Each eruption lasts about twenty seconds, subsides, and builds again, and O'Hara sits through a dozen before the R arrives.

Four stops later, O'Hara gets out at Times Square. Unlike the Village, it's streaming with New Yorkers and visitors. The locals ply familiar routes in silence. The tourists move in thrilled packs, chirping in their native tongues. O'Hara is swept along in the flow, barely participating in her own locomotion, until she starts up the stairs and sees five feet in front of her the back of a tall red-haired man carrying a guitar case and a tiny amp and realizes it's Axl.

The stairs lead to a mezzanine, with a walk-in newsstand to the left. In the sprawling subterranean archipelago, it occupies its own level, floating above the Queens-bound tracks from which they just ascended and below the pedestrian thoroughfares that lead to the shuttle, the 1, 2, and 3, and the A, C, and E. Just short of a railing overlooking the tracks, Axl puts down his guitar and amp, and O'Hara ducks behind a column.

When she looks back, Axl is crouched on one knee. He plugs in his old Fender, fiddles with some knobs, and casually strums a few chords as if alone in his room, picking out a melody. From the track below come the hiss of brakes and the recorded female voice: "This is a Queens-bound R train. The next stop will be . . . Forty-Ninth Street."

As passengers sweep by, O'Hara makes out the start of Aerosmith's "Walk This Way," and despite her precarious state, the riff lightens her heart, just as it would if she stumbled across it on a radio dial or it dropped on a jukebox. It has the same effect on three young skateboarders. When Axl reaches the chorus, using a wah-wah pedal to simulate Steven Tyler's wail, one puts his hands on his hips and performs a cocksure urban strut. In the midst of the second verse, another train pulls in. Rather than compete with the clamor, Axl stops playing and talks to the skaters, cultivating his little audience, keeping it intact. When enough quiet returns, Stevie Wonder's "Living for the City" snags a couple more travelers. So does Joan Jett's "I Love Rock 'n' Roll."

O'Hara is mortified to see her one and only son busking in the MTA, not even in a good spot. At the same time, she is in awe of the stones required to take out a guitar and play in front of the passing crowd. She couldn't do it in a million years, not with a gun pointed at her head, but Axl can. He's good at it and likes what he's doing, and people can tell. It puts them at ease and inclines them to linger, and after every song newcomers outnumber deserters. In fact, the spot he's chosen isn't half bad. With the

airiness of the space and the tiles on the walls, put on during the eighties, when the city was awash in cash, the acoustics are excellent. And of
course she approves his choice of covers. Maybe this is not such a bad
development, she tells herself. Maybe this can all work out.

"There's something I should tell you," says Axl when the subways
cooperate. "If anyone out there is tempted to steal my tips, you should
know that my mom is with NYPD. In fact, she's a homicide detective. No
shit. Not too many females in homicide. When she had me, she was young
and crazy. She still is, but that's another story. When I was colicky, or
refused to fall asleep, she sometimes put this on the stereo. Whenever I
hear it, I think of her."

The song builds slowly and takes a minute or two to morph into ZZ
Top. As a fresh surge of travelers scale the stairs, Axl sings.

Hot, blue and righteous
an angel called me aside
Hot, blue and righteous
said, "stick by me and I'll be your guide tonight."

O'Hara's love for her son buckles her knees, and she grabs the column for support. By the time she collects herself enough to peer out,
Axl has unplugged and packed up, and is descending the stairs. O'Hara
is proud of her son and scared to death for him, and as she watches his
shaggy head disappear from view, she knows that her worst fears and
fondest hopes have both come true.

ACKNOWLEDGMENTS

To Detective Keith Flannery from the 7th Precinct, Detective George Taylor from Manhattan Homicide South, and Ret. Detective Irma Rivera formerly of Homicide South, for continuing to let me sit around, watch, and listen. To Bradley Adams, forensic anthropologist for the office of Chief Medical Examiner in New York City, and Ret. Detective Bob Geis, formerly of the NYPD Special Frauds Unit, for the benefit of their experience and expertise. To my agent, Todd Shuster, for support; to my wife, Daina Zivarts, for support plus affection; and to my editor, Claire Wachtel, for saving me from multiple embarrassments, then putting a gun to my head. Most of all to Detective Donna Torres from Homicide North, without whose generosity neither this book nor the one that preceded it would have been possible.

ABOUT THE AUTHOR

Peter de Jonge is the author of *Shadows Still Remain* and the coauthor of three *New York Times* bestsellers with James Patterson: *Beach Road, The Beach House,* and *Miracle on the 17th Green*. He has been a reporter for the Associated Press and a contributing writer for the *New York Times Magazine*. His work has appeared in *Best American Sports Writing, National Geographic, Harper's Bazaar, Details,* and *Manhattan, Inc.* He lives in New York City.